HARMONY AT STRATHMORE

A JANE HARMONY MYSTERY

GAIL BALENTINE

*This book is dedicated to those
who told me they enjoyed visiting Winslet...
and wanted to go back.*

PROLOGUE

FRED FLORES SAW them through a small gap in the bushes. In the fading light, he could make out two figures. A tall man, who was obviously in charge, wore a long black coat, a gray fedora pulled low over his brow. He was dressed like a businessman, but his ramrod posture was more that of a soldier. The man did not speak; he simply held out a gloved hand.

The second man, in uniform, handed over a large white envelope trimmed with red edging. He was the shorter of the two, had dark hair, wore glasses, and was based at Strathmore—Fred didn't know his name, but had seen him in Winslet. None of his motions were smooth and he was constantly looking around, everywhere but at the tall man. Fear radiated from him.

After the man in black took the envelope, he nodded and turned to leave. Fred knew he had witnessed something important; he could feel it in his old soldier's bones. He believed the meeting and contents of the envelope were about the men on the second floor of the army's Strathmore Hospital, those behind the window bars. He had to get to a telephone.

He tried to quietly move back, deeper into the bush, but while doing so, stepped on a twig that made a loud snapping noise. The soldier looked toward him and then ran in the opposite direction like a spooked deer, while the tall man headed directly toward the sound at a fast pace.

Fred knew he couldn't outrun him, so he grabbed his stout walking stick and held his breath. The man came to a halt near where he was painfully crouching and pushed back the brush. Gazing into the stone-cold eyes of a killer, Fred didn't hesitate.

He jumped up and brought the walking stick down on the pursuer's head with all his might, causing the man to stumble and fall to the ground.

Then he ran. Even though he knew with his clumsy left knee and unsteady gait the tall man would easily catch up once he regained his footing, he tried.

His mind raced as he kept going, disregarding the shooting pains from his knee. How could he alert someone *now*? And who? Then he thought of Micah.

He heard the fallen man curse, get up, and start running. He tried to move faster while reaching inside his coat, between his shirt and underwear. The feel of cold metal reassured him as he tore the object loose and flung it as far as he could. *Please, Micah,* he silently pleaded, *find the medal, understand the signal.* He staggered but managed to right himself.

Fred's breath was coming in gasps now, his knee pulsating.

In what seemed like seconds, the man was making up the distance between them. He heard him call out *halt!* The last time anyone had shouted that word at him was in 1918 when he was trying to get away from the German soldier who'd shot him, shattering his kneecap.

He'd reached his limit. He could run no longer, barely able to stay on his feet at this point. He sensed the motion behind him before the pain struck. As he fell to the ground, Fred's last thought was of his Iris—the best thing that ever happened to him.

———

CHAPTER ONE

"Life's what you make it, always has been, always will be."
Eleanor Roosevelt

FRIDAY, DECEMBER 24, 1943 – BEACON HILL
HOUSE, BOSTON

TWO SUITCASES WERE CRAMMED full and waiting for a final check before they went downstairs. I was likely taking more than I needed, but in truth, I wasn't sure how long I'd be gone. As I walked down the stairs and headed toward the dining room, I could hear my Uncle Frank's latest rant about Franklin Roosevelt, a frequent topic during mealtimes. It seemed railroads and a possible nationwide strike had been added to the breakfast menu. According to my uncle, the President should concentrate on the war and leave the running of the country to others, whose responsibilities my uncle changed weekly.

"Good morning, Aunt Margaret."

I gave her a quick kiss on the cheek and settled into my usual seat.

"Good morning, dear. You look lovely. That green sweater brings out the red highlights in your hair. And look, the skirt matches it so well."

I smiled. I knew my aunt. What she wanted to say—but didn't—was she was glad to see me wearing something other than the slacks I favored. Katherine Hepburn and women's war jobs had made wearing pants in public popular, and my aunt's generation did not approve.

My uncle ignored the fashion discussion and continued ranting about the President.

"Uncle Frank, remember your blood pressure, and the fact the President can't hear your opinions anyway."

My aunt and I smiled at him, and he growled in response. We went on to the main topic of the day: our trip to Winslet.

"Jane, I'm so excited for TJ's wedding."

My brother, Staff Sergeant Thomas J. Harmony, better known as TJ, and a wonderful girl named Aggie Liddings were to be married in a Christmas Eve candlelit ceremony at the Carriage Lantern Inn in Winslet. And we were going to be there.

My aunt, who reminded me so much of my mother, looked forward to returning to the town where my brother and I had been raised until I was twelve. Me? I was ambivalent. When I'd left from Winslet station on that rainswept night so long ago, a frightened twelve-year-old, I'd sworn never to return. My mother, brother, and I had left quickly after my father died in what some, including the law, called a tragic accident while others insisted it was murder.

My trip back two months ago, the first in sixteen years, had been bittersweet. I had broken my vow about returning in order to prove ` the police had made a mistake in arresting my brother for the murder of the town's Chief of Police. I'm not sure what it was I'd expected I could do, but before I knew it, I was knee-deep in the chase for a killer.

During the weeks I was there, old issues resurfaced; some were resolved, but not all.

I made myself come out of the past and think about my aunt and uncle and how they were feeling. "I know you two haven't been back to Winslet very often in the past few years. I wonder what you'll think of the changes in the town now we're at war?"

She laughed.

"If Winslet has changed a lot from the quiet little Berkshire town I left, I'll..."

Before she could finish her sentence, the phone rang.

Uncle Frank went to answer it while my aunt and I finished breakfast and talked about what we still needed to do if we wanted to be on the road by 11 a.m. I sensed she had something else to say, but Uncle Frank came back at that moment and sat down.

He was unusually quiet, and had that *I hate to say this* look he got when he had to deliver news he knew you didn't want to hear, such as the time he had to tell me he could not come to my nursing school graduation because of work obligations.

"What is it, Frank? Tell us."

"That was Ida. It seems a body has been found in the woods beside the old Strathmore Estate—you know, that place the army has turned into a temporary base? Though God knows why. All leaves have been cancelled and the soldiers ordered to return to base, and that means the wedding has to be postponed."

"Dead body? No wedding?"

Aunt Margaret looked at me as if I had the answers. I shook my head and thought about how disappointed TJ and Aggie must be.

When she spoke next, my aunt was obviously agitated. "Jane, you must promise us that you will not get involved if this person was murdered. Either that, or we can all stay home."

I sighed. My family had held strong feelings about my involvement in murder investigations since the two I had been part of in October had nearly got me killed. I understood what she was saying, but also realized that without my intervention, an innocent man—my brother—may have gone to prison. We'd had this conversation many times and it always ended in a stalemate, her with concerns about my safety, versus me and my sense of justice.

"Aunt Margaret, please. I think you're getting ahead of things." I turned to my uncle, "Was there any talk of murder at all?"

"No, none. Ida knew very little. She didn't know who the person was or how he or she died."

"There, see? Please don't worry."

Trying to improve the mood, I changed the subject. "The important question now is do we still want to go to Winslet for Christmas with the family? I vote yes."

Uncle Frank replied first. "Of course, we will go."

Aunt Margaret hesitated. "Yes, yes—we should go. But Jane, I'm not only concerned about this body, although that is a terrible thing. What is going to happen when you see Captain Maitland again? You haven't said..."

This time, Uncle Frank had had enough.

He stood, leaving the rest of his breakfast untouched.

"Margaret, would you leave the girl alone—please! She is twenty-eight years old and more than capable of making her own decisions. I'm tired of these round-robin discussions that get nowhere. When she decides about her future, she will let us know, I'm sure. Now, I'm leaving here at 11 a.m., even if I have to go alone!"

My aunt was more than able to stand up for herself; the two of them were a good match in that department, but this time she backed down and sighed.

With that, he left the room.

"All right, I'm outnumbered. I'll stop. It's just that this whole world has turned upside down what with this horrible war and the awful news coming out of Europe... and those Pacific islands with strange names, and TJ, Russ, and James all in the service, and people getting killed in Winslet. And you up to your ears in patients, a flu outbreak, and murder investigations! It's hard not to be concerned about the people you love."

She laid her hand, which felt cold, on mine and squeezed gently.

"I know what you're saying, and I agree it's a crazy world right now and I am worried, too. But I also know we each must decide for ourselves what is right and concentrate on those things we can control—like deciding we will still go to Winslet and have Christmas with family. Please, have faith that all that time my mother and then you and Uncle Frank took to raise us wasn't wasted. TJ and I know how to be careful and will do what we think is right."

"Come on, you've got to see to our road lunch and pack the gifts while I go and play Santa to Margie and the staff."

With that, I stood up, gave her one more hug, and breakfast was over.

UNCLE FRANK DROPPED me off near the center of the main Boston shopping district, home to department stores such as Jordan Marsh, Filene's, and Gilchrist's. There were also smaller, more specialized stores, restaurants, souvenir shops, and street vendors selling everything from gifts to wreaths to roasted chestnuts.

The war, of course, had subdued things a bit, but the streets were still filled with last-minute shoppers, rushing from store to store, their arms filled with packages.

Soldiers and sailors mixed in with the young and old. I couldn't help but wonder what lay ahead for these young men.

I looked at the decorations on every building, smelled the roasted chestnuts, and listened to the sounds of Christmas carols from a chorus of costumed singers with red noses from the cold. Salvation Army 'soldiers' and their kettles were on each corner, ringing their bells and wishing each donor a Merry Christmas.

I felt myself relax and smile.

Christmas and all that went with it was my favorite time of year.

The crowds, dressed up in their holiday finery to shop, were part of the fun of it all. Most of them were smiling, too, although a few scrooges had somehow slipped in among them. At the hospital, I worked with very ill patients and enjoyed any opportunity I had to see people having a good, if slightly harried, time.

As they had been for the past several years, signs were posted in many windows to remind shoppers not to forget those fighting for us and to support them by buying Victory Bonds. Our family had a stack of them, most of which were going to TJ and Aggie as a wedding gift.

Mothers tried to pry wide-eyed children from Jordan Marsh's *Enchanted Village* holiday window displays that showcased animated scenes, including toy soldiers, dolls, talking stuffed animals and, of course, Santa's elves decorating the tree, and the man himself in a sleigh full of toys. Normally, I would have loved to pause and enjoy the windows and the children's reactions, but today I had to move along.

It took time to maneuver through the crowds, cross Washington Street, and enter Filene's. Bypassing the main floor, I went down to the basement where bargains waited, and you could get a nice dress for half price. Sadly, there was no time for browsing. Instead, I squeezed around two women playing tug-of-war over a coat and hurried to the Customer Help Desk to pick up the package waiting for me.

Before we could leave the city and head to western Massachusetts, I had to deliver gifts at work. As I emerged from the stairs leading to the street, I looked up at the large clock on the corner: 9:30 a.m. It would usually be a brisk fifteen-minute walk from the shopping area to where I worked but I picked up the pace and made it to the hospital in ten minutes, panting a bit.

As I walked, Winslet came to mind. How were the residents reacting to yet another dead body? Were they worried whoever the person was had been killed? Did they think their small town wasn't safe anymore? As to my safety, I understood my aunt's concern—she had voiced it many times—but I was not looking to become involved in another murder investigation.

The problem I needed to focus on was my future. And

what would it be like to see Hank again? We'd had several arguments while talking on the telephone over the past weeks, mostly about how, when, or if we were ever getting married.

We had very different opinions about what a marriage should be like.

MGH

Massachusetts General Hospital was made up of a series of large buildings in which patients had been taken care of since the early 1800s. It had an international reputation for excellence, and I loved nursing patients alongside the top doctors and nurses that MGH attracted. The hospital's architecture, history, and solid feeling were already impressive but with the war, we had expanded to over 900 patient beds, eighteen of which were on Langdon East, the Orthopedic and Surgical Ward where I worked as the Assistant Head Nurse. The rest were scattered throughout buildings with a footprint the size of a small city; thousands of people came and went through its doors every day.

By the time I had walked through the White Building door and ridden the elevator to Langdon East, I was shivering a bit. Our recent mild weather was finally turning seasonably cold and odds of the *White Christmas* that Bing Crosby sang about were increasing by the minute.

I was cutting my time close and knew my uncle would have started wondering where I was.

When I entered the ward, I could, as always, feel the electricity in the air. Our patients were very ill, with multiple ailments. We were a step down from the Special Care Unit and doctors and residents made rounds several times a day, often changing patient orders. Our ward secretary Frances—a woman who juggled multiple tasks and made it look easy—saw me, smiled, and then continued writing while she listened to whoever was on the other side of the telephone call. I left the box of homemade cupcakes and cookies for the staff on her desk and turned toward Margie Malone's office but heard someone call my name. It was Mary Anderson, a nurse I was training to be the charge nurse on the weekends I did not work. She was young and smart with a lot of potential, but she lacked in self-confidence.

"Jane, I thought you had left for vacation already!"

She grabbed my arm. I knew she didn't realize how hard she'd squeezed it.

"What's the matter, Mary? You look really upset."

"Neil Cameron developed sudden, severe abdominal pain this morning. His blood pressure plummeted, and we had to transfer him to the Special Care Unit. I wish you had been here!"

"I'm sure everything went very well."

"Not like it would with you. You can handle anything."

It was obvious she needed to talk. "Come on, let's sit down for a minute."

Langdon East had a small area set aside with two comfortable chairs and a side table over by a window at the front of the ward. It was where we sat with family members or patients when we could make the time.

"Tell me exactly what happened from the time you discovered the problem to the time you moved him to SCU."

Mary and I had been through several patient emergencies together and I knew it was calming for her to review what had happened, step by step. She did that and I watched her visibly relax, but she still ended her recitation with a confidence-lacking comment.

"It all went fine, I think. But it would definitely have gone much better if you'd been here."

I knew that was Mary's anxiety talking so I wanted her to try to separate fact from feelings. Nobody who really knew me would call me a patient person but with new nurses, students, and patients, I had the ability to resist my usual need to move things along quickly.

"Two things, Mary. First, why don't you tell me what you think I would have done differently?" She bit her lower lip and thought for a minute but came up with nothing.

"And second, what did Dr. Eldridge have to say when you were leaving the SCU? He always has a comment or suggestion." I again watched carefully as Mary thought back.

"Well, he said we did a good job. But he always says that, right?"

I laughed out loud, a little too loud. People turned to stare at us.

"Um no, no, he definitely does not always say that. If he had any concerns about what you did, he would have said it then or worse, told you he wanted to speak to you later."

She thought about that but then frowned. "But even if I did what I was supposed to do, I was too nervous. Past nervous, Jane, *scared*. You're always so calm."

"What do you think? Did Mr. Cameron know you were scared?"

"No... no I don't think so. I hope not. I tried to sound calm and talk in a reassuring voice like we were taught."

"Good. Now let me share something with you. When I was as new as you are, if there was an emergency, I would do what I had to do for the patient, then go into the staff bathroom and be sick. Later, when I went home, I would write down every single thing I could remember before I even changed out of my uniform. I did that so I could review it with Miss Malone, who was my charge nurse at that point. It…"

I was interrupted and turned at the sound of Margie's voice and the laugh that went with it.

"I can testify to that story. It got to the point where if anyone asked for Jane in the ten minutes after a crisis, the rest of us would answer in unison that she was indisposed."

Margie's bright eyes and huge grin could light up a room. She was my best friend and missed no opportunity to tease me, according to her, 'to keep my ego from getting swollen'. She was also the nurse whose opinion I trusted most.

Dr. Eldridge was with her and nodded his head to Mary. "You did a fine job today, Miss Anderson. Mr. Cameron is being prepped for surgery as we speak. I'm sorry to interrupt your conversation, but I need to have a quick word with Miss Harmony, if I may?"

The two of them left and, as Mary and I stood, she leaned over and whispered to me. "I didn't realize he knew my name!"

"He makes it his business to know everyone's name. Now you go back to work, believe that you are doing a good job, and I'll see you after my vacation. And Merry Christmas."

She smiled, thanked me, and I made a quick stop to ask Frances to call my house and let them know I would be late. I told her if my uncle answered, to be sure to hold the phone away from her ear.

As I caught up with Margie and Dr. Eldridge walking

toward Margie's office, I wondered what kind of conversation was ahead of me.

WE DIDN'T SIT down in Margie's crowded office. We all had places to go.

"Miss Harmony, I would have spoken to you before this, but I got the approval I needed to begin a new project yesterday. I have a job offer to make to you and would like your permission to call you while you are away to explain it to you. I don't mean to be cryptic, but I don't have time right now to get into it. I'm due in the OR."

For a surgeon, Dr. Eldridge was generally a very calm man.

While some others of his specialty lost their tempers at the drop of a hat, he only raised his voice if he thought someone had made what he considered a stupid mistake. He would have his say and then go back to being calm again. Where others demanded immediate attention— everything was a crisis—he quietly asked for what he needed and, as a result, grateful nurses got it to him quickly. But now, there was a definite twinkle in his eye I was not used to seeing and an excitement in his voice I was not used to hearing.

"Of course, you can call me, Dr. Eldridge. Miss Malone knows the number."

He thanked me, wished us both a good holiday, and rushed off toward the operating room and Mr. Cameron.

I turned to Margie. "A job offer? Do you know what that was about?"

She shook her head. "I've heard rumors about a new ward, but details were vague, and it sounded like it would be a while from now. I thought it was another rumor; there always seems to be a new one circulating."

"I haven't heard of any new wards popping up." I thought for a minute. "Do you remember when we had those two young soldiers all trussed up in splints and traction?" She nodded. "Well, Dr. Eldridge said their fears and nightmares were as big a problem as their wounds. I remember him saying something had to be done. Maybe it's that."

I was still trying to think what it could be that Dr. Eldridge wanted my help for when I saw Margie steal a quick look at her watch, so I said, "Look, you've got to go, I've got to go. My uncle may send out the rescue dogs if I don't get home soon."

"Jane, I do have things to do but first—well, I am concerned about what happens when you see Hank again." She held up a hand to stop my protesting. "I know you haven't gotten along too well lately, but please don't make any rash decisions. You two are perfect for each other and I hope you can keep that in mind as you work something out." She paused and then quickly added, "Look, I'm not trying to put any pressure on you, but I do need to know your plans almost as soon as you do. If you decide you are giving your notice and only coming back for two weeks after your vacation, I will need to replace you, and that will not be an easy task." Her smile was sad. "And if you decide to move to Winslet, I want to say that that town seems to be nothing but trouble for you. *There,* I've been wanting to say that for a long time."

She was right, it was time Hank and I made up our minds as there were other people who would be affected by our decisions. As far as Winslet went, I thought about telling her about the latest body they'd found, but since she would likely take the same leap my aunt had and caution me against getting involved—even though there was no hint of murder—I decided to spare her that concern.

We needed to wrap up so I told her that I understood what she was trying to say to me and that I would not make any hasty decisions. After swapping Christmas gifts wrapped in the newspaper's funny pages, we hugged each other, and she waved goodbye as she was picking up the telephone.

———

CHAPTER TWO

"There is nothing... so hidden that we cannot discover it, provided only we abstain from accepting the false for the true."
Rene Descartes

FRIDAY, DECEMBER 24, 1943

WHEN I ARRIVED HOME, I went quickly to my bedroom, looked around for forgotten items, and then brought the bags outside for my uncle to load them into the trunk of his '39 black Ford sedan. Our cases took up the whole space and Uncle Frank slammed the trunk of the car shut. My aunt came down the front stairs, picnic basket in hand.

Muttering all the time, he took the basket from her and shooed my aunt into the front passenger seat, then me into the back where I shared the space with the presents and the picnic lunch. Aunt Margaret rolled her eyes and we both smiled. We had agreed not to let my uncle's growling upset us. After all, it was Christmas Eve Day and we were leaving the hustle and bustle of Boston for the quiet of a small town to see family, wedding or not.

Uncle Frank went back into the house for his own final check. He always had to have one last look at the locks on the downstairs windows and doors, as well as check that no burners on the gas stove were lit, even though they'd all been checked at least twice already.

Sometimes, when I looked at my aunt, I could see some of her sister, my mother, Hannah. It was bittersweet to think how my mother would have looked as she aged, had she not died too young. But looks were where the resemblance ended. Where my mother was shy and quiet, my aunt was not. The way in which they were the exact same was that they were both loving mothers. She and Uncle Frank had been protective, caring, strict adoptive parents from the first day they'd taken TJ and me into their home.

As soon as we were on our way, Aunt Margaret began 'helping' Uncle Frank with his driving, pointing out when he was too close to another car or when to turn.

My attention turned to the people we passed as the car merged into the Beacon Street traffic. Servicemen and women dominated the landscape, young people who came and left the city so quickly. How did they handle the fears they must have? Where would they be sent to fight? And what about after the war, whenever that finally came? Would they be able to pick up their interrupted lives when they returned—*if* they returned?

They each had people who worried about them, as did our family about my cousins, Russ and Jimmy. We never knew where they were or what they were doing. I was so grateful that both TJ and Hank were stationed here, or, as the newspapers called it, *stateside*.

We saw the soldiers in the city only for a short time before they departed South Station for Battery Park in New York City. From there, they embarked to Europe. These young men roamed Boston in a frenzy of activity to seemingly take in all the sights before they faced war, snapping pictures and flirting with pretty girls.

Sailors, too, swarmed the city when their ships docked at the Boston Navy Yard. I'd heard they headed directly to Scollay Square in downtown Boston, lured by its lively night life and racy reputation. Clubs, bars, tattoo parlors and well-known landmarks like the Old Howard burlesque theater were doing a rousing business. Some of the younger girls who came into work bleary-eyed on Monday morning repeatedly assured the rest of us they only went to the Square "for the famous hot dogs at Joe and Nemo's". Margie said that was like saying you went to a bar because you liked peanuts.

While we waited in holiday traffic, my aunt turned to me and asked, "Jane, dear, are you curious about the dead man that Ida told us about?"

My uncle sighed and looked at me in the rearview mirror.

It took a few seconds to switch gears from thinking about the soldiers and sailors to thinking about the body found in Winslet.

When I answered her, it was with questions of my own. "Well, aren't you interested in who it was? What if we know him?"

"Of course, of course. But that isn't what I'm asking, and you know it." She paused and then decided to go on. "I remember when you returned from Winslet in October, it took a long time for you to stop talking about your time there. Not so much about TJ, the flu epidemic, or even Winslet itself. No, you talked about the investigation process, about putting the pieces together to find who killed Chief Connawell and his cousin. It was—it was as if you *enjoyed* doing it. And I'm concerned you will feel that way again!"

If anyone else had asked the same question, I might have given them a flippant answer, but I knew Aunt Margaret was concerned for my safety. She always had been and was obviously not going to let the subject go, so I took a minute to decide how to word my answer.

"I have always enjoyed a challenge, you know that. At work, I do not enjoy a patient's illness, but I do take satisfaction when I help to find a solution. It's like the war. In my heart, I believe that this war is about justice and doing the right thing. I know there are more factors involved, but that's what I believe is at the core. A mob of cruel people want to run the world, eliminating all those who disagree with or offend them.

"And, to a much more limited extent, it was the same in Winslet. A mob of angry people had decided TJ was guilty, mostly because of our past with the town. I reacted to that anger because of TJ, but I still wanted justice for Chief Connawell." Sometimes, my pale coloring betrayed me, and I could feel the blush on my cheeks. "I know that sounds corny, but this man, whoever he is, would deserve that justice too if his death was violent."

I could see Uncle Frank nodding his head in agreement, though he wisely stayed silent.

My aunt made one last try. "This man may have died of natural causes for all we know. And if he didn't, don't you think Chester capable of getting that justice for him?"

Chester Fielding was not only the new Chief of Police in Winslet, but he and his wife were also dear friends of Aunt Margaret and Uncle Frank.

"Of course, he is. I didn't say I was going to get involved — I may not even know the man. But, if my help *is* needed, I wouldn't turn away. I'm not made that way and deep down, you understand that because whenever my mother got upset with me, she always said I was as stubborn as you."

"Ha! She's got you there, Maggie, me girl!"

Aunt Margaret seemed to give up and I looked out the window and went back to reflecting about the changes in my adopted city. For the second year in a row — along with dimmed streetlamps and car headlights — Christmas lights and store display windows would not light up Boston at night. It was all part of the blackout required of coastal cities since the war began. At first, people, especially businessmen, had thought the regulations too strict because, after all, the war was *over there*, not over here. But the discovery of German U-boats off the Boston coastline in 1942, and the sinking of supply ships with subsequent loss of life had soon put a stop to all that talk.

A hand-made sign in a storefront window said it all: "End the war in '44!"

WE PASSED through Kenmore Square and started driving west on Route 20, which would take us most of the way to Winslet. I loved the idea of traveling on a road that had been one of the first postal routes between Boston and New York back when mail was delivered on horseback.

We drove for an hour and, after a quick stop for our picnic lunch, we were back on our journey. Route 20 was like watching history go by from the backseat of a car. We drove past a mixture of 18th-century homes, farms, colonial inns that advertised rooms for soldiers and their families, and old and new businesses such as an auto shop next to a harness maker, next to an old barn being converted to a salvage outlet for the government.

As we drove, my aunt and uncle talked quietly with each other in the front seat and the thought came to me that, in all parts of the country, Americans had people and places they loved enough to fight for.

CARRIAGE LANTERN INN

We'd left Boston at 11:15 a.m. and three-and-a-half hours later, turned onto Main Street, Winslet. I felt myself relax as familiar houses and buildings came into view. I had always loved this small town; it was some of the people who lived there I'd had a very hard time even being civil to. Some of the old ghosts of childhood were buried two months ago, and I hoped I could now enjoy my former home for what it was, a haven from the hustle and bustle that was Boston, tucked into the western corner of Mass-achusetts.

We soon had to stop and wait while a shiny fire engine, Winslet's only, was backed into its station. Winslet had always celebrated holidays with parades of marching boy scouts and girl scouts, balloons, and a small ragtag band consisting of high-school students and former students alike. Even though the festivities were more sober everywhere due to the war, they still went on, with veterans leading the line. It looked as though we'd arrived after it was over since people were scattering in all directions.

All along Main Street, flags large and small waved in the December sunshine, rippling with the breeze;

Christmas wreaths were attached to each lamp post and large red bells were suspended from holly-covered wires overhead.

Holiday Inn was playing at the Paramount Theatre and war bond posters hung in store windows. Due to the same short supplies of gift items that the entire country was experiencing, the shop windows were filled with small Christmas scenes rather than wares for sale.

The street itself was wide enough to accommodate two lanes of traffic with parking for cars at right angles to the sidewalk in front of the stores.

A few people were walking with paper-wrapped bundles and some waved at us. I smiled when I realized that if a little snow were to be added to the scene, downtown Winslet at Christmastime would make a lovely cover for the *Saturday Evening Post*.

Thomas and Aunt Ida's Carriage Lantern Inn was on Main Street, next to Veterans Memorial Park. I loved the graceful Victorian-style home built at the turn of the century, a place that had been my grandmother's family home for years. She had left it to Thomas, and he and my aunt had converted it to an inn. When we arrived, we all took a moment to admire the greenery decorating the sweeping porch and the baskets of holly and berries lining the stairs and the walk. It felt simple, warm, and welcoming.

I opened the front door and called out a greeting.

Only Victor, the resident cat, answered me. He came running around a corner in a black blur and launched into my arms from a few feet away. I'd known what was coming so I was prepared but Aunt Margaret and Uncle Frank were surprised and a little taken aback.

"Hello, Vic, how are you?" I scratched under his chin and when he started purring, the sound was much louder than his small size would lead you to expect. I turned to my aunt and laughed, "It's all right. This is how he greets people he loves, and since we got very close in October, he can go right on doing it as far as I'm concerned."

Loud voices coming from the kitchen interrupted the reunion. The conversation sounded heated. The three of us left our suitcases at the door and quickly headed down the hallway, past the parlor with its huge Christmas tree set in the front window, past the family pictures on the wall that separated the dining room from the hall, and on to the small area that led to the kitchen on the left and family bedrooms on the right. The guest rooms were upstairs.

When we entered the kitchen, Winslet's new Chief of Police, Chester Fielding, was nearly nose-to-nose with Micah, a good friend of my uncle's and a lifelong resident of Winslet. Both of their faces were scarlet and my uncle Thomas was trying to insert himself between them while my Aunt Ida wrung her hands, and Micah's friend Johnny Birdcage stood there, shock radiating from his face.

"Are you calling me incompetent?" growled the usually mild-mannered Chief.

Micah answered in a voice just as angry. "If the shoe fits..."

The cat jumped out of my arms and ran out of the room. Smart cat. Without thinking about it, I used the charge nurse voice I reserved for patients acting out and said, loudly, "Stop it you two, right now! You're both going to have heart attacks if you keep this up!"

That grabbed everyone's attention.

The Chief and Micah each stepped back, and Thomas and Johnny quickly moved between them. My words had the effect of throwing cold water on the combatants and when they turned in my direction, they both had the grace to look embarrassed, the Chief more so than Micah.

In the silence that followed, *Happy Holidays* began playing on the radio.

Uncle Frank, never shy and retiring, pushed his way past Aunt Margaret and me to get closer and glared at the two men. He then turned to Thomas. "What the hell is going on here?"

Everybody started talking at once until my Aunt Ida stepped up and said, "Let's everyone calm down. Go into the dining room and have a seat. Thomas and I will bring out something to eat and we can discuss this quietly, like the friends we actually are."

After that, she came over and gave each of her new arrivals a hug, leaving her ever-present fragrance of vanilla floating after her. As far as I was concerned, my Aunt Ida had been a savior for TJ and me during the childhood years we'd lived in Winslet and during our recent troubles. Whenever we needed it most, she would turn the inn into a haven for us and I associated her scent with love, warmth and safety. Thomas was right behind her.

He shook Uncle Frank's hand, kissed Aunt Margaret's cheek, held me in a warm embrace for a full minute, and then immediately returned into his usual gruff self and told us to leave the kitchen so they could get something done.

Aunt Margaret, Uncle Frank, and I left the room to put our coats in the front closet. Micah and Johnny went into the dining room, and the Chief went out onto the back screened porch. My guess was he sorely needed a breath of fresh air. A few minutes later, we were all seated around the dining room table with coffee or tea in front of us and the tension between the Chief and Micah somewhat lessened.

· · ·

"AUNT IDA, I'm amazed you can still get coffee after the army moved out. We're even having trouble at the hospital."

"Truth be told, Jane, that Captain Maitland of yours is a very generous man. He stocked us up with some hard-to-get items for the holidays."

My mind drifted for a moment when she said "... that Captain Maitland of yours". Would he still be mine after we talked?

It was Thomas who took the lead in getting our discussion started.

"Glad to have you folks here." He nodded to his sister, brother-in-law, and me. "What you saw was a difference of opinion..."

"Not a difference of opinion, Thomas." Micah was angry, tension radiating from him.

"The Chief refuses to listen to facts."

"Micah." This time, it was my Aunt Ida who spoke up, with a smile that nobody I knew could resist. "Please let Thomas explain what has happened so everyone is up to date. One person can get through the story quicker. These folks have traveled from Boston to join us for Christmas and I'm sure they would like to have a chance to rest before supper tonight."

He mumbled something which I didn't catch, and then nodded. Thomas continued. "As we told you this morning, a body was found at that new army hospital. It was an older man, lying face down in the middle of a path leading out in the woods. Captain Maitland," he looked at me, "called the police to report the crime, and then called Father Fitz to see if he could identify the man since nobody at the base had recognized him."

Thomas paused to light his pipe and another of my favorite scents filled the room—peppermint.

"When Father Fitz saw him, he knew right away that the man on the ground was Fred Flores. Chief, maybe you should take over now."

The name was unfamiliar to me.

A much calmer Chief Fielding—the personality I was more familiar with—continued the story. "Apparently, there was a strong smell of alcohol coming from Mr. Flores..." Micah made a growling sound, but Johnny was able to quieten him. "The scene my officers saw looked as though a drunk, homeless man had tripped in the woods, hit his head and, well, the worst had happened.

"Their focus quickly went on to how the man got so close to a secure facility and why he was there in the first place."

Micah couldn't stay quiet any longer. "You said 'they'. Where were you?"

"I was giving a deposition in Boston in one of my former cases."

"Well, that may be what your deputies and the army were worried about, but *I* want to know what really happened to my friend!"

"Now Micah..." This time, it was Thomas speaking to him in a calm voice.

With that, everybody started talking again. I was trying to decide how to help when the doorbell rang. It was a relief to leave the room to answer the front door. I quickly greeted Father Fitzgerald, affectionately known as Father Fitz, the Catholic priest from St. Agnes'.

"Boy, am I glad to see you!"

I hung up his coat and escorted him into the dining room, where voices were starting to raise again.

"What's goin' on in here on this fine Christmas Eve Day

—a boxing match?" His voice was hoarse, making his brogue sound a bit stronger than usual.

The priest's presence calmed the men down. My aunt introduced him to Aunt Margaret and Uncle Frank, and then gestured to the coffee. He fixed himself a cup, all the while keeping a watchful eye on those around the table. Father Fitz was a man who exuded confidence. From former conversations with him and the little information he reluctantly shared, he had a past in Ireland that included activities not generally found on a priest's resume.

And he was as physically fit as any soldier could hope to be, a fitness that had once saved me from two would-be attackers.

"Finally! A person who makes sense!" Micah looked as though he wanted to get up and hug the cleric. "Father, you knew Fred Flores pretty well, didn't you?"

As he took a seat between Aunt Ida and me, the priest nodded. "As well as he let anyone, except you and Johnny here, of course." He smiled at both men and sipped his coffee.

"Yes. Did you ever see him drunk?"

Father Fitz immediately shook his head. "A drink now and then, sure, but drunk? Never. And I'm Irish—I *know* drunk!" His attempt at humor fell short in the face of the serious situation. "On top of that, whenever I would offer him one for the road, he would refuse it. Why would you ask me that?"

The Chief jumped in. "Didn't you smell the alcohol on Mr. Flores when you went to the scene?"

At that point, Father Fitz turned away to sneeze into his handkerchief. "Pardon me. No, Chief Fielding, I did not. I haven't been able to smell anything for a week now. Truth is, that day I had a fever and stayed at the scene as short a time as I could."

"The Chief here thinks Fred fell down drunk and died of the cold." Micah looked from the priest to the Chief and back to the priest.

Father Fitz shook his head. "I don't know from what he died, but I'm willing to swear it was not because he was drunk." A second sneeze punctuated his words and I added my 'bless you' to the chorus that followed. "I've seen my share of men losing their lives to the drink. They are usually unable to get out of a bed somewhere, tucked up in the corner of an alley, or stretched out on a park bench. What they are not doing is running in the woods beside an army base."

"Hear that?" Micah didn't pause. "And another thing, did anyone see his walking stick near his body?"

He was leaning so far across the table now that he was almost standing up.

Father Fitz thought back. "No, there was no stick. Da... darn, I must be getting old, I should've noticed that for myself. Never saw him without that. No sir."

"Of course you didn't because he can't get more than thirty feet without it to lean on! I can't imagine why he would leave it behind." He turned to the Chief, eyes flashing, as he sat back in his chair. "That's what I was trying to say! Something is wrong here and I want to know what it is."

There was a soft curse from the Chief as he got up from his seat and headed to the hallway where the telephone was located.

He made two calls. The rest of us waited in silence but we could hear his side of the conversations. The first call was to someone at the police station. He went over each point that Micah had raised and listened quietly to the answer. He made a second call, this one to Hank, and repeated the same questions as he had asked on the first call then listened silently to whatever else Hank was telling him.

My aunt took the opportunity to take muffins out of the warming oven and returned to pass them around. Most of us ate but Micah waited. Thomas had once told us that Micah was not in the habit of raising his voice and the fact that he had done that made it clear to me how upset he truly was. He sat there, looking downward, tugging at his bushy eyebrow. I doubted he was aware he was even doing it.

When the Chief returned, he said, "I'm going back to the scene. Micah, I want you and Johnny here to come with me. Captain Maitland will join us when we get there." He paused and a look of pain passed over his face. "And I want to publicly say, after talking to the responding officer, that I am sorry if a hasty judgment was made, and I will do everything in my power to rectify it."

He held out his hand to Micah who shook it without hesitation. Every person in that room knew the Chief was a good man—they also knew good people could make mistakes.

————

CHAPTER THREE

"A hidden connection is stronger than an obvious one."
Heraclitus of Ephesus

FRIDAY, DECEMBER 24, 1943

AUNT MARGARET LOOKED at me as the men rose to leave and, if I had to guess, I would say she was willing me to stay at the inn. Never mind that I had not been invited to go to Strathmore; that had not stopped me before and we both knew it. Curiosity and questions bubbling up in my mind aside, it so happened that this time, I agreed with her. I said nothing and started to clear the table.

"One more thing." Everyone stopped when Micah spoke. He looked to me and then turned back to the Chief, saying, "I want Miss Harmony to come with us."

Both of my aunts gasped, and I was surprised, too, as he continued.

"Fred knew all about the help she gave you in finding Jack Connawell's killer and he told me one night that if anything suspicious ever happened to him, he wanted her 'on the case', as he put it. When I look back on it now, I think he was sure something was *going* to happen to him, and he wanted me to know how he felt."

I doubted very much that Chief Fielding would ever use the word *help* to describe my part in solving the former police chief's murder. Everyone voiced their opinion of this new development, loudly, but no one asked me what I thought.

My relatives and the Chief seemed of one mind in saying that this crime, if it *was* a crime, was nothing like two months earlier when my brother had been accused of murder. They pointed out that I didn't even know Fred Flores. And, that it was plain wrong—and dangerous—for women to get involved in such things as investigations anyway.

Strangely, as I listened, I found myself uncharacteristically reluctant to get involved, too. Not for their reasons, though. I had come here to talk with Hank about our future and I felt I owed him that courtesy before committing to another investigation. And my family was right. I didn't even know Mr. Flores. As much as I wanted to respect his wishes—and wanted justice for him—I told myself that Hank and the Chief could handle this murder, if indeed it was that.

I was about to express my wish to be on the sidelines when the Chief said, "Miss Harmony, did you know Mr. Flores?"

I shook my head.

The Chief nodded and continued. "Whether Mr. Flores wanted her there or not, Micah, is beside the point.

Captain Maitland asked me if Miss Harmony knew about the body. When I told him yes, he made me promise to keep her away from Strathmore in case there was foul play. He doesn't want her to get involved and I happen to agree with him."

I looked across the table at Aunt Margaret and raised an eyebrow.

She started to say something, thought better of it, and shrugged her shoulders. Uncle Frank cleared his throat and looked away.

Hank making decisions for me went to the heart of our problems. I wanted a relationship where we could discuss things and then, knowing his input, decide what I was going to do. And he could do the same. I was looking for something like I had with my brother, TJ, as far as making career and 'sideline' decisions such as investigations went.

"It's not true that she doesn't know him." Micah turned to me. "Miss Harmony, you met Fred once. Don't you remember?"

I stopped thinking about Hank making decisions for me and turned to Micah. "I'm embarrassed to say that I don't. When would that have been?"

"I can understand it slipping your mind. A lot had happened in Winslet, and you were headed home to Boston. He told me he was one of the people who went to the train station to see you off after you helped with the flu epidemic and solved Chief Connawell's murder. He got a chance to thank you personally for what you did for me *and* everything else. He said it was only for a few minutes, but after that, he told me he felt like he knew you and that you had an 'old soul'."

I caught my breath and so did my aunts, Uncle Frank, and Thomas.

People used to say that about my mother. It was on my seventh or eighth birthday that I asked her what being an *old soul* meant and she said people called someone that who showed wisdom beyond their years. Well, in my eyes, my mother was the smartest, kindest woman I knew so I asked her if she could give me an old soul, too. She laughed and said she was sure one day, I would become one. It was one of those family stories that was repeated and enhanced on my birthday every year, until she died. It had been years since I'd heard that term and I suddenly missed my mother and her wisdom terribly.

When I recovered, I could picture an older man standing right in front of me and shaking my hand before I got on the train. He had the weather-worn, lined face of a man with much experience and the deep blue, haunted eyes that said it wasn't all good.

"Oh yes, of course! You're right. His hand held mine gently, but he looked at me intensely. I never knew his name, but have not forgotten his face, and he gave me the gift you sent. I'm embarrassed I forgot to send you a thank-you note."

Micah looked confused. "Gift? I didn't send you a gift, Miss Harmony. What was it?"

"You know, the wooden carving." Micah still looked confused. "Let me get it."

I retrieved my handbag from the front hall and took out my keys. Attached was a keyring with a wooden disc the size of a quarter hanging from it. On one side of the disc was a Florence Nightingale lamp, carved in relief. On the other side was etched the word *Resolute*.

I showed it to Micah. "I meant to write to you the moment I got home. I often rub the lamp and it's become a symbol to remind me to continue to follow what my heart tells me to do, like when I became a nurse and when I came back to Winslet because I believed TJ needed me."

He smiled sadly and shook his head. "That isn't from me, it's from Fred. He could whittle better than anyone I ever saw." Johnny nodded his agreement. "Miss Harmony, he very much admired and appreciated what you did for the town and me."

I thought for a minute about the look in Fred Flores' eyes and wished I had taken more time to talk with him. While it was true I didn't actually know the man, I wished very much I had. The peace I felt each time my finger outlined the lamp he'd carved was precious to me—the kind of gift a friend gives a friend.

Father Fitz had not said a word. I turned to him, smiled sweetly, and asked, "And what do you think I should do?"

He laughed, took out his silver flask, poured a small amount of whiskey into his coffee, and replied, "Jane, darlin', if there was one thing I learned in October, it was that you will do what you will do. Short of locking you up in jail, these folks have no way of stopping you from fulfilling Fred Flores' request, if that's what you have a mind to do."

My finger gently rubbed over the lamp.

———

CHAPTER FOUR

"*Every man has his secret sorrows which the world knows not and oftentimes we call a man cold when he is only sad.*"
Henry Wadsworth Longfellow

FRIDAY, DECEMBER 24, 1943 – STRATHMORE

WHEN CHIEF FIELDING, Micah, Johnny, Father Fitz and I arrived at the gate to the army base and hospital, the light was beginning to fade. It was getting much colder, and the wind was picking up. It smelled like snow in the air.

The guards asked us to back up off the property, to wait. They had been expecting two people, not five. We would have been four, but Father Fitz had invited himself along because he said there might be a shortage of cool heads when Hank saw me there.

I was sitting up front with the Chief and it was not long

before Hank's long legs ate up the path from the converted hospital to the gate. My friend, PFC Martha Billings, had a hard time keeping pace with him. My heart tripped a bit at the sight of him, so handsome in his uniform, but his jaw was set, and he looked every bit like the officer-in-charge.

He looked my way and, briefly, his face registered his surprise at seeing me. He started to smile as he headed toward me, but I could see the moment he realized why I was there. The smile turned to a frown as I rolled down the window.

"Jane, maybe you didn't get my message. I specifically asked the Chief not to let you get involved in this. Will you please go back to the inn?"

His tone was gentler than I would have expected, but I had no doubt there was steel beneath it.

"No, Hank, I can't. We need to talk about this."

He looked at me for another minute and then went to speak to the Chief who had left the car and stood a few feet in front of it.

I could feel emotion radiating from him. I'd known Hank as a patient, a boyfriend, a fiancé, an *ex*-fiancé, and as a man who had recently apologized and wanted me to forgive him enough to marry him. I had seen him with a gun, very ready to kill in my defense. I had seen him giving orders to the two or three soldiers who seemed to accompany him everywhere. But I had never seen him as the man in charge of a base and hospital and would have liked time to react to this new aspect of his personality before dealing with it.

His greeting to Chief Fielding was abrupt for a normally polite man, just a nod of his head.

"Didn't I make myself clear, Chief? This is a secure base. I only allowed you and Micah here as a courtesy."

We had no trouble hearing the conversation.

"Yes, Captain Maitland, you did."

"Then why are you here now, with all these extra people?" He waved toward the car.

I reached to open the door but felt a restraining hand on my shoulder. "No darlin'. Let the Chief handle this round. This is a game of chess, and he has the advantage of calm thinking on his side."

I exhaled, decided Father Fitz was right, and settled back to watch. I felt conflicted, not exactly sure who I was rooting for.

Chief Fielding calmly replied, "Because Micah would not come without them, and I need him here."

From the back, "That would be *check*."

"Well then, I'm sorry you've wasted your time, but none of you will be coming in today because the army owns the rights to this property and..."

Continuing in the same calm voice, the Chief said, "Actually, Captain, the army leased the Strathmore home and the grounds from the town for the duration of the war. The woods, however, were not included in the lease, which is why the town maintains them. As recently as two months ago, the town removed dead limbs and brush, including a fallen tree near the border of the leased property."

He let that settle for a moment before continuing.

"Since that is the case, Fred Flores may or may not have been a victim of foul play on town property, which means it comes under my jurisdiction."

"And that would be *checkmate*," came the hoarse voice from the back, followed by a soft sneeze.

The two men stood there, staring at each other, until the Chief said, "Look Captain, seems to me we have an equal interest in finding out what happened to Mr. Flores. Why don't we work together, share information, and not get into a territorial battle over who should do what?"

After a short pause, Hank held out his hand and they shook. It was too bad all disagreements—including the terrible war—couldn't be handled that way.

Our car was allowed onto the grounds. We drove around in a semicircle and parked near the entrance to the woods on the other side of the property, almost directly opposite the front gate. A half-dozen soldiers were milling around the spot; they came to attention and saluted when Hank and Martha arrived on foot.

I thought it was interesting that there was no wall between the woods and the hospital grounds. Instead, a very thick, neatly trimmed hedge about my height with a tall, solid, wooden gate which led to the path and woods beyond. The gate had what looked like a shiny new padlock and was clearly marked *Gate 2*.

Hank looked at the soldiers. "Two of you men wait here, the rest come with us."

With that, we passed through the gate and walked about twenty yards into the woods until we came to a small clearing. From that area, three paths—one forward, one to the left and one to the right—went deeper into the woods. We went right and only walked about ten yards before we stopped. In the middle of the path lined with trees and shrubs was a flattened area with broken twigs, crushed leaves and footprints all around it. A soldier was standing on guard there, and stakes in the ground outlined the body-sized area.

"This is where Mr. Flores' dead body was found, face down. The only visible injury when he was turned over was a nasty wound on the right side of his forehead. It was clear that when he fell, he hit that rock."

Hank pointed to a large rock with a dark red stain on one side. Micah couldn't look at it. Hank continued, "There's also another clearing farther ahead you will want to see."

We followed him to a small area bearing many footprints. Another guard and more stakes were there. This time, the marked area was an approximate circle, maybe eight feet in diameter.

"This area was not identified as important when the police first came. They thought they were dealing with a man who had frozen to death and..."

"Yes, Captain, we know. How did you discover it?" The Chief's face held a calm expression as he asked but his posture had stiffened into what looked like a painful position.

"When I came to see the body, I didn't recognize the man. He was not in uniform. I wanted to know what he was doing in the woods and how he'd got here. We started following the trail and came to this clearing.

"It had rained earlier in the week, and the ground was soft. From the footprints, it was clear there had been more than one person here for a meeting. At that point, I was concerned there could be another dead person, so I ordered a search of all three paths."

Micah stepped closer, looked around, and said to Hank, "Where does this path start?"

Hank pointed straight ahead as he answered, "At Gate 1, at the back of the kitchen and dining area."

The Chief addressed himself to Micah. "Looks to me like Mr. Flores came along this path. There are other footprints but there were soldiers all over here once he was found and everything is blurred."

"Why was he found? What made the soldiers come down this path?" I asked.

"Several men entered the woods looking for a Christmas tree to cut down and that's when they found him," Hank answered.

Johnny bent down to look closer at the footprints, but Micah whispered to him and pointed to several spots. They both turned around and started looking at the clumps of surrounding bushes. They found nothing where they first checked but Micah called to the Chief from behind the second.

"See that?"

Micah pointed to what looked to me like an ordinary short stick. He bent over to pick it up, but the Chief stopped him. He was wearing gloves and pulled it out from partway under the brush. It turned out to be the lower part of a hand-carved walking stick with a splintered end. The top part, with a well-worn leather handle, was on the ground farther under the bush.

"That belongs to Fred, and he needed it to walk. He couldn't get very far without it."

Everybody looked from the shrubs to the clearing and back to the shrubs.

The Chief spoke next. "Looks like he saw something over there." He pointed to the clearing. "Something he wasn't meant to see, something someone thought he had to die for. A meeting, maybe? After that, it looks like one person came after Mr. Flores and he hit whoever it was with the stick, breaking off the top part. He left the pieces here and tried to make it to the gate where we came in, but only got as far as where the body was found."

His friend's last few minutes of life were becoming clearer and the look of pain on Micah's face intensified.

At this point, both Chief Fielding and Hank were frowning. A soldier came through a small opening in the shrubs behind Hank and spoke to him quietly. Hank signaled for us all to follow and we did, except for Father Fitz who stayed where we had found the stick.

Not too far from where we had been standing was a lean-to under a huge willow tree, mostly hidden by the long branches. It was built from an odd mixture of wood and crates with a blanket for a door. None of us went inside except the Chief and Hank but it was obviously a storm shelter. From the doorway, I could see two cots with blankets and pillows, one against the left wall and the other against the right. One crate on top of another made a crude table between the beds, candle stubs in sardine cans resting on the top surface. Several books lay in one stack and a pile of newspapers along the back wall. The only other item I could see was a map of Europe pinned to the back wall, with Berlin circled in red and a green line starting in Italy.

Hank and the Chief each bent down to look under a cot. The Chief stood up quickly, but Hank pulled the cot on the right out and called for the flashlight one of the soldiers had brought. He got onto the bed, reached down, and removed a bulky envelope so dirt-smudged it would blend against the stick and wood walls. It was amazing he had seen it.

He stood up and handed it to the Chief, a gesture acknowledging who oversaw the investigation. It was the kind of thing that I admired about Hank—that he always tried to do what he saw as the 'right thing' whether it was what he wanted or not. The Chief looked inside and then showed it to Hank. They came out to see us.

The Chief looked piercingly at Micah and said, "And

what use would a seemingly homeless vagrant have for an army-issued gun that looks to be in pristine condition?"

Micah looked back at the Chief and said nothing.

Hank turned to the Chief.

"The clearing done this fall? Do you know when that was?"

"I didn't come here until October, so it was sometime after that. And before you ask, nobody reported to me that they saw this hut and certainly not this gun."

Johnny cleared his throat. "Excuse me, but I was part of the town clean-up crew those two days. The shed was here but nobody thought anything of it."

Hank's eyebrow almost reached his hairline and Johnny looked nervous.

"And why was that?"

"Because we all knew it was Fred's shack that he sometimes shares with his friend, Cede. He has one in the woods near the park in South Winslet, too. If you look at that map on the wall, you'll see they're following the allies' progress on their way to Germany."

"Who the hell is this Cede and where is he?"

I could hear the frustration mounting in Hank's voice.

Micah answered for him. "Cede is a friend of Fred's who came to Winslet now and then and stayed here with him. I don't know nothin' else about him because Fred never talked about him. I only met him the once and he didn't say a word."

The silence stretched out and became uncomfortable as I could see Hank processing the fact that not one man, but two, had a hut on property next to the base. It was good for this man Cede that he was not within Hank's reach at that moment.

Finally, he turned to the Chief. "I'll need a list of the

people on that clean-up crew. At least we can narrow down who knew about this hut and…"

Micah interrupted Hank and said, "You'd have to put half the town or more on that list, Captain. We all knew. Some of us helped him build it."

In a menacingly calm voice, Hank asked, "If it's such common knowledge, then why did no one ever tell *me*?"

Micah shrugged his shoulders and calmly said, "You never asked."

Hank was out of questions at that point so Micah continued, sounding very sad when he said, "All Fred wanted to do was to live long enough to see the allies bring the German war machine to its knees. As veterans of the Great War, we thought we'd done that in 1918. It was difficult to admit that we had been wrong, *dead* wrong."

IT WAS GETTING VERY COLD, and the light would be gone in a matter of minutes. We headed quietly back down the path. When we got to the place where Fred had died, we stopped and I turned to Hank. "If someone called for help from here, would anyone on the base hear him?"

His response was to call out for the soldiers who remained at the gate to join us. We waited. No response. He shouted again, even louder—still no response.

Micah had one last question for the Chief.

"Did the police make a list of everythin' Fred had on him?"

"Yes, that's standard procedure."

"What did they find?"

"He had four dollars, some change, a train schedule, a handkerchief, and a pair of socks in his pockets as I remember. That was it."

"They found no medal?" asked Micah.

"Medal? No, why?"

Micah and Johnny looked at each other and then started looking around the area as he gave his response. "He wore a Silver Star pinned to his undershirt. Always. He'd never leave it anywhere. We were each awarded one during the last war and we made a pact that if one of us were ever in trouble, we'd send ours to the other. He might have tried to use it to warn me."

At that point, we all spread out to look. I was using the flashlight I had brought with me and was lucky, finding the medal about twenty feet away from where Fred had fallen. It had landed in a bush and tumbled down inside a way, but my flashlight reflected off the metal.

I reached in and unsnagged it from a branch, then called to the others and held it out the palm of my hand. In the beam of the flashlight, the attached ribbon was a bit shredded on the edges and half-covered in leaves, but the shape of the medal was visible. Micah took it into his hands and gently brushed away the debris to reveal the Silver Star.

"Chief Fielding," said Micah, "if Fred threw this, his most prized possession, into the bushes, he was not expectin' to come out of these woods alive."

———

CHAPTER FIVE

"It's never wrong to do the RIGHT thing."
Mark Twain

FRIDAY, DECEMBER 24, 1943

IT WAS a somber group of investigators who left the woods and headed toward the Chief's car. At the gate into the woods, several jeeps were positioned in a semicircle with their headlights on since it would be dark in minutes. The field lights could not be used during blackout hours.

Hank gently touched my arm and asked me to wait for him—he wanted to talk with me and would see I got back to the inn later.

As he went over to wrap up with the Chief, I sought out Father Fitz. Micah and Johnny joined us.

"Who is Cede?" I asked Micah and Johnny.

Micah answered, "All I know is what I told the captain. He's no trouble, doesn't even talk."

Johnny shook his head. "I never met the man and don't remember Fred talking about him."

I made a mental note to learn more about this Cede.

It was getting colder by the minute, and we were pressed for time. I turned to Father Fitz. "Why didn't you come to the hut?"

"I've seen it before, with Mr. Flores. I brought him some food when he was sick."

"You did? How did you get past the guard?"

He laughed. "Same as he did. There's a back way into the woods that I'll tell you about later." He could see I wanted to pursue the discussion, but he held up his hand, and changed the subject. "That small clearing near where Micah spotted the walking stick?"

I nodded.

"I took a good look," Father Fitz said. "There were two sets of prints on the ground different than the others. Deeper. You know how the weather has been warmer than usual this past week? At least until today, that is. Because of that, we can see these impressions. One was a soldier's boots, smaller than the rest. One was civilian shoes, and the wearer leans heavier on his right leg than left. You could see that they went separate ways—the smaller prints toward the house, running, and the larger, deeper prints toward the bush where Fred was hiding."

Micah said, "I don't know how you figured all that out, but we need to tell the Chief."

"Tell me what?"

The Chief and Hank had quietly walked up to us.

Father Fitz repeated what he had seen.

When Hank started to ask why he hadn't shown them,

he replied that Hank and the Chief were in the hut until it was too dark to see the ground, but he did show the soldier on guard at the clearing.

"And why would a priest need to learn how to read footprints?" asked the Chief, trying, but failing, to sound casual.

"Well now," said Father Fitz, "I wasn't always a priest and in some parts of the world, it is important to know who has been where."

He turned away to sneeze and winked at me.

"And where would you learn such a skill?" The Chief wasn't quite ready to let it go.

He exaggerated his brough and said, "Ah Chief Fielding, darlin'. Sure, I learned at my father's knee, where all the important lessons in life are taught."

After that, Micah, Johnny, and Father Fitz got into the car. The Chief nodded to me, slid into the driver's seat, and slowly drove toward the gate.

Hank and I walked silently to the house's main entrance, with Martha several feet behind us. Hank's hand rested gently on my back, and I could feel the tension radiating from him.

We walked through the over-sized wooden door and from the dark into a large, brightly lit foyer. It took my eyes a moment to adjust.

There was a desk directly to the left and Martha went right to it. From there, she had a clear view of the door, the stairs going up to the second floor, and a series of doors down the corridor, all closed at that moment. Martha had told me she checked the credentials of those entering, escorted visitors to their destination, kept a record of how long they were in the building, and answered calls for Hank. Basically, nobody wandered around unknown and unescorted. I thought of the numbers of people who came and went daily at MGH and smiled at the idea of someone trying to do Martha's job there.

Hank led me farther down the hallway to a door on the right that opened to his office. Before I had a chance to take my coat off, he put his hands on my shoulders, smiled and said, "Let me look at you." Then he kissed me soundly and scooped me up into a bear hug.

His kiss, his arms around me, being pressed closely against him, the smell of his aftershave mingled with a pine smell from the woods—they all led to a pleasant buzzing in my head. I didn't want him to ever let me go.

We stayed that way for a minute until, smiling, I slipped my arms around his neck, looked up at him and said, "I thought you didn't want me here."

"The soldier in me didn't. The man who loves you couldn't wait to see you, although I had hoped it would be in different circumstances."

He continued holding me for a minute longer and then helped me off with my coat; the two of us sat on a couch along the left wall. Before we could start talking, there was a knock on the door. Once he'd stepped outside the room, I took the opportunity to examine where he worked. Hank as an army captain was a man I had only seen in glimpses.

Directly opposite the door, facing it, was a long desk with the few items on it aligned neatly, as I would expect from Hank. Behind it was what must be a large window, but blackout curtains covered it, and beside the window, on brass poles, stood the US flag, an army flag, and what was likely a regimental one. In front of the desk were two wooden chairs, the kind that did not invite lingering, while across from the couch was a wall of file cabinets, each with a lock on it. The room had a very official feel since there were no personal pictures or mementos. Serious business was conducted in a room like this.

Hank came back, sat down, and took my hand. "Jane, I didn't want you in the middle of this mess. Why did you come?"

Rather than answer him, I asked my own question. "I heard that you told Chief Fielding not to bring me. Tell me, why didn't you ask to talk to me instead of making that decision for me?"

"At that point, there were a group of people in here, and another call on hold from Washington. I couldn't take the time."

"All right." I didn't like it, but understood it. My job had very busy moments, too. I had leapt to the conclusion that he was telling me what to do, and I needed to be more careful about doing that. "Look, I realize this is a bad situation for you, and I'm sorry for that, but it's a lot worse situation for Fred Flores and Micah and I'm here for the two of them."

I probably should have let it go at that for the moment, but didn't.

I took a deep breath and plowed ahead. "Hank, whether I'm your girlfriend, fiancée, or wife, you need to know that *I* have the final say about what I will or will not do—not you. And I do not expect to be telling *you* what to do, either."

He ran his right hand through the hair that the army had left him, stood, and paced back and forth.

"I've thought of what it was going to be like to see you again and this is nothing like it, believe me. When I talked with the Chief, all I could think about was how close I came to losing you in October, and I don't want to ever feel that way again."

He paused and I could see the worry in his eyes. I

wanted to say something to make him feel better, but didn't know what.

"This is no game, Jane. There are things going on here," he waved his hand to indicate the building, "that you know nothing about. Things that make what may have been a clandestine meeting and murder very, very important and dangerous. You were lucky you made it through your last stab at playing detective. I need to know what happened in those woods and I will need to give it my full attention until we find out. I can't be worrying about my fiancée while..."

"Fiancée? Aren't you getting a little ahead?"

"What? The last time we spoke on the phone, before that silly argument, you said you had some good news to tell me. I assumed that was what you meant."

My conscience tweaked a bit because that was exactly what I'd meant at the time. But I had not actually said it and since then his behavior had set off all the old warning bells in my head. We'd argued during several phone calls. He'd said everything would be fine when we could sit down in person and talk but I knew I could not live a life in which someone else—even someone I loved—wanted to tell me what I could and could not do.

We needed to resolve the issue.

Another knock sounded on the door. Hank swore softly and opened it. I could hear Martha apologize for interrupting, but he was needed upstairs.

I stood and put on my coat. When he came back to me, I said, "Right now, neither one of us has time to talk. Do you think you will be able to come to the inn for Christmas dinner tomorrow?"

Hank quickly kissed me on the cheek and answered, "I'm hoping to be there," on his way out the door.

Martha waited as I quietly closed the door to the office.

We were walking toward the front door when I heard a scream from upstairs.

"Qualcuno mi aiuti!"

I watched as Hank, taking the stairs two by two, reached the top and disappeared.

"What language is that?"

"Italian. These men are often in pain, and they cry out. It's heartbreaking to hear."

"Yes, it is." I hesitated and then said, "Look Martha, nobody around here is stupid. With all the security, the bars on the second-floor windows, and so many soldiers posted in a small place, there are rumors in town that you're holding prisoners of war here and the army is afraid there may be an attempt to break them out."

She stared straight at me but didn't answer.

I blew out a frustrated breath and waved my hand in a dismissive gesture. "All right, all right. You can't say anything. I get it. But if anyone in town, like Thomas and my aunt, were in any danger from those men upstairs, you would tell me, right?"

"Yes, if any one of the men upstairs were a threat to you or the town, I would tell you, I swear." She changed subjects. "How did it go with the Captain? Good to see him again?"

Martha and I had become friends in October when she had helped me prove that TJ was innocent, and we'd gotten to know each other quite well. She knew Hank from the viewpoint of a soldier and commanding officer, worlds apart from my own view.

"Different time, different circumstances, same problem. Honestly, I don't know what we're going to do. If I didn't love the big lug so much, this would be easier." She laughed,

I sighed, and asked, "Are you available to drive me to the inn or should I call Thomas?"

She shook her head again. "Captain Maitland might need me for whatever is going on up there. I dare not leave. But I can call the garage and Sergeant Richmond or one of the others will drive you home."

As she reached for the phone, I said, "No, please, let me call Thomas. You do what you need to do. I'll walk down to the gate and wait there for him."

I called and he said he would be right along to fetch me.

I said goodbye to Martha and stepped outside, smiling at the word 'fetch'. My mother never told us to 'go get' anything, TJ and I were always sent to fetch whatever she needed. I walked along, musing at how one simple word could bring back a flood of memories. Lost in thought, I had reached the halfway point to the gate, the darkest part of the road, when suddenly, a large shape came out of the shadows and stepped in front of me.

Before I even thought about it, or could properly position myself, I called out for help, and then wildly swung at the shape with my right arm, completely missing, and falling forward.

Two strong hands grasped my wrists, firmly. "Whoa, whoa. Slow down, ma'am."

As I pulled back, bright lights came on all along the path, and several armed soldiers rushed toward us.

It turned out the dark shadow was a sergeant named John Richmond, known to the men who had come running. They stopped pointing their weapons at us and began to laugh and taunt him.

"What's a-matter, Richmond, can't get a date? Gotta scare 'em into it now?"

"What happened, Richmond? Did the lady tell you to take a powder?"

He ignored them and continued to look at me. He was a tall, handsome man who obviously had no need to resort to attacking a woman to get her attention. I could feel myself blush from my overreaction.

"Strathmore has become a dangerous place lately, ma'am. You need to watch where you are going—you never know who might be around. But I'm here and always ready to help, all right?"

Everything he said was appropriate but instead of being relieved, I had the feeling the man was toying with me; I didn't like it. And he held my wrists longer than necessary. I was about to reply when one of the soldiers called, "Attention!"

Suddenly, Hank was beside me, looking at the men in front of him. They all saluted.

He turned to me and said, "Jane, what happened here?"

"It's obviously a misunderstanding. I was walking to the front gate and thinking about something when the sergeant here was suddenly right in front of me. I thought he was going to attack me so swung out at him."

He turned to Sergeant Richmond. "Anything to add, Sergeant?"

"I was walking along the path, saw the lady, and said good evening to her. I thought she had seen and heard me coming but apparently, she did not." He turned to me and said, "I am sorry, ma'am, I had no intentions of frightening you."

Hank looked at me. I apologized too, and the incident was over. "You men are dismissed."

Hank turned to Martha, who was behind us, and told

her to have the lights turned off before the Air Raid Warden came around yelling about rules and regulations.

As he did that, I heard one of the soldiers whisper to Sergeant Richmond, "Sure, scare the hell out of the Captain's girlfriend. Nice way to..." The rest was lost as they walked away.

Hank and I started walking toward the gate.

"What were you doing out here in the dark alone?"

I explained about calling Thomas instead of taking the ride Martha had offered. I didn't need to see the look on his face, Hank's jaw set loudly. My first trip to Strathmore ended as it began, with Hank frowning at me.

THOMAS WAS WAITING at the gate. I thanked the guard who had come to help and slid quickly into Thomas' truck.

"Everything go well with you and the Captain?"

"Why are things always so complicated between men and women?"

He laughed and we drove back to the inn in silence.

Soft snowflakes began to fall on the windshield as we drove. After a week of unseasonably warm weather, it looked as though the children might get that *White Christmas* that Bing Crosby sang about. I smiled.

He dropped me off at the front door and drove the truck to park it at the side of the inn while I walked up the inn stairs to speak to the man sitting there.

CARRIAGE LANTERN INN

"Hello, Jane." Mike Evans, the town doctor, stood up

from the chair on the right side of the large porch and came over to where I stood. "Hope I didn't scare you."

Fortunately, the dim streetlights had cast enough of a glow for me to know he was there. Being startled twice in a row would have unnerved me.

I smiled and said, "No, Mike, I saw you. What are you doing out here? It's cold."

"Waiting for you. I have news. I called a friend, a pathologist at Sedgwick Hospital. He went to the morgue and did an external exam on Mr. Flores. He fractured his skull when he hit a rock on the ground, like the officers said, but that didn't kill him. Jane, there's a knife wound in his back. It's pretty clear to my friend and me, it was murder, intentional or not."

"Why would someone kill him? And why didn't the officers notice a knife hole or blood?"

"I think he was killed because of whatever he saw in the woods. As for the police, my friend said Mr. Flores' jacket was old, dirty and tattered, with many holes. Easy to miss a single hole."

"Does Micah know?"

"He's the one who asked me to tell you." He paused for a minute and then said, "Are you going to get involved in another murder investigation? Because I'm sure the Captain and your aunts and uncles and even TJ won't approve."

"Tell me, would that stop you?"

"Hell, no!"

"Well, it won't stop me either as long as I think I can help."

"Thought you'd say that. I'm available for whatever I can do."

I knew it would cause problems with Hank, but I was indeed going to investigate Mr. Flores' death, with or without the Chief's or Hank's help. I started thinking about how to proceed when Mike coughed, and I snapped out of my reverie and opened the door to the inn. It was time to try to share as normal a Christmas Eve as was possible during wartime, never mind the start of a murder investigation.

THERE WAS excitement in the voices coming from the dining room. We hung up our coats and followed the happy sounds to family and friends who were sitting down to eat. Mike sat beside Catherine, my cousin and his future wife, as well as the mother of his child. I went to my place near the head of the table, between Aunt Margaret and where Aunt Ida would sit.

"What's happened? You all sound delighted."

It was a wonderful thing to hear people sound so cheerful, so unlike those dealing with a war, the end of which nobody could predict.

Aunt Ida brought in the platter of turkey at that point, set it on the table, and said, "Jane, you missed it! Russ called! He sounded so well it was wonderful to hear his voice. And he has leave coming in two weeks!" She was laughing and crying all at one time. "He plans to get here for however long he can during his leave or Thomas said we could meet him wherever would work better."

She used the hem of her apron to wipe away the tears that she couldn't stop. Thomas, who had been standing behind her, moved forward. He put his arm around her shoulders and kissed her cheek in a rare display of public affection.

He continued. "Russ said he spoke to James a week ago, quite by accident, but couldn't tell us the circumstances. He said James is well, sends his love to all, but isn't sure when he will get leave. He asked if the aunts could keep the cookies and socks coming and they both wanted to know if Jane had seen or heard about any of their friends."

I couldn't speak for a few minutes. Thomas and Aunt Ida's sons were younger than TJ and me, but we were still close growing up. Somehow, when they too had enlisted right after Pearl Harbor, it had made the war so much more personal to me.

Blackouts, rationing, and inconveniences were nothing like the worry of having someone out there, some in places we'd never even heard of. It was Jimmy's room that was assigned to me each time I came to the inn and when I touched the bureau or lay on the bed, I could picture his shy smile and mop of unruly red hair.

Thomas got the Christmas Eve dinner started. "Mother, let's sit down, say grace and eat this good food with family and friends."

Father Fitz was at church, but we read the grace he had written for Christmas.

Dear Father in Heaven,
Thank you for the food we have before us,
thank you for the people with whom we share it,
and thank you for giving us the strength
to carry on and do our part
so that right will prevail.
Amen.

TWENTY-FOUR HOURS EARLIER, my life had seemed simple, organized. We were coming to Winslet for

TJ's wedding. I had thought I could pass on being involved in the latest investigation.

And, I had hoped that somehow, Hank and I would work things out so that we could marry, even though I couldn't see how it was possible.

Then, in one day, the wedding could *not* take place; I'd been asked to help in what was turning out to be another murder investigation and I realized that Hank and I had an even longer way to go than I had thought if we were ever going to get married.

———

CHAPTER SIX

"There are some things you learn best in calm, and some in storm."
Willa Cather

SATURDAY, DECEMBER 25, 1943 – CHRISTMAS DAY

CHRISTMAS DAWNED COLD. The night before's snowflakes had turned into several inches of snow that blanketed the town, making it look like that Currier and Ives print I had pictured in my mind. People in their Sunday best headed toward churches in horse-drawn sleighs, in cars, or on foot. Someone had recently said there were no atheists in foxholes, and it looked as if that was true for those waiting for the troops to return, too.

TJ had called early to wish us all a Merry Christmas and it had been wonderful to hear his voice. When it was my turn to speak with him, I asked what they were doing at Strathmore while they were all confined. All he had a chance to say was that they were beefing up security and then it was time to let the next soldier call home.

My aunts, uncles, and I, snuggly in our warm coats, walked to church. Breakfast and exchanging presents would wait until after our arrival back at the inn.

We passed children already outside at 8:30 a.m., wearing what looked like new hand-knitted hats and mittens and sliding on sleds or large cardboard box pieces that had been broken in for them. They laughed and called out *Merry Christmas* as we passed, and we returned the greetings.

It was so idyllic, the best of small-town life. For a few moments, it was possible to forget about war and murder, and about problems that were wanting solutions.

We waved to other families heading to the lovely old church. I was a 'lapsed' Catholic for lack of a better term. I had decided that the church of my childhood was the perfect place and this visit the perfect time for me to find out whether that was going to be a permanent or temporary state; I had been angry with God since my mother died and realized I owed it to her to at least try to make peace.

ST. AGNES' CHURCH

St. Agnes' was a small, white, wooden building with two huge front doors bordered by tall, slim, stained-glass windows on both sides. A large wreath made of pinecones and finished with a red bow hung in the center of each door and organ music drifted softly through the open door each time people entered the church.

A stone path led to the church and on the lawn, to the

left of the entrance, was a large hand-carved creche scene, the same one that had been there when I was growing up and attending Mass with TJ and my mother. I walked closer to examine the paint on the blue robe of one of the Three Wise Men. The scratches left by Freddie Quill's sled had been repaired. I smiled as I remembered that day. He was fooling around with two other boys and his sled skidded right into the statue, knocking it down. The other boys ran but Freddie stood there frozen, terrified his name would be on the priest's bad list.

I was standing back a way, but could sense his dread. Luckily, his fears did not materialize. After numerous Our Fathers and Hail Marys, and a summer of mowing the church lawn, his trespass was forgiven. But I did see Freddie's name on a list this October—the large display board covered with glass in front of the park named those Winslet residents currently in military service, those who had been killed, and those missing in action.

I cried when I saw that Freddie had lost his life in Sicily.

As we joined the line to enter the church, I saw that Father Fitz was nodding good morning to people but not chatting much. He kept looking over at me and I got the sense he was waiting for me. When I reached him, he took my hand and leaned a little closer.

I could hear the urgency in his raspy voice.

Father Fitzgerald was not your average priest, not by a long shot. His dark-brown eyes twinkled when he was either being funny or intense. It was the latter at that moment.

"I need to talk to you after Mass, Jane. Please wait for me."

He gave no indication of what he wanted, and my aunt

and uncle had moved along so I joined them. Nodding my head yes, I proceeded into the church to attend my first Christmas Mass in fifteen years. I looked around at the familiar sights. The altar was draped in new cloths, but the same candlesticks my mother and I used to polish were there; in an alcove to the right of the altar was a statue of Mary with several tiers of devotional candles in front of her. Most were lit even before the service, likely for those away fighting. There was a similar alcove on the opposite side of the church, with a statue of St. Agnes, the patron saint of young girls. I used to light one of her candles every Saturday after confession, praying that my father would not come home drunk again that night. Sometimes, but not often, my prayers were answered.

Father Fitz was as efficient at serving the Mass as he was at everything he did. Even with the hoarseness still in his voice, you could clearly hear the Latin words. Somehow, the Irish lilt added to them made them seem warmer, more meaningful. For his sermon, he did not go to the pulpit. Instead, he stood halfway between the altar and the congregation with the members of the all-female choir gathered behind him. He read the Christmas Story according to St. Luke, then added his rich baritone as the choir sang *Angels We Have Heard on High*. It was a beautiful sound that filled the small church and my heart. I sensed my mother's presence and felt a gentle easing of the anger toward God that I had been harboring for too long.

I knew Mother would be pleased.

As soon as Father Fitz finished shaking hands and wishing his parishioners a Merry Christmas, he came over to join me. My aunts and uncles had gone on ahead to the inn.

He smiled gently and asked, "And how did it go, being at Mass?"

"It was a very peaceful feeling. I'm glad I came."

"'Tis a start, a good start."

I was hoping he would let the subject of religion go at that, and he did. His smile changed to a serious expression.

"Now, to other things. I've asked around, thinking about those shoe prints we saw, the ones not made by army boots. No strangers have been seen in Winslet this past week, but once I mentioned Fred Flores, I learned a lot about the man.

"It seems Micah and our Mr. Reddy were both in Mr. Flores' squad in France in 1918. After Mr. Flores was wounded, he went to a hospital in England and then nobody saw or heard from him until after the war. Because of the strong friendship that the three men had developed, Mr. Flores and his wife, Iris, relocated to Springfield, down the road a way, and the trio saw each other over the years until Iris died. After that, Mr. Flores gave his house to the veteran who had been boarding with them and became a recluse, living in huts, earning whatever money he needed at odd jobs. The two men I spoke to had nothing but good things to say about Mr. Flores, especially his heroism and patriotism."

I stood there, absorbing the information, adding to my knowledge of Mr. Flores the man, rather than the victim. Then a thought came to me.

"I'm surprised Hank didn't make you promise not to help me, too."

I watched the twinkle come back into his eyes. He started fingering the rosary beads he held in his hands.

"Sure, he did call and ask last night. I do remember saying something like I could understand why he would feel that way."

I arched my eyebrow.

"Well now, I didn't exactly swear to secrecy."

"Father, what do you mean by *exactly*?"

"Coincidentally, I had myself a true coughing fit right at that moment." He smiled as he patted his chest.

"That coughing fit will cost you five Our Fathers and ten Hail Marys, *Father* Fitz. Remind me when I ask you for a promise to make sure that your fingers aren't crossed."

We both laughed but I sobered quickly as I again thought of Mr. Flores.

Father Fitz and I said goodbye and I headed back to the inn, thinking how the new information fit in with the picture I was building about Winslet's most recent murder victim.

My mind raced as I navigated the streets. I was so lost in thought I walked right into a tall, heavy-set man who had exited a black car and stepped directly in front of me. I would have fallen backward if not for help from a second man, in uniform, who had rushed around from the other side of the car in time to catch me.

Before I could apologize, my 'victim' immediately started berating me, in inappropriate language. Christmas or not, I was about to let him know what I thought of him and his heritage until I looked at his face and gasped. It was Albert Winslet.

He recognized me at the same time and scowled. "Of course, it would be someone like you who would walk right into me. You never did know your place. What are you doing back in Winslet? Did they kick you out of Boston?" He didn't wait for a reply, instead turning away quickly, as if I had a contagious disease.

I called to his back, "And a Merry Christmas to you, too, *Uncle* Albert."

There were all kinds of things I thought of adding but before I could, the army major who had rescued me said, "Am I right in assuming you are Jane Harmony, Mr. Winslet's niece?"

"Yes, I am."

"Well, Mr. Winslet said several times on the drive here that the last two people he wanted to see in Winslet were you and Doctor Evans. He is expecting to see the doctor when he goes into the house which has put him in a bad mood—and now, he's seen you, too. His reaction fit his words." He smiled at me. "Please don't let him get to you. Hopefully, we won't be in town for long."

I turned and watched my uncle walk up the stairs to his former house, where Catherine, Mike and the baby now lived.

CARRIAGE LANTERN INN

There was no way I could warn Catherine of what was coming so I thanked the Major and hurried on my way to the inn as quickly as I could. I burst through the door, out of breath, not even stopping to take off my snowy boots. My heart was pumping hard, and I needed to see Thomas.

They were all in the kitchen and turned when they heard me.

"Jane, dear, what is..."

"Thomas! Your brother Albert is at his old house with some soldiers. I couldn't warn..."

Without a word, he headed to the coat rack to get his jacket.

Aunt Margaret removed her apron and headed to the front closet. "Don't you dare leave without me! There's no telling what that... that man will do."

I turned to Aunt Ida. "I'm going with them. I'll help with dinner when we get back."

"Jane, this meeting has been coming for a long time. It's personal. Maybe you should leave it to them."

"I won't interfere with anything they have to say but Uncle Albert made it personal for me, too."

My Uncle Frank started singing *We Wish You a Merry Christmas* in his distinctive, croaking voice, and Aunt Ida threw a dish towel at him.

The three of us piled into Thomas' truck and drove to Catherine's in silence. When we walked up the path and started to climb the stairs to the house, we could hear the baby wailing through the closed door. We hurried in without even bothering to knock.

Right there, in the foyer, it was as though Albert Winslet was holding court, directing orders all around.

"Catherine, do something with that screaming child. Evans, get out of my house and don't ever come back. You two," he pointed to two soldiers who had come with him, "make sure he and anything he owns is out of here. You can throw it all in the street for all I care."

Mike was struggling to get past the guards to reach Albert and I could tell it wasn't giving him a hug that Mike had in mind.

Aunt Margaret pushed her way through to Catherine and baby Elizabeth and escorted them into the parlor, where she helped settle the crying infant down.

"Exactly who do you think you are, Albert?"

Thomas' softer tone was in sharp contrast to Albert's loud commands, but it got people's attention. Everyone froze in their places and turned toward us.

"Well, of course you would rush right over here. You and Margaret always did defend Hannah's... *child*."

Everyone knew he had not used the word he was thinking.

"Answer my question."

"If you must know, I had to leave my loving family and come here on Christmas Day because an incompetent Captain Maitland can't deal with a falling-down drunk hobo dying on a small, temporary US Army base."

I gasped at his cruelty and wanted to give him a piece of my mind, but Thomas gave my arm a warning squeeze.

"And what does the self-described 'financial whiz of Washington' have to do with the army base?"

This time, Albert threw back his head and laughed.

"Shows what you know! I *am* the Strathmore Army Base. Now get out of here, all of you, and leave me in peace."

The soldiers moved Mike out of the way and Albert headed through the parlor toward the dining room, but Catherine rose from the sofa, holding the now sleeping Elizabeth, and stood in his way.

"Father, what has happened to you? Where is the man who was very good at his job but still valued his family? Where is the man who spoke to me about the war so honestly it brought me to tears in Washington? And why haven't you spared even one glance at your granddaughter?"

Catherine was struggling hard not to cry.

Albert got into Catherine's face and said, "Nothing has happened to *me*. It's you who have changed. You used to be the kind of daughter a man could be proud of but now... now you choose to associate with people like them." He gestured toward Thomas and me. "And you're a married woman living with another man. As to that child? Your mother and I have no interest in it. As the old saying goes, you made your bed..."

Thomas, Mike, the Major, and I all moved toward him, but Aunt Margaret got there first.

She slipped around Catherine and slapped Albert hard across the face.

"I should have done that years ago. And after this performance, you should be grateful I don't carry a gun."

The soldiers let Mike loose and went to grab my aunt but the Major stepped in.

"Stand down." He turned to the rest of us. "This has gone too far. I'm asking you all to leave, now. Take what you need for the child and go."

Mike glared at him. "Is that an *order*, Major?"

"At the moment, it's a request and I would like to keep it that way."

"*He* may be making a request, but *I'm* giving you all an order," said Albert. "You have twenty minutes to get your-selves and anything you need out of here or I will bring charges for trespassing and assault."

He proceeded to the dining room and sat down, but not before he got in a final jab.

"Oh Catherine, by the way, Joseph Hoffman is on his way to Winslet to plan the future with *his* wife and child."

Thomas took a minute to call Aunt Ida at the inn and the rest of us got to work putting together those things that Catherine, Elizabeth, and Mike would need. We were out of the house in the required twenty minutes, and back at the inn in a few more.

Aunt Ida was waiting for us at the front door. The ladies entered first. Behind us, Mike and Thomas brought in suitcases and several boxes. Mike was reluctant to leave but he needed to join Father Fitz for joint Christmas rounds on his sick and elderly parishioners. He kissed Catherine goodbye and left by the front door.

Catherine spoke to Aunt Ida. "Thomas invited us to stay here. Do you mind the extra people? We'll try not to..."

Our aunt hugged her and said, "Oh hush. Of course, we don't mind. Jane, could you help them move in while I finish the preparations for dinner?"

Knowing she was giving us a chance to talk alone, I appreciated her thoughtfulness. And, it seemed, allowing private time for us was also on Aunt Margaret's mind.

She had her coat off and stepped up to take the baby from Catherine. "And I'll settle this little bundle of joy in the bassinet in James' room for a nap while you two get the bedroom ready." I heard her cooing to the baby as she walked away. "Did that mean old Albert scare you?"

Thomas, Catherine, and I had the suitcases and boxes upstairs quickly. He turned to leave but Catherine asked him to wait.

"That was a really unpleasant scene with my father. Do we have to discuss it at Christmas dinner?"

"If I know Margaret, she'll have my wife and Frank caught up in no time. And Mike will do the same with Father Fitz. I'll take the Chief aside and tell him." Thomas gave her and Elizabeth one of his rare big hugs and gave me one for good measure. "Albert is not going to ruin this Christmas, don't you worry. Major Genese—he introduced himself when he came outside and spoke to me—asked me to update Captain Maitland, to warn him that Albert was here and angry so I'm going downstairs to call him now."

AFTER THE REST of the guests arrived and we'd sat down to eat, it seemed that Catherine had worried for nothing. We were all determined to share our meal as pleasantly as we could. Father Fitz repeated the lovely grace he had written, and conversation centered on the delicious meal. It was turkey and all the familiar trimmings. In exchange for Thomas bringing a local farmer's produce into Haymarket Square in Boston once a month, the man provided turkeys for the inn on holidays. The vegetables came from the inn's large Victory Garden. The herbs for the stuffing had been dried by hanging them off the rafters in the unheated pantry where the potatoes and squash had been stored in bushel baskets since they were picked, while the green beans and onions had been canned late in the summer. Aunt Margaret and I had made the two apple pies along with the stack of mincemeat turnovers waiting in the kitchen and brought them with us. From some mysterious source, Father Fitz produced two bottles of wine. We were grateful for everything we had and that we were together.

Aunt Margaret asked if she could toast her friends in Boston. We all looked a bit confused until she said, "My friends at the Boston Red Cross Volunteers told me it was lovely that we got to leave the big, bad city and come to the sleepy little town of Winslet, where nothing ever happens. Perceptive, weren't they?"

We laughed and raised our glasses to preconceived ideas.

———

CHAPTER SEVEN

"Only one link of the chain of destiny can be handled at a time."
Sir Winston Churchill

SATURDAY, DECEMBER 25, 1943 – CHRISTMAS DAY

WITH THE TOAST FINISHED, conversation turned to our heartfelt relief and gratitude that Winston Churchill had recovered from his second bout of pneumonia. The radio announcer said he had been well enough to meet with General Eisenhower and other allied commanders at his headquarters in Tunis, Tunisia, today. The idea of having to continue the war without him was unthinkable, especially since we were all hoping the invasion of Europe would come soon.

After dinner, as we served pie, Christmas pudding, and

coffee in the parlor to the menfolk, they began talking about the anticipated allied forces' invasion of Europe that would occur as soon as weather over the English Channel permitted—likely May or June.

Rumors were rife and the newspapers and radio shows were full of speculation about what would hopefully be the end of Hitler. We frequently talked about it at home and, when I was at work, questions swirled through almost every conversation as I passed by tables in the cafeteria at work. When would it happen? What would be the allies' attack route? How many of our men would go? And most importantly, how many would come home? Anxiety had been with us all during the war years, but now, war-weary people were grasping at hope—hope for peace—and the only way to get it seemed to be an all-out invasion of Europe by the Allies.

We left them to talk and made short work of the cleaning up. When we rejoined the men, Thomas gave a brief account of Albert's return to Winslet, including exactly what Albert had said about Fred Flores' death. I had heard that Albert's attitude and words often made people angry, but this time, I watched it as it happened.

"That man has needed a horse-whipping and I should have given it to him a long time ago."

Uncle Frank's face was red as he spoke, but nobody argued the point. Frankly, I think we all agreed with him.

Chief Fielding, sounding disgusted, said, "We got a call several days ago notifying us that Albert was coming to Winslet and that my office should be 'on call' for whatever may be needed."

That was the cause of some not very Christmas-like comments from the group and it took the combined charms of Aunt Ida and Father Fitz to calm people down and send them on their way to enjoy the rest of the day.

Thomas let us know he had already called and warned Hank what was coming. I planned to call him later if he was not able to come to the house.

By four o'clock, everyone except those staying at the inn had left.

Catherine and the baby were upstairs for a nap so my aunts, uncles, and I decided to exchange Christmas gifts. With the war on, and the fact that none of us really needed anything, we'd agreed to keep gifts down to one each and had decided who bought for whom based on whether someone had something specific in mind.

Aunt Margaret received a beautifully framed photograph Aunt Ida had discovered in the attic, a shot of her together with her brothers and sister when they were all in their teens. It was easy to identify each of them—Aunt Margaret, Uncle Albert, Thomas, and my mother, Hannah.

She thanked us and said, "This picture will help me to remember what seemed like more innocent times."

Uncle Frank was an avid fisherman and Thomas had found a specific rod that Uncle Frank had wanted for a long time. He tried to explain the intricacies of why it was so wonderful but—upon receiving only blank looks in return— he finally thanked Thomas and let it go at that.

For Aunt Ida, Uncle Frank had to go out to his car and bring in the gift we had purchased. It was wrapped in the funny papers and a red bow. The look on Aunt Ida's face when she realized what we had brought her was priceless. It was a radio for the kitchen, where she spent so much time, and Thomas brought in a small table he had refinished to put it on.

"Oh my, this is such a luxury! I can listen to music or

one of my daily shows while I work. All I need is more sugar and I could bake up a storm!"

She cried happy tears and hugged each one of us. It was so rare to see her or any of my relatives cry that I didn't know what to say or do.

Thomas' gift came from all of us. For years, he had been working on a large diorama of Winslet as it looked in the summer of 1915. He had converted a broken-down pool table into the base for his town and painstakingly added handmade houses, stores, benches or churches to it each year. As children, TJ and I had loved it, especially after he added the working train, the engine of which sent out puffs of steam and the streetlamps that illuminated downtown in a soft glow when the lights in the cellar were turned down.

Thomas had let us paint our own house the year he made that.

The grandson of one of our neighbors in Boston taught Uncle Frank, Aunt Margaret, and me how to make scale models from the pictures of two older Winslet houses and St Agnes' Church that we drew from memory. Model rail-roads came in different sizes and Thomas' was in what was known as HO scale. It was very exacting to make everything the right size but it turned out to be a fun project for us all as we listened to music on the radio. All three of us had a part in each project, and we gave them as much detail as we could, including curtains for the windows. Aunt Ida made the stained-glass windows for St. Agnes' Church out of melted candy.

Thomas was delighted and didn't even try to hide a big grin.

Vic appeared, came over to me, rubbed my leg, and sat down. My gift was last and, while very nice, was also bitter-sweet. They gave me a wristwatch with a leather strap.

Some of the nurses I worked with had them but most on my ward still preferred pendant watches, the kind that women, especially nurses, had been pinning to their uniforms for many years.

The faces were upside down—the twelve at the bottom —so you could see the time or count a pulse by looking down, even when both hands were occupied. My mother had given me her pendant watch shortly before she died, and I had worn it every day since. I looked at it attached to my sweater, and while it was certainly showing signs of wear, I loved it. I would decide which I'd use at work later.

"Thank you, it's lovely."

"We know you love your mother's pendant watch, Jane, but we thought maybe you could save that for work and have this for home."

The look on Aunt Ida's face was so kind that I nodded and told her that sounded like a way to enjoy both.

Everybody hugged everybody, pleased with the gifts and with being together. It was what I thought of as the pleasant finish to a day filled with ups and downs.

———

AS WE STARTED to clean up the paper and bows from the gifts, I heard a car stop out front and a door close. It was an army staff car and Hank was coming up the path to the inn. I went quickly to the front door and opened it.

He stopped at the bottom of the stairs and looked up at me. Neither of us spoke for a moment and then he asked, "Would you like to take a walk?"

I nodded and put on my coat, hat, and boots. I told my family I was leaving, and Hank came halfway up the stairs to meet me, holding out his hand. We walked to the park entrance in silence. He cleared the snow off a bench, and we sat close together, still holding hands.

"Hank, I've been worried. What happened today? Did Albert Winslet go to Strathmore? Are you in trouble?"

His expression was grim. "He didn't condescend to come to me. He 'summoned' me to his house to talk about Fred Flores. The good news is, remember the officer who stopped you from falling when you bumped into your uncle? That's Major Paul Genese, my friend, and my commanding officer. He's the one who got me into the army in the first place."

"Your friend seemed like a good man. But what did 'uncle dear' have to say?"

"He started to bluster but when I brought him up-to-date on what we now know, and emphasized that the investigation was legally under Chief Fielding's direction, he stopped talking and started pacing back and forth. Next thing I knew, he was waving his hands and carrying on about how *that's what you get when you deal with amateurs.* I assumed he was speaking about me because in the next breath, he said he would have to talk with *Franklin* about taking over the whole investigation and how people like me would lose the war for us, and other things I won't repeat. I didn't respond. When he finally ran out of steam, Paul asked me about security measures moving forward and we discussed that."

"That man is such a... such a..."

Hank smiled and briefly touched my cheek with his gloved hand.

"I'm okay. Don't worry, Paul will handle him when the time comes. I've met his type before and when I left to come here, Paul walked me to the car and confirmed I was right about him."

"Meaning?"

"Your uncle somehow bullied his way into the Strathmore project, and they listened because he knew of an ideal site for the base. Seems these days, he considers himself more of a general than a financier, but Washington will only tolerate him so long as he's useful. War brings out people like this. Instant power, or the thought of it, goes to their heads."

"He told Thomas that Joseph Hoffman was coming to Winslet."

He nodded. "He'll be here tomorrow, and before you ask, I can't tell you why he's coming. Confidential."

I was trying to digest this information when he squeezed my hand.

"Jane, I didn't come here to discuss all that. I came here to discuss *us*." He gained my complete attention. "We both know we have problems to work out. I need to know if you're willing to try."

When I looked into his eyes, I saw the turmoil reflecting what I was feeling.

"Yes, I want to try. Of course, I do." I touched his cheek. "I've thought about this for months and come to realize that loving you isn't the issue here. I do love you, very much." He would have kissed me except I went on, "From my point of view, the real problem is that what I want is to be able to love you *and* continue doing other things that matter to me, things that help people. You've known since you were my patient, before we started courting, how much nursing means to me. As much as your family's business means to you, I would imagine."

He sat back and waited, watching me warily.

With a deep sigh, I charged ahead. "If I marry you, I'd have to give up hospital nursing, during wartime, when there is a terrific shortage of nurses. And what would I do? Set up an apartment for us and bake cookies without sugar, waiting for you to come home? Or spend my days volunteering?"

He let go of my hand as if I'd burned him. "Is that what you think marriage to me would be like?"

I sighed. "Hank, married nurses can't work in hospitals. You know that."

"Aren't there other places you could work? Visiting Nurses or an office nurse maybe?"

"Yes, I could. And those are important jobs, too, but I have spent years building up an expertise that is sorely needed right now and it seems un-American to waste it."

We both paused for a long moment. I felt soft snowflakes fall on my face, but not the cold.

He reached into his pocket and took out a small box, a green ring-sized box.

I jumped up. "Hank!" I could feel my face turning beet red and I hated that feeling.

"Didn't you listen to a thing I said? You..."

"Jane, open it."

"No, I am not going to accept a..."

"Jane, open the damn box... please."

When he changed his tone, I relented and opened the box. I looked down at him questioningly.

He asked me to sit. "I did go shopping for a diamond ring but then I got talking to the nice Irish lady who owns the shop. I told her about our situation, and this was her suggestion. She said they call it a Claddagh ring."

"Cladder?"

"It's spelled C-L-A-D-D-A-G-H, but she pronounced it *Clad-duh*.""

I sat back down and looked at the lovely ring nestled on

a bed of green velvet. It was gold with a heart in the middle, held by two hands, and a crown on top.

"She said the ring symbolizes love, in all forms. The heart represents love, the hands are for friendship, and the crown for fidelity. Now the part that is perfect for us; how you wear it matters. If you put it on your right hand, heart pointed away, that means friendship. On your right hand, heart pointed inward, that means a special relationship, kind of like when you're going steady. But, if you wear it on your left hand, heart pointed away, that means you are engaged, and when the heart is pointed inward, it is your wedding ring."

I again looked at him. "And how is it you thought I would wear it?"

He tilted his head and those chocolate brown eyes that I loved looked into mine. "I had *hoped* this would be our engagement ring but it's clear you are still not ready for that step. Instead, would you do this?" He gently took my right hand, removed my glove, and slipped the ring on, heart pointing inward. It fit perfectly. "If you would wear it like this for now, you can switch it to your left hand when you're ready."

It looked beautiful and felt right but there were two questions I needed to ask before I could leave it on my finger.

"When did you buy this? What about our conversation yesterday?"

"I'm a practical man in love with a stubborn woman, Jane. I made two purchases days ago." He flashed his little-boy grin and put his hand in his pocket. "Want to see the other one?"

"No, no, this ring is perfect. However, does this ring mean I'm the one who decides what I do, including where I work and if I help with investigations, or whatever should come along?" I held up my hand before he could answer. "Of course, I would still discuss these things with you since your opinion really does matter to me. But I need to have the final decision."

Now it was his turn to sigh.

"Jane, I love you, but you don't make it easy. I'm trying to figure out how we can each get what we need, I really am. Let's finish this discussion over a dinner as soon as we can, okay?"

I would have preferred to keep talking but Hank had to get back to Strathmore. So, I nodded and savored his hug. We were two tall people, Hank over six feet and me five foot seven, higher in the boots I was wearing. When he hugged me, my head rested comfortably on his broad shoulder, making me feel warm and secure.

I could not imagine living without his hugs.

When he left, he must have taken the warmth with him because I started to feel the cold. I looked down at the ring on my right hand and wondered for the millionth time what our future would be before I slipped my gloves back on and headed toward the inn. It was bittersweet that putting my future with Hank on hold meant I could return to work at Massachusetts General and, for the time being, totally focus on Fred Flores' murder. As a matter of fact, I was so focused on my thoughts that Augustus Reddy, Winslet's Air Raid Warden of 'Reddy's always Ready' fame, was walking beside me before I knew it.

"Miss Harmony, I understand you are going to help the police find out what happened to Fred Flores?"

The speed of small-town news transmissions, even on holidays, never failed to surprise me. They seemed to know what I was doing before I did.

"Yes, Mr. Reddy, I am. Is there something I should know?"

"Fred Flores was a good man. During the Great War, he put the lives of the men he led in front of his own. I know, I was one. I helped get him to the medical tent after he was shot. He had made sure we all got out of this ramshackle shed we had taken over and then he took the bullets in the back of the knee as he turned to leave, with Germans chasing right on his tail. When Micah and I got to him, it looked as if the Krauts had shot his leg clean off and it was good to see, after the war, that he could still use the leg."

I nodded as a picture of Fred Flores saving his men formed in my mind.

"What I wanted to say was that I'd had a conversation with him a week back that bothered me. I told the Chief this morning and I'm telling you now. I saw Fred at St. Agnes'. He was so focused on what he was looking at that he woulda walked right past me if I hadn't spoke up."

Lately, I, too, had been more focused on my thoughts instead of where I was going.

"Really? What was he looking at?"

"A grocery list, of all the fool things! The man never shopped for more than one or two things at a time. He ate with friends, earned a meal working, or went without."

"Then why did he need the list?" I asked.

"That's exactly what I asked him, and he said he hoped to be able to tell me soon. Then he walked away. Now what do you think of *that*?"

————

CHAPTER EIGHT

"Courage is resistance to fear, mastery of fear, not absence of fear."
Mark Twain

SATURDAY, DECEMBER 25, 1943 – CHRISTMAS DAY – CARRIAGE LANTERN INN

WHEN I RETURNED to the inn, I sat down on the bench inside the door to remove my boots. As I started on the second one, the telephone rang and Aunt Ida answered it.

"Oh, Aggie! And a Merry Christmas to you, dear. Yes, yes, TJ called here, too." Aggie continued talking, and my aunt gestured for me to stay. I waited for my turn and, after a few more minutes, she said, "Yes, she's right here."

Aunt Ida turned to me and pointed at the door opposite the parlor which led to the bedroom she and Thomas had converted to their private study.

"Jane, why don't you two talk in there, so you can have some privacy?"

I nodded, went into the room, and closed the door. Then, I sat down at the desk and picked up the telephone as my aunt was saying goodbye.

"Hi, Aggie, Merry Christmas! How is Boston? And your grandfather?"

"Merry Christmas to you, too. Boston is more crowded with soldiers and sailors than I would have thought possible, and church was a sea of uniforms today. Grampa and I are fine except I miss TJ terribly." She sighed. "But I under-stand I'd better get used to sudden changes in plans. On a more positive note, Grampa and I are starting a new project. When we are a bit further along, I'll talk to Thomas and Mrs. W about it. We're going to write a history of the town, which will of course make it mostly about the Winslets."

"Uh-oh. Thomas hates talking about his family history."

"I know, but we're going to base the book on articles my grandfather and the staff wrote and published in the *Winslet Daily Chronicle,* along with resident interviews. It'll be kind of like those 'Remember When?' books so it isn't really new information. Grampa will talk him into it.

"The other thing I wanted to tell you was that when I told him that Mr. Flores' body had been found in the woods and that's why TJ and I didn't get married as planned, Grampa said he knew him. He told me a lot of things about him that will be in the book, but what I thought you'd be most interested in is that during the Great War, after he was shot in the knee, Mr. Flores didn't stop serving. He didn't even head home. As soon as he got out of the hospital in England, they moved him to someplace in Scotland and he started doing intelligence work with the British Secret

Service Bureau. I guess there were other Americans there, too."

"Does your grandfather know what he did for them?"

"No, like a lot of other men, Mr. Flores never talked about what he did in the war. When Grampa found out he had saved the men in his squad and been given a medal, that news didn't come from Mr. Flores—it was from an article in the New York Times! I'm telling you all this now because TJ told me that they believe he saw something he shouldn't —a meeting, an exchange or something—and that's why they think he was killed. Seems to me, with his background, Mr. Flores would have realized—more than most—the potential of a clandestine meeting on a military base whose mission is kept secret."

My mind started racing, trying to factor in what she was saying with what I already knew. "And what if there had been other meetings before that one?"

"Yes! We're both thinking the same thing." She coughed and said, "Grampa said to be sure I stayed with facts and logical assumptions only, not overly dramatic theories, when I told you."

Even though she couldn't see it, I shook my head as I answered her. "A man's dead. I'd say *that* provides the drama, not your words."

Because Aggie was two years younger than me, TJ's age, I sometimes forgot what a thoughtful, intelligent women she'd grown into and how much managing her grandfather's newspaper since his illness had influenced her. It was a reminder that I also had to stop thinking of TJ as my baby brother. People grew up quickly in wartime.

"Amen. TJ thought you were planning to help solve Mr. Flores' murder and that Captain Maitland wouldn't like that. Is all that true?"

"Yes, I have agreed to help and no, Hank doesn't like it. He can't seem to understand that helping with the investigation, in whatever way I can, is something I really feel I have to do."

As I looked at my new ring, I caught her up on the latest decision Hank and I had made. She wanted to know how I felt about it.

"Truth be told, I would like it to be *settled.* It seems that all anybody does anymore is wait—for the invasion, for the war to end, for the men and women fighting to come home, for food to come back to the stores and, most of all, to feel *safe* again."

"Yes, I know what you mean. TJ and I thought we could squeeze the wedding in but it wasn't meant to be." Another sigh.

After that, we hung up, promising to keep in touch.

MY AUNTS and uncles were having a late supper in the dining room after I finished talking with Aggie. I went to the doorway.

"Jane," said Aunt Ida as she started to rise from her chair, "Join us. I'll make you a sandwich and..."

"No, no. Please sit down and continue, all of you. I'm very tired and not hungry. I'm going to go to my room, take a bath, and then start working on trying to solve Fred Flores' murder." I put my hand up against the protests that started immediately. "Please, stop. That decision is made. And another decision you should know about is that Hank and I have put our relationship on hold for a while because we realize we have differences to resolve. Neither one of us is happy about it and yes, it's mostly because of me, but I have to do what I think is right." I paused for a minute and then said, "All over the world, lives are on hold until this war is done, for many reasons. Now ours may be, too."

I waved and headed to my room. A warm bath and a little pampering went a long way toward relieving some of the stress of the past two days. Forty minutes later, dressed in a nightgown and bathrobe, I sat at Jimmy's student desk in his former room with Vic purring on my lap. The cat had been waiting for me, always seeming to sense when I needed him around.

Now that I was about to see if I could help capture Mr. Flores' murderer and find out the reason for his death, I took a moment to think about why I had changed my mind about getting involved in the investigation. After remembering the train station meeting with Mr. Flores and the peace his gift gave me, I felt I had a personal connection to Fred Flores.

And because of everything that had happened during the investigation into Chief Connawell's murder, I had first-hand knowledge that serious crimes had long-term consequences and that the reasons for them were not always obvious. I had also come to understand that the law had limits that ordinary citizens could sometimes circumvent to discover the truth. Most of all, I wanted to know why a decorated veteran of the Great War had wound up dying alone in the woods at Strathmore and I wanted to see his killer brought to justice. I felt that those who knew the man, and the kind of man he was, *owed* Mr. Flores that.

I opened the notebook I had brought with me and began writing down what I knew at that point. While doing so, I munched on the turkey sandwich my aunt had left on a tray with a glass of milk and a slice of apple pie, despite my insistence that I wasn't hungry. My Aunt Ida believed any situation improved with food and, of course, she was right since I devoured every bite of it and felt ready to tackle my task.

. . .

IN OCTOBER, when I had worked to prove TJ innocent of
murder, I had written things down in a notebook Chief
Fielding had given me. Rereading it during that time helped
keep me on track. I planned to repeat the process. This book
was brand new, about four inches by six, and fit inside my
purse. I started writing down what I knew about Mr. Flores'
murder.

As I wrote, I could hear Christmas Carols playing on
my aunt's new radio while she and Aunt Margaret cleaned
up the kitchen. Like war, murder didn't pause for Christmas. I couldn't stop the war but maybe I could help stop the
murderer.

FREDERICO (FRED) FLORES (FF): Age: 53. No
family.

1. Bad left knee, needed walking stick.
2. Veteran—never the same after war. Distressed
   that Germany was again the aggressor.
3. Locals knew him by sight, some gave him food
   or temporary shelter.
4. Lived rough in a lean-to shed in the Strathmore
   Hospital woods and another one in South
   Winslet woods. Police found gun in good
   working order in shed.
5. Sometimes had male companion called Cede,
   who stayed with him. Cede was mute.
6. Micah, FF's good friend, identified the body.
   Johnny, Father Fitz, Thomas, Mr. Reddy and
   Aggie's grandfather knew him.

7. Aggie's grandfather thought FF had continued to work for government. ???

MURDER:

1. Pathologist said he was stabbed in the back. Could have been killed either by <u>a man or a woman</u>.
2. Chief Fielding originally thought it was an accident because the report said the body reeked of alcohol, was dressed in old clothes and alone in the woods. Looked like he tripped and fell while running.
3. Micah was sure death was not an accident from the beginning: FF <u>didn't drink</u> and needed to use a walking stick <u>for balance</u>. <u>Stick was found</u> —broken as if FF had hit someone with it.
4. Fr. Fitz saw <u>regular shoe prints</u> and smaller <u>soldier boots</u> at the clearing.
5. Pockets contained four dollars, some change, a train schedule, a handkerchief and a pair of socks.
6. FF tossed his war medal into a nearby bush. Micah believes that was a message—a warning —to him from his friend.
7. Mr. Reddy mentioned a <u>grocery list</u> FF had.

QUESTIONS:

1. Where is FF's other hut? Anything important there?
2. Who is this Cede? Was he there the day FF was killed?
3. What sort of meeting in woods on an army base between at least two people (2 sets of footprints) would get somebody killed? Espionage?
4. What, if any, secrets are there to know at Strathmore?
5. Who are the patients behind those barred windows?
6. Is the grocery list Mr. Reddy talked about important? Is it some kind of code?
7. How could I see a copy of this grocery list?
8. How can I get Hank to let me talk to soldiers who found FF at Strathmore?

I WENT TO BED EARLY, my head swimming with facts and questions. Surprisingly, I fell asleep instantly.

SUNDAY, DECEMBER 26

We woke to a cold, clear December morning. As children, TJ and I would have been outside on a school vacation day like this one—all day if possible—shoveling stairs and walks to earn a little money and then sledding with our friends. And Mother would have had a pan of milk on the stove, ready to make cocoa when we came inside. Those were the kind of pleasant Winslet memories I hoped in time would replace the not-so-pleasant ones.

By 8:30 a.m., Aunt Margaret and Uncle Frank were

ready to leave for Boston. In a surprise decision, Catherine and baby Elizabeth were going with them.

I spoke to Catherine. "Are you sure you want to leave Winslet?"

"It's only for a week or two—however long my father and Joseph are in town. Mike and I agreed it was a good time to go. I'll miss everyone here, but I've been wanting to visit with Uncle Frank and Aunt Margaret, so this seems like a good opportunity." She looked lovingly at my niece, Miss Elizabeth Jane Harmony. "And I'd like to do a little shopping for this one. Mike's planning to drive to Boston and bring us back when the time comes."

I gave them each a kiss and helped them settle into Uncle Frank's car. At that moment, Mike arrived to say goodbye to them.

He sat in the backseat and put his arms around Catherine and the baby.

My aunt, uncle and I moved away a few feet to give them some privacy. As soon as we did so, my aunt spoke up. "Jane, why don't you come home with us, too? Like Catherine? I hate the idea of leaving you here with a killer on the loose and..."

"Now Margaret, leave the girl alone. She's smart as a whip and she's made up her mind."

In all the years TJ and I had lived with them, my aunt had been our champion and the more liberal voice while Uncle Frank tried to wrap TJ and me in cotton batten to protect us from any harm. She had explained to him over and over, with infinite patience, that we had to learn things for ourselves to become strong people. From the look on her face, I think she felt we'd learned our lessons too well. And if I knew my aunt, my uncle would hear about his decision to switch tactics as soon as they were alone in Boston.

"Thank you, Uncle Frank, I'm glad you understand. But I'm curious, what made you decide it was right for me to stay?"

"As I said, you're a smart one. And Thomas and I went over to Micah's house and spent some time talking with him and Johnny last night. Good men. They explained what kind of man Fred Flores was and how much he admired you. They also told me how much you did for the town and for your brother in October. Seems you left out a lot of details about your trip to Winslet, young lady." He smiled and wagged his finger a bit. "Of course, I want you to stay safe, but I also want you to get the bas... person who did it. You get him for Fred."

I gave them both heartfelt hugs, promised to call soon, and waved goodbye to all of them.

MIKE CAME over to talk with me after the car had disappeared. "Got a minute?"

"Do you want to go inside?"

He shook his head, so we went up on the inn porch and sat down on the glider. Aunt Ida kept a thick blanket there for such conversations, so we were able to fend off the cold for a while. I waited for him to talk.

"I got a call from a Dr. Minnegan, the physician at the army hospital at Strathmore."

I'm sure I looked as surprised as I felt. "Physician, not psychiatrist? With the bars on the windows, I thought it was a psychiatric hospital?"

"Not quite. From what I can gather, it's a hospital for men recovering from bad wounds who also have some serious psychiatric problems—battle fatigue, specifically."

He could see from my expression that a list of questions

had popped into my head, but he raised his hand to stop me. "Before you ask for more, that's all I know about the place so far. He called me because of the medical needs. I guess the army decided the hospital was too small for a full-time psychiatrist and doctor, so the doctor was transferred out. That's where I come in. He wants me to provide the medical care on a part-time basis."

"But Mike, you're not in the army."

"No, and neither is the psychiatrist."

"What did you say?"

"I said I had my hands full in Winslet, but I might be able to make rounds a couple of times a week—*if* I had someone to help me." He paused. "I thought that someone should be you. And while you're there, maybe you could figure out who killed Fred Flores or at least why he was killed?"

Mike looked like my brother had when we were kids and he thought he had come up with a brilliant idea.

"And, Dr. Evans, what do you think Captain Maitland will have to say about that?"

Now he was laughing. "Quite a bit, I suspect, quite a bit."

We were both laughing when Thomas opened the door and said I was wanted on the telephone. He went back into the house, and I got up.

"Are you in? Do you want the job?" Mike asked.

"Can I call you in the morning and give you my answer? So much has happened, I'd like to think about it today and overnight, if that's all right?"

"Certainly. Call me."

.   .   .

INSIDE, Thomas pointed to their study. I went in and picked up the telephone. "Hello?"

"Miss Harmony? Dr. Eldridge here. Is this a bad time?"

"No, Dr. Eldridge, this is fine. Did you have a nice holiday?"

I removed my coat, hat and boots and waited to hear what he wanted to talk to me about. As soon as we finished exchanging pleasantries, he started with the purpose of the call.

"Miss Harmony, since the war began, I've been proposing a ward to some of my colleagues where we can treat the wounded who return home with severe wounds *and* what's known as shell shock or battle fatigue. During the Great War, I went with a group of doctors and nurses from here to France and worked in the hospital's mobile unit, where we saw many patients like that.

"At present, the army and navy hospitals take care of the bulk of those who return but, as you know, we admit some with specific needs we can best meet here. I've been in meetings with our closest military hospitals to expand that number to include more special cases, specifically those I've described. On our proposed ward, Dr. Rubens would oversee the medical care team, Dr. Johansen the psychiatric end of things, and my group will handle the surgical cases. Once the physical injuries are in check, the psychological work that starts here can continue at McLean Hospital. The point is not to let these men get lost in the medical system and to get them the help they deserve."

He paused. "How does all that sound to you?"

"Very exciting, Dr. Eldridge. And badly needed."

My head was swimming a bit. It felt as though Dr. Eldridge had been listening to my conversation with Mike. I was surprised that he had chosen to talk with me about the new ward in the planning stages, but he quickly made his reason clear.

"I was hoping you would feel that way, Miss Harmony. You see, there's nobody we can turn to for advice on how to get this kind of ward up and running, what protocols we need, and all the rest. So, we're putting together an advisory board that will start meeting right after the New Year to create our own, which will obviously change as we go along and learn more. We need input from the best nurses we have, which means we would like you and Miss Malone to be the nursing representatives on the board, and perhaps work on the actual ward when the time comes. What do you think?"

Now, I was both flattered and speechless, a rare event in my life. Two jobs, in two very different places, concerning the same kind of patients, offered to me in a ten-minute period. I shook my head to try to clear it. Was someone trying to tell me something?

He waited a few seconds and then said, "I realize this is a lot to ask you to commit to, especially when you are on a well-earned vacation. So, I took the liberty of sending some information to you in Winslet about work that's being done with individuals. If you could find time to review it, to get a better sense of what treating these patients will entail, then you could give us an answer when you return to the hospital. Does that seem reasonable?"

I found my voice. "Yes, Dr. Eldridge, that sounds like a good plan. And thank you for thinking of me."

We said our goodbyes and I sat back in the chair, my head filled with questions. *Am I going back to Boston and MGH? Am I staying in Strathmore? Am I able to make any kind of commitment right now and if not now, when? And what about Fred Flores?*

. . .

AUNT IDA, Thomas, and I went to Sunday Mass. The church was still decorated for Christmas and would be until the Epiphany on January 6th. As a child, I loved this tradition because it felt as though Christmas lasted longer than a day. We didn't have many gifts back then, but my mother fostered the spirit of the season in TJ and me and that warm feeling had stayed.

After the service, we waited for Father Fitz outside. It was cold and the sky promised more snow. I was glad for the knitted bright green hat and matching scarf in a complicated stitch pattern that Margie had given me as a Christmas gift. I had told her more than once that if she ever got tired of nursing, a wonderful career as a designer and knitter awaited her.

When Father Fitz joined us, we complimented him on the sermon he'd given about maintaining faith in a time of war, with all the fear and sorrow that it brought. His sermons made you think, and I knew I would remember his words later. And then Thomas and Aunt Ida tactfully started walking slowly back to the inn, giving us a moment of privacy.

"And you, Jane, anything new since yesterday?"

I mentioned the job offer at Strathmore Hospital.

Rather than the enthusiasm that I expected from him, he made some sort of a *tsk*ing sound and said, "That seems like you could be headed straight into what soldiers call 'harm's way', girl. Are you sure you're ready for that?"

There was no time for further conversation because his parishioners were waiting to speak with him. I hurried along the path home and caught up with Thomas and Aunt Ida. We came to Winslet House and paused. The army sedan was gone, likely at Strathmore. I shuddered, slipped my arm through Aunt Ida's, and we walked the rest of the way to the inn in silence while I pondered Father Fitz's response to me taking a job at Strathmore.

Once we got there, I offered to prepare lunch and suggested Aunt Ida take a seat in the parlor with Thomas. I didn't cook often but thought even I could handle a ham and vegetable casserole made with leftovers from the day before, accompanied by warmed bread. We ate in the kitchen as the snow started falling. It was quiet inside and out.

Much of the rest of the day was spent in the parlor, with Vic sleeping on my lap, and Aunt Ida and I knitting socks for soldiers while Thomas read the newspaper. The radio was on for war news and then music.

It was a good chance to think. The job offers from Mike and Dr. Eldridge—and Father Fitz's comment—never really left my mind. I went to bed that night not knowing what I wanted to do.

———

CHAPTER NINE

*"Never in the field of human conflict was so much owed by
so many to so few."*
Sir Winston Churchill

MONDAY, DECEMBER 27, 1943

AT BREAKFAST, I showed Aunt Margaret and Thomas
the Claddagh ring. My aunt knew about them and said, "So,
you and Captain Maitland are 'special friends' for now?"

"Yes, we are, and we postponed further discussing our
future until the time is right, likely when the war is over."

I knew it wasn't the news she wanted to hear but it was
all I could tell her at that point.

After breakfast, we cleaned the guest rooms Aunt
Margaret and Uncle Frank, and Catherine and the baby
had used. The sheets went downstairs to be washed in the
utility room off the kitchen. After Aunt Ida put them

through the wringer, we hung them on lines strung from one end of the porch to the other, where the top half of the walls were screened, allowing fresh air in, and the bottom half were wooden panels. It was very cold out there, but the clothes dried rather quickly. They would be stiff when brought in, but a little shaking out and time in the kitchen on a rack took care of that.

I had been awake long into the night before, so the cold air and activity were good to help me wake up. I had gone to bed confused about what I wanted to do but the more I thought about Mr. Flores, the clearer things became. I realized that the job at Strathmore was the one I needed to accept, for the time being at least. It would indeed allow me to pursue Mr. Flores' killer, the most immediate need before someone else was killed. My experience had taught me that once a person killed a human being, they didn't hesitate to kill again—and that thought cemented my decision. I hoped Chief Fielding wouldn't object to my help because he was going to get it one way or the other.

There would also be the benefit of learning more about patients with battle fatigue and how to treat them. I knew I wanted to be part of the Advisory Board for the new ward at MGH in some way and the information I gleaned would be invaluable for that.

The last thing I did before I finally fell asleep was to promise myself I would not surprise Hank by showing up at Strathmore unannounced. I would not want that done to me twice, and I knew he had his hands full of problems, my Uncle Albert included.

Once Aunt Ida and I finished with the morning chores, I called Mike and told him I wanted to accept the job, at least on a temporary basis. I also insisted he call Hank and tell him what was happening. He gave me a half-hearted argument—he had wanted to see the surprised look on Hank's face again—but reluctantly agreed it was the right thing to do. I told him I had an errand to run, I'd be out for about an hour, and could talk with him after that.

WINSLET PUBLIC LIBRARY

The library was on Main Street and though smaller, it was as impressive as the town hall directly opposite. One of oldest libraries in the area, it was built of brick with a half-flight of marble stairs leading to a Greek portico entry housing an oversized oak door.

I tugged hard at the door and entered first through the small anteroom and then a swinging door, the top panel of which was glass. Miss Smithers' desk was directly ahead. She met me halfway and gave me a huge hug.

When I'd returned in October, I had been surprised by her gray hair, new glasses, and weight loss during the years I had been absent. But despite those changes, today she looked better, more energetic, more like the 'old Miss Smithers'.

"Jane, it's so good to see you." She held me away from her by the shoulders. "Is it for good this time? Are you back? Are there wedding bells in your future?"

The library was deserted so we sat down to talk at a table in one of the two main rooms. I told her the status of Hank's and my relationship and showed her the Claddagh ring on my right hand, explaining its significance. She listened quietly, without interruptions.

"Sounds like the Captain knows you better than you know yourself."

I didn't want to go down that road, so I moved on to Fred Flores and asked if she knew him.

Her face took on a sad expression. "Fred? I knew him well. Every two weeks, like clockwork, he returned three books on the day they were due and picked up the next three, which I had set aside for him. He had a friend in South Winslet who knew how to repair torn bindings, so the books that needed repair always came back in better condition than when they left." She heaved a heartfelt sigh. "Both the library and I will miss him terribly."

I patted her hand, and we were silent for a moment. Then I said, "So, that means that Mr. Flores was here in Winslet at least every two weeks?"

"At least."

"How long has this been going on?"

"Well, off and on for years. I'd see him mostly when he came to visit Micah. But the last few months, it's been regular as clockwork."

"Since, say, the army has been renting Strathmore?"

She thought for a minute. "Well, I hadn't put the two together but yes, he's been here regularly since September. As a matter of fact, sometimes, he stays here in the library."

I raised an eyebrow. She stood and said, "Come with me."

We left that room and went to the area behind Miss Smithers' desk. I had been as far as the card catalogs immediately behind her desk when I'd lived in Winslet, but this time, we kept going down a short corridor. She opened the door into a small room that barely had space for an overstuffed chair, a small table, and a reading lamp beside the only window. On the largest expanse of wall were pegs for coats. A woman's blue coat was hanging there, and boots sat side-by-side on a rubber mat below. An open door on the opposite side of the room led to what looked like a closet converted into a bathroom.

"He spent time here, especially if he was researching something. This used to be a storage room, but Fred attracted attention that he didn't want out in the main rooms, what with the way he dressed and all, so we fixed this up for him. And some nights when it was too cold or snowy for his shed, he stayed here."

"Oh, he did?" I couldn't keep the surprise out of my voice.

"Jane, what the Town Council doesn't know won't hurt them."

Coming from the most honest woman I knew next to my aunts, the statement made me pause for a minute but then we both laughed. Before I could comment, she stopped laughing and stared at the chair. She walked over to it and bent over. Partially hidden behind it was a knapsack, old, battered, and brown. She picked it up, looked at it, and nodded her head.

"This is Fred's. I haven't been in this room since I heard about him dying until today. I wonder what's in here?"

She started to unbuckle the straps until I stopped her.

"Don't you think you should call Chief Fielding instead of opening that? There may be evidence in there."

"Evidence? Evidence of what?"

I paused too long.

"Jane Harmony, are you trying to tell me that the Chief thinks Fred was *murdered*?"

My mother used to say that sometimes, my mouth worked before my brain, and she had been proven right again.

I sighed. "Mr. Flores did fall and hit his head but there was a knife wound in his back. It has not yet been officially confirmed, but it's likely that your friend was murdered. I'm very sorry, Miss Smithers."

She sat down in the chair. Because of the sad look on her face and the fact that the large chair engulfed her small body, for the first time since I'd known her, the independent, outspoken, and caring Miss Smithers I knew looked vulnerable.

Even when she'd been quite sick with the flu, she hadn't looked this bad.

After a few minutes, she asked me to tell her what we knew so far, and I did. I held nothing back. I took my notebook from my purse and showed it to her. She read it, thought a minute, then stood and held up the bag.

"Come on, let's go call Chief Fielding and ask him to come over here. I want to see what's in this knapsack and I'm sure you do, too." I nodded. "We have to find the person who did this awful thing. For Fred. And for Winslet. People are going to be very upset when they hear about another murder. It hasn't been that long since October, you know."

While we waited, I asked if she knew the man called Cede.

She shook her head. "Not really. I met him briefly, once. I remember mostly because I thought he was odd."

"Why?"

"I met the man, but can't tell you what he looks like except he was tall and slim and moved as though he was younger than Fred. He had his hat pulled low, his collar high, and he kept his eyes on a book that he leafed through."

"Sounds like he was interested in it. Maybe it's a clue to his identity. Do you remember the title?"

"I certainly do, we had to wait a while for it. The name is *Make Way for Ducklings*."

I looked at her askance, but she smiled, shrugged and added, "And one other thing, he didn't talk."

"Maybe he was just quiet?"

She shrugged again.

Chief Fielding entered the library at that point. Miss Smithers told him about Fred taking out books, showed him the room, and, finally, the knapsack.

"That's quite a story, Miss Smithers. First off, I'm going to need a list of those books that Mr. Flores took out, and their subjects."

Miss Smithers opened a drawer in her desk and handed him several handwritten pages with books listed on them, along with dates and comments on some.

"I kept this list so we could be sure he wasn't asking for the same book twice."

"Oh, well, um... thank you."

Chief Fielding looked a bit flustered. I doubted that all his witnesses were as organized as Winslet's well-loved librarian.

"Second, I'm going to take this knapsack over to..."

"Now just a minute, Chief, I want to know what's in this knapsack, as does Miss Harmony. She shared what you saw at Strathmore, in the woods." That earned me a sideways glance from the Chief, but Miss Smithers was having none of that. "Now don't you go blaming her. If she hadn't explained all that to me, I would already have opened that bag and you might never have gotten to see whatever is in it.

"Either you open it here and we all see what it contains or Jane and I will march out of the library and follow you to the station, talking loudly to draw attention. That would be a sight that people will talk about. You know it, and I know it. Take your pick."

I worked very hard and managed not to laugh.

Miss Smithers put a closed sign on the library door while Chief Fielding slowly unloaded the contents of the bag onto the table in the main room where we'd been sitting earlier. Nobody talked as he separated them, shaking things out one at a time: a brown sweater, a change of underwear, two pair of socks, a comb, a bar of soap and a razor with extra blades. There was an old map of Massachusetts, a flashlight, two extra batteries, and a pocketknife larger than a boy scout's knife. One hidden pocket contained a $5.00 bill.

There was also a piece of paper with what appeared to be grocery items listed in a column.

I spoke first. "That must be the grocery list that Mr. Reddy told us about."

There were seven items on the list: Baked Beans, Turnip, Ice Cream, Onions, *Tomaten,* and Cranberries.

Frowning, Miss Smithers said, "Fred didn't need a grocery list."

"Is that his handwriting?" the Chief asked.

Miss Smithers gave the list a cursory glance and replied. "No, it's not."

"You seem very sure."

"I am. It's simple. Fred didn't write things, he printed everything except his signature. He said his writing was like hen scratch." She smiled for the first time in a while. "He was right, that was exactly what his signature looked like, a hen scurrying across the page. No, whoever wrote this list, it wasn't Fred.

"And, if he *were* to write a list, the letters would never be... well, this fancy. And precise. A schoolteacher would be pleased with the writing style." She paused, reading it again. "But she wouldn't like the mistakes."

"Mistakes?"

"Look at the items. Fellows Market does not have a freezer so you could not buy ice cream there. And one of the words is spelled wrong. See the word 'Tomaten', I bet that's meant to be tomatoes. No, Fred would never..."

She stopped, covered her mouth, lost all color in her face, and quickly sat down.

Both the Chief and I went to her and asked if she was all right. She nodded her head and spoke as soon as she could. "That word *Tomaten?* That's the German word for tomatoes."

There was a short pause while we all absorbed what she had said.

"Did Mr. Flores speak German, Miss Smithers?"

"Why yes, he was quite fluent... wait, what are you suggesting, Chief Fielding?"

More quickly than was good for her blood pressure, she stood up. Her eyes narrowed, she turned beet red, and her hands curled into fists. I moved a bit closer to her, to where I could hold her back if needed.

The Chief held his hands up in a surrender pose. "Now Miss Smithers, you calm down. I'm not suggesting *anything*. It's my job to get the facts, as I'm sure you are aware. And that's all I'm doing."

That took the wind out of her sails, to use an old family expression.

"That's one of the things I wanted to ask you about today, Miss Smithers," I said. "I think it could be some kind of a coded message and wanted to know if you had any books about secret codes."

"Of course! You're right, Jane! That's a message, a code of some sort. And I know Fred was thinking it might be."

"Why do you say that?" the Chief asked.

"Look at that list of books. In the past month, he's taken out three books, at least, on writing codes. I remember asking him why and he said he used to work on codes and wanted to brush up on them. I didn't believe him. He had a mind like a steel trap. I knew he was looking for something specific."

A random thought popped into my head. "Chief, have you talked to Mr. Flores' friend Cede yet?"

He shook his head. "Still looking for him."

He was ready to leave.

"Before word gets around that Winslet is harboring a German spy, I want to look into this more. And talk with Captain Maitland." He stared hard at each of us in turn. "It goes without saying that neither of you is free to mention this to anyone without my permission, correct?"

"Chief, what about Micah and Mike Evans? They are both active in this investigation."

He sighed. "Use discretion, ladies, please."

We nodded and Chief Fielding started to take everything to the police station—once Miss Smithers copied the grocery list, spelling errors and all.

When he got to the door, he added, "You know, one of the reasons I left Boston for Winslet was because my wife and I thought the police department in Winslet would be a nice calm way to ease into retirement in a few years. I'm beginning to rethink that decision."

After he left, she made a second copy of the list and gave it to me.

"I didn't want to say it in front of the Chief, but Fred and I talked on some snowy nights about his experiences in Germany during and after the war. Not specifics, mind you, but he said there were two things he admired about the German people. One was their precision. Clocks, trains, meetings—everything was on time. Captured soldiers in torn uniforms marched in straight lines, shoulders back when possible. The other thing was music. He said that once in a while, someone on the German side played a harmonica at night. It was what Fred called 'longing for home' music and it made him long for home, too."

I didn't know what to make of what she said. Everything in the newspapers, on the newsreels, and on the radio depicted all Germans as terrible people out to conquer the world. Somewhere in my mind, I knew that was not true but the good things about Germany had been pushed to the background among all the pain and losses of war. I wondered if after the war was over, and hopefully the allies had won, whatever the new Germany looked like could include trains on time and beautiful music. For Mr. Flores.

My reverie was ended when Miss Smithers said, "I'm going to continue looking through the books Fred read and some war novels that I know used coded messages in their plots. Do you have any idea what this list could be about?"

"It's only a guess but it could be related to the patients at Strathmore Hospital, the ones behind bars on the second floor."

"So, names maybe? Or information they'd have? Why don't you discuss this list with Micah and see what he can make of it?"

I said what I felt sure we were both thinking, "If we find out what the list says, then we may be able to figure out who might have wanted it enough to kill for it."

MONDAY, DECEMBER 27 - CARRIAGE LANTERN INN

When I got back to the inn, Mike was waiting for me in the kitchen, eating toasted cheese sandwiches and home-made tomato soup with my aunt and uncle. I apologized for being much later than I had expected but he waved it off as I helped myself to some lunch.

"Your sometimes fiancé is not happy with either you or me, but said he's stuck. He has to have a doctor and since I won't come without you, it looks like you have a job if you want it."

"You two are going to work at the army hospital?"

Aunt Ida looked from one of us to the other.

Mike explained about his new job and said he needed my help, at least at the beginning.

She turned a hopeful glance to me. "So you're staying in Winslet? Will this change what you said earlier?"

It broke my heart to know I was going to take that look away.

"Yes, I'm staying, for a while at least, Aunt Ida. But no, this changes nothing. I'm sorry to disappoint you..."

Thomas, who'd been quietly studying me, went right to the heart of the matter when he softly said, "This job will provide you with the perfect opportunity to investigate Fred's death. Am I right?"

I nodded.

"Oh, dear," was all my aunt said.

I grabbed at the first thing I could think of to change the conversation. "Do any of you know a tall man named Cede who was a friend of Mr. Flores?"

They shook their heads no. It was Thomas who wanted to know why I asked.

"Oh, he's someone Miss Smithers mentioned, and I had never heard of him."

MIKE'S CAR

We quickly finished lunch without further conversation

and left. It was a relief to be in the car. I loved my aunt and uncle but at that moment, I wished I lived anywhere except the inn.

First, I caught Mike up on what Miss Smithers had told me. We discussed the grocery list and the man Cede for a few minutes and then I asked my questions about his family.

"Have you heard from Catherine?"

He laughed. "Yes. She and baby Elizabeth are being royally spoiled by Margaret, Frank, and some of their friends. She didn't bring Albert or Hoffman up and neither did I and it was nice to hear her happy."

"That is good news; I'm glad she went to Boston." I hesitated a few seconds and then said, "Sorry to have to switch to a not-so-good topic, but about Mr. Flores—what specific things will they be looking for during the autopsy today?"

"Fred Flores' alcohol content and the cause of death— the fall or the knife wound in his back?" He paused to light a cigarette and I rolled down the window despite the thirty-degree weather. "One other thing. My friend who looked at his back for me said something odd. He noted that for a man everybody described as living *rough* and eating here and there, he was in good physical condition under those old clothes, his left knee being the exception."

I knew that autopsy report was going to be very important to us and our search for an answer to Mr. Flores' death, but it would have a huge effect on Hank and his investigation as well.

———

CHAPTER TEN

*"The mind that opens up to a new idea
never returns to its original size."*
Albert Einstein

MONDAY, DECEMBER 27, 1943 – STRATHMORE

WHEN WE ARRIVED, we were stopped at the gate and
told to park the car in a nearby space, some fifty or so feet
from the front door. We were also informed that we would
have an armed guard assigned to us while not in the building, Captain's orders. Mike took this in stride, but I felt it
was Hank's way of knowing what I was doing and didn't
like it. As if he had sensed our presence, a sergeant armed
with a rifle appeared at our side, nodded, and fell into step
with us. He was tall, well-built and very friendly. Almost
too friendly.

"Good afternoon, Miss Harmony, Doctor Evans. My

name is Jenkins and I have been assigned to escort you whenever you go in or out of the buildings. Captain Maitland has requested that he be informed if you wish to go anywhere except the main building, and that either he or I accompany you.

"Taking good care of you, Miss Harmony, isn't he?" I could have sworn he winked but he had turned his eyes forward so quickly I couldn't be sure.

I started to protest that we didn't need a guard, but Mike squeezed my arm. I got the message and decided to hold my comments for Hank. In private.

Mike and I both returned the sergeant's hello and started walking toward the main building. I expected him to fall into step behind us, but he stayed right beside me.

"Is there anything I can help you with today, ma'am?"

"We're fine, Sergeant. If we need anything, we'll let you know."

With that, I turned to Mike, "How long are you able to stay today?"

"Not sure. I'll have to check with the office."

TO OUR LEFT was a large lawn that at one time likely held croquet wickets but was now used as a parade ground. A flagpole stood directly in the middle of the area, its flag flying at half-staff.

Even though there was still a coating of snow on the ground, there were at least thirty men in three separate groups, running relays, doing squats, or performing jumping jacks. As they were exercising, they were singing some chants that I could barely hear, likely just as well.

I craned my neck a bit and saw that at the end of the property, beyond the green and opposite the hospital, was a large garage with four bays and a full story above it. Trucks and jeeps were lined up in a row, precisely at right angles to the structure.

I had barely noticed the building when we had come to examine the site where Mr. Flores died, but seeing it in the daylight emphasized the size. Looking around the outside of the former estate, the garage was the only place where there were Christmas decorations, and those were limited to wreaths over each bay.

The only time I had ever been on the estate as a child was one day when Thomas had been asked by the watchman to help him load some furniture from the main house onto the back of a truck. The pieces were going to Boston to be sold at auction. TJ and I had begged to go with him, and he'd agreed but we had to stay outside. Still, even though it had been deserted for many years, it was easy for us to see what a grand home it once must have been.

We'd played tag around the green and passed by the stables, which the army had converted into the garage space. As children, we'd thought that grand old house must have been as big as the White House in Washington, D.C.

I turned to look at the elegant structure that was now the army's temporary headquarters and hospital at Strathmore. The large, graceful white building had been repaired and painted, bringing it back to what was likely its original beauty. A large wing had been added to the building's right, between the house and the woods.

Rumor had it that the second floor had been converted into a small hospital. It all would have been lovely, except that the hospital had bars on the windows.

We went through the large front doors and Martha was waiting for us at her desk. She stood when we came in.

"Thank you, Sergeant Jenkins, I'll take it from here and I'll call you when they are leaving."

I did notice that while I felt a sense of relief to see him and his rifle leaving, she flashed him a brilliant smile—and he returned it in kind. Sergeant Jenkins was a handsome man, I had to admit.

Mike knew Martha from when she had been one of our patients at the inn, so the formal introductions were dispensed with. I asked her about the flag flying at half-staff and Martha said that Hank had had it lowered in honor of Fred Flores. He said the man was awarded a medal for bravery and deserved the recognition. I agreed with him.

Before going upstairs, we were required to remove our coats and hats. I also removed my boots and put on shoes I had brought with me in the knitting bag borrowed from my aunt. Mike removed his rubbers, and we were ready to go.

Martha walked us the short distance to the staircase. She lowered her voice and told us that Albert was in Hank's office, along with Joseph Hoffman and Hank's senior officer and friend, Major Paul Genese. Mike and I moved quickly and quietly up the stairs, out of sight.

At the top of the stairs was a wire mesh fence about six feet tall stretching across the hallway from wall to wall, and a gate with a prominent lock directly in front of us. A soldier who had been sitting to our left at a desk like Martha's, located in a small area in front of the fence, rose and asked our names. Mike responded.

Private S. Barnett checked his clipboard, placing it back on the desk.

He asked for Mike's medical bag, checked it, and returned it. Mike was required to remove the contents of his pockets and allowed to return everything except for what looked like a boy scout knife, for which he apologized as the soldier confiscated it. I had no pockets except in my wool slacks. I turned them inside out to show they were empty. This exact same routine would be followed when we left and each time we returned. The army took nothing for granted. One thing was clear to me, if Mr. Flores had seen an exchange of some sort in the woods, whatever was exchanged had not come through this gate without an explanation.

Once he opened the gate, the private walked about six feet with us to another door, this one wooden with a glass top panel. The private rang the buzzer and an army nurse responded. We identified ourselves through a speaker, and she opened the door, let us through, and then closed and locked it. I found myself wondering whether that door was protecting the people outside or the people inside.

That thought didn't stop me from continuing, but I admit my senses were on full alert.

The nurse, her nametag reading Lieutenant Shrug, silently led us down a short hall. We passed two closed doors and turned a corner to enter the clinical area. Bars on windows outside had conjured up rooms resembling prison cells in my imagination.

What we saw shocked me. It was unlike any ward I had ever heard of, let alone seen.

One very large room was right in front of us and a smaller one beside it. The center of the first was a fully furnished parlor—two sofas, two easy chairs, reading lamps, and end tables stacked with magazines, all arranged in a spacious central area. The furniture formed three sides of a rectangle, making the area almost an island unto itself. The fourth side was an open passageway. Two men in pajamas and bathrobes sat in the chairs, reading.

They didn't look up as we passed by.

Around the perimeter of the parlor furniture, but back at least eight feet from it, were hospital beds. At one of them, assisting a patient to get out of bed, were two male caregivers. One waved to me. It was Calvin, a medic who had helped us at the inn with the flu epidemic.

A quick count showed eight beds in all, five occupied at that point, and all visible from the nurses' station beside us.

It wasn't only the furniture in the center that was different. Gone were the drab green and white walls that hospitals everywhere had. Instead, there was deep, rich brown woodwork with a satin finish on the lower half of the walls while the upper sections were painted a soft sky blue. No customary hospital white bed coverings, either. Instead, there were bedspreads in shades of blue and green and the furniture was upholstered in a soft blue and green floral print. I walked closer to the empty bed near to us and looked at the equipment on the bedside table. All modern, new-looking. My fingers itched to touch everything, but I refrained. Directly ahead of where Mike and the lieutenant stood, at the opposite end of the room, was a double-door-sized opening that led to what appeared to be a covered, screened porch. Soft music played in the background.

I heard Mike mumble, "Holy..."

As soon as I recovered from my initial shock, I looked around at the patients still in their beds and realized this was indeed a hospital ward. Not usual by any stretch, but still a place to treat ill patients nonetheless. From the way the men looked and the amount of equipment surrounding them, they were in varying stages of severe illnesses.

We walked to the nurses' station and the lieutenant addressed Mike, telling him that the resident psychiatrist would be there shortly to talk with him. Then she turned to me and the full force of her emerald-green eyes bored into me. She was shorter than me but still managed to assume a condescending attitude, as if looking down her nose at me.

"Miss Harmony?"

"Yes, but since we'll be working together, please call..."

She continued as if I had not spoken. "Miss Harmony, I am confused about your role here."

Mike jumped in before I could answer.

"She will make rounds with me, assist with treatments, respond to calls from you when I am not available, keep records, and generally help me tend to these patients."

It seemed Mike had a voice he'd kept hidden from me until now, one that he could use to intimidate caregivers, the same way as many doctors I had known.

I wondered if they practiced that voice in medical school.

"Precisely my point, Dr. Evans." The woman certainly did not back down easily. "Those are the duties I and the other nurses already handle. Miss Harmony is not needed."

"You handled those tasks when you had a physician in residence. I am not going to be stationed here. I have an entire town to provide medical care for as well as Strathmore. Sometimes, Miss Harmony may be called upon to respond to a patient's needs if I am otherwise occupied. Since I have total confidence in her judgment, I want my own assistant and liaison, and when I accepted this job, that was all a part of the agreement. If you have an objection to that, I suggest we go see Captain Maitland right now."

Unfortunately for Lieutenant Shrug, she had very fair skin like mine. I could feel her frustration as her face turned crimson. Behind me, I heard a faint snicker and a door closing. But I didn't dare turn around.

"Looks like you've met your match, Avis, old girl."

A very tall, reed-thin man wearing a brown tweed

jacket, blue checked shirt and red striped tie with a large grease stain on it, joined us. He had come from one of the rooms we had passed on our way to the ward.

"My name is Alex Carlson and I am the psychiatrist in residence."

"Mike Evans, physician not in residence."

He shook hands with Mike and then held his large hand out for me. His grasp was solid and his skin warm. He was not a handsome man but his dark brown, almost black, eyes were mesmerizing, and he looked like a man you could trust. I could easily see how he would be good in his chosen profession.

"Don't mind Avis here. She's a great nurse, but she's used to being in charge and giving orders. Army through and through. Can't quite get used to the fact that the army is using civilians when needed."

"Dr. Carlson!"

He laughed, turned to Mike, dropped his voice lower and said, "Let's go to my office. We have to have a conversation."

On the way there, I suddenly felt the need to reassure myself that I knew how to exit Strathmore Hospital.

————

CHAPTER ELEVEN

"Very few of us are what we seem."
Agatha Christie

MONDAY, DECEMBER 27

THE OFFICE to which we were led looked much like an extension of the man himself—relaxed, comfortable, and in no way coordinated. Either of my aunts would have had a hard time not immediately cleaning up the stacks of books and cartons that seemed to spring up from tables, the overstuffed bookcases, and the floor itself. At the small conference table reposed the remains of several meals. Lieutenant Shrug left and came back with a cleaning lady who shifted the debris efficiently and then turned to Dr. Carlson.

"Would you like coffee and donuts for your guests? Chef made them this morning."

She grinned as if she knew a secret.

"Donuts? Bless the man! Yes, Maude, we would love coffee and donuts. But you get one of the boys in the kitchen to bring it up, okay? Too heavy for you."

She left smiling and we all took a seat.

"First, I apologize for the state of my office. We're in the process of removing books and bookcases to make way for a new project."

He got no further before the door opened and Hank walked in. Lieutenant Shrug moved to stand but Hank gestured her back to her seat; the rest of us stayed where we were.

He approached the table, avoiding eye contact with me, and spoke directly to Dr. Carlson. "I'm sorry to interrupt. I meant to do this before they came up here." He turned to us and waved two papers. "These are nondisclosure forms that you must sign to be allowed onto the patient areas and to treat patients at Strathmore Hospital."

Dr. Carlson looked as though he wanted to interrupt but changed his mind and remained quiet.

Hank handed us each our own form and stood still while we looked them over.

"It's a standard form. With your signature, you swear that you will keep all matters relating to Strathmore Hospital and its patients confidential for at least the duration of the war. Should you break this contract, your privileges here will be immediately terminated, and the United States Army reserves the right to prosecute you for crimes against your country in a time of war, up to and including treason, if warranted."

I caught a glimpse of the quick smile that came and went on the lieutenant's face as Hank said those words. I think she was hoping I'd give the local newspaper an interview all about Strathmore Hospital as soon as I left the building.

We each signed, I more reluctantly than Mike, who was used to army talk.

Hank thanked us and quietly left after he held the door open for a very young soldier to deliver our coffee and donuts.

"Let's begin, shall we?" said Doctor Carlson. "Mike, would you please tell me what you have been asked to do at Strathmore Hospital? And what you know about our mission here."

Some people ask questions in abrasive ways, while others seek to make you feel at ease in the hopes you slip up. It had been my experience that the people who used the latter technique could get you to say things you didn't think you would. Dr. Carlson seemed like an old pro at putting you at ease if defending me from the lieutenant, providing donuts, and now looking only mildly interested in our answers were any indications.

Everyone reached for the coffee, some for the tempting donuts.

Mine was jam-filled and delicious.

Mike passed on the donuts and answered him. "As far as your mission goes, I know nothing. As for my duties here, your former physician, Captain Minnigan, called me this morning. He knew I had gone to England in '39 and treated wounded soldiers. He said that this, and my experiences as a patient after that, made me a perfect fit.

"He wanted me to provide medical coverage beyond the basics that you handle and said he was very concerned about two of your patients specifically.

"Shortly after we hung up, I got another call, this one from an adjutant at the War Department in Washington, who reinforced the invitation to join this hospital staff to the point where it sounded more like an order than a request. And so, here I am."

"But neither one described the mission here?"

Mike shook his head.

"And you, Miss Harmony, what do *you* know about us?"

"Just guesses and rumors. With the bars on the windows, I assumed it was a psychiatric facility but everyone in town thinks you have prisoners of war here and some are nervous about that. Even when we came to start looking into the death of Mr. Flores—the man found in the woods—nobody talked about what you were doing here. And before you ask, yes, Captain Maitland and I have a relationship. But no, he at no time has given me any information—despite my clever attempts to get him to talk."

Even Lieutenant Shrug chuckled at that one.

With that, Dr. Carlson said, "That's perfect, just what I needed to hear. In order to have the fewest people involved from outside the army, things are going to change from the way it was with Dr. Minnegan. I was on the telephone with Washington as you were coming up the stairs. Rather than have you come here, we'd like to do our communicating regarding patients' medical issues over the telephone. The way it would work is that Lieutenant Shrug notifies me of the issue, I see the patient, and then call and discuss it with you." He turned to me, "Miss Harmony, it turns out the lieutenant was indeed correct. Your services are in fact not needed."

He said all this kindly but firmly. Lieutenant Shrug had the good grace not to smile.

Mike recovered quickly. "And does Captain Maitland know about this turn of events?"

"It's very recent. He's being informed now."

"If this is what you planned, why bring us here? Why did we sign those forms?" I tried to keep the frustration out of my voice. When was Hank going to trust me?

"That was bad timing, I'm afraid. The original plan was to bring you on board but that changed with a telephone call I received as you were coming up the stairs. By the time I hung up, you had already arrived and seen the hospital layout, the way our patients were being treated. Since we don't want any information whatsoever getting out, I didn't stop you signing the forms. Besides, it may be necessary sometime in the future for one or both of you to come here again."

He waited for any replies and since none came forth, he continued with, "So, with all that said, I think this meeting is..."

The door opened without a knock. Uncle Albert, Major Genese, and Hank came in.

Albert turned to Dr. Carlson and said, "I have spoken with the War Department in Washington several times." He pointed at Mike and me. "Those two people will have nothing to do with this facility. Having dealt with both, I know that they are of poor moral character and not trustworthy. Doctor Evans is involved with another man's wife and Jane Harmony interfered with a murder investigation. I evicted them from my home, and I want them away from here with no delay, and henceforth, no contact whatsoever. Do you hear me?"

Hank stepped up.

"Mr. Winslet, this decision was made higher up the chain of command and Dr. Carlson and I are working out a plan to meet our needs. Until their role is agreed upon, Dr. Evans and Miss Harmony are our guests, and I would appreciate it if they were treated with respect."

I could see the telltale tic in Hank's cheek that signaled his anger; with me, it was my fists, which were clenched so tight they hurt. I also recognized from my childhood the look of disdain on my uncle's face; it had been the same expression whenever any member of my family had happened to be 'in his way' in downtown Winslet. This time, its force was directed at Hank.

"You said higher up the chain of command? There is no such thing at Strathmore." Albert's face turned beet red, and his arms started flailing as his voice became louder. "You heard what I told the adjutant who called. This whole base, the hospital, finding the funds for it—all of it was *my* doing. If I don't want someone here, by God, they will not be here! And that may include you, Captain!"

He turned to Major Genese. "We are going downstairs and make another call to Washington to take care of this mess once and for all. This time, it will be someone above the rank of adjutant I speak to, I can assure you!"

They left. Before Hank followed, he apologized to all of us, his gaze lingering on me for an extra second.

Nobody said a word for at least a minute. It was usually Mike who broke the tension at awkward moments but this time, it was Dr. Carlson.

"You can certainly tell me to mind my own business, but that rant seemed far more personal than whether you should be given a job. Am I correct?"

I looked at Mike, he nodded, then spoke. "I am engaged to marry Albert Winslet's daughter, Catherine, as soon as she is able to get out of the marriage her father arranged."

"And Albert Winslet is my uncle. I am the daughter of his youngest sister, who he turned into the black sheep of the family."

Dr. Carlson whistled and sat back in his chair.

Lieutenant Shrug's eyes grew huge, and she blurted out, "I will never, ever complain about my relatives again. And that includes Cousin Filomena who religiously bathes annually, with her clothes on, whether she needs it or not."

We all smiled at that, and it was Dr. Carlson who spoke next.

"Knowing how the army works, you two may want to go home and wait until one of us calls."

"And what about the patients Dr. Minnegan was concerned about? Don't they need medical care right now?" Mike asked.

"Yes, Mike, they do."

Having seemed to make up his mind, Dr. Carlson stood up. "Dammit, that's what I hate about bureaucracy; it makes you forget what's truly important sometimes. Avis, if you will go out and cover the ward, I will go downstairs and wade in where angels fear to tread." He opened the door before he spoke to Mike and me. "Please be patient. I will be back as soon as I can."

They both left.

I turned to Mike, "What are you thinking? Was our coming here a bad idea?"

"Why? Do you think it was?" he asked.

"It's causing problems for Hank. Who knows what my uncle will do if he gets mad enough?"

"He's all talk, Jane. Look, if you want to leave, that's fine, but don't do it because of him."

"He *isn't* just talk. He made my mother's and our lives miserable when we were growing up. He can do the same to you, Catherine, and me."

·   ·   ·

IT WASN'T that long before Dr. Carlson, Hank, Major Genese, and Lieutenant Shrug came into the room, their facial expressions somber. Nobody sat down.

We heard a car door slam out front.

Major Genese nodded toward the window.

"That sound is Albert Winslet leaving Strathmore. We called Washington and this time the message was clear enough that he got it. He has no say in what happens here or who works here."

I let out a breath I didn't even know I'd been holding.

"And Miss Harmony, Dr. Evans, on behalf of the army, I would like to apologize for this morning's fiasco. Like it or not, Albert Winslet is a force to be reckoned with and has some important friends in Washington, including the President. I would not blame you if you walked out the door right now. However, there is still a very important job to be done here and if you are willing to join us, we want to have you. I'll leave you to discuss it."

Hank spoke next. "I want you to know that you *both*," he looked at me, "have my full confidence and, if you decide to stay with us, I think you would be a welcome addition to our staff."

With that, Hank and Major Genese left the room. Dr. Carlson and Lieutenant Shrug sat back down and the doctor turned to us.

"I guess the next question is, do you two still want to work here and do you need some time to decide?"

Mike answered first. "Yes, I do. I want to do anything I can to end this blasted war for Catherine's and Elizabeth's sakes." Then he turned to me. "But for you, I could very well understand you changing your mind. You could go back to Boston and your old job and nobody would blame you." He paused for a second. "One thing that has not been mentioned today is the danger involved to all those who work here."

He nodded to Dr. Carlson and Lieutenant Shrug.

"For you and me, it may be worse even than for them because we will be leaving the base and will be on our own at times."

His brows furrowed, he pushed his glasses up, and the concern was hard to hide.

Hank had entered the room again, on his own, as Mike was speaking. He sat down quietly beside Dr. Carlson and listened.

I nodded my head. "I, too, am starting to understand the dangers involved. I realize there are people who would give a lot to know what is going on here. Maybe that's why Fred Flores was here, trying to ferret out a spy, and that's why he was killed. Or his death may not be connected at all. Who knows at this point? But if that is why he was here, someone at this base may already be leaking information."

People readjusted their positions in their seats but kept their eyes on me. My heart was pounding in my chest, but I put every ounce of energy into sounding as calm as I could.

"However, as Dr. Carlson said, we have already seen the hospital. My mind has begun putting two and two together so as far as I'm concerned, I'm already in danger whether I go on working here or not. There are people who want to know what I already know."

I looked at each person, but my eyes rested on Hank when I said, "I'm staying."

Dr. Carlson nodded. Hank left again but not before he asked to see me when we were finished meeting the sickest patients.

"All right then, from the beginning." Dr. Carlson went into team mode, and Mike and I were now part of that team.

"You are, of course, aware that all the allies' hopes of victory in this war are based on a successful invasion of Europe. There are many people working on when and where that will occur. Some hope it will be as early as March, but even though we don't yet know the specific date, multiple things are being done to prepare. We, and other places like us, have a role in that preparation."

"How, exactly?" asked Mike, right before I could.

"Excuse me for a minute, will you?" Dr. Carlson left and came back in five minutes with my brother, TJ, who was carrying what looked like a rolled-up map.

It was so good to see him that I couldn't resist getting up and giving him a quick hug. When I sat down again, I looked at Dr. Carlson and gave him what I hoped was a *couldn't help it* smile and he smiled back.

"TJ, I've started telling them what we are doing here but I thought you could explain it better." Dr. Carlson leaned back and lit a cigarette.

TJ and Lieutenant Shrug cleared off the table and spread out a map of Europe that was about four feet wide and three feet high.

"Before the war began with England in '39, Hitler and Mussolini had all the maps available in Germany and Italy gathered up and the printing of new ones was stopped. They did the same thing in each country they took over, wanting to make it hard for an invading army when war came, something they did with typical German precision.

"This map is dated 1935, and comes from a collector in Washington who donated most of his maps to the army as soon as he saw what was going on in Europe. The problem is that years of war have changed the landscape and when the invasion does occur, an invading force needs the maps to be as up-to-date as they can get them."

He turned to Doctor Carlson, who continued.

"And that is where we come in. Our patients are not prisoners—quite the opposite. Each one of those men is an American or British spy placed into various locations around Europe. Some have been over there for years, others for months. They have lived and worked among people in France, Italy, Germany and Austria. As well as the work of war such as sabotage, they are also experts at gathering intelligence.

"Each of these men was severely wounded and brought to hospitals in England, identified, and then transferred to New York. Then, as soon as we were ready, they came here. Mike, you need to know their wounds are at various stages in the healing process.

"Some have had complications, but they all have another problem. Along with their physical wounds, every one of our patients is suffering from what used to be known as *shell shock* but is commonly called *battle fatigue* today. Locked in their minds is a great deal of valuable information and it's our job to get as much of it out as we can.

"We need to help them remember about roads, troop installations, troop movements and possible paratrooper landing sites. We need them to identify who will help us—partisans—and how to reach them when the invasion comes. They were our eyes and ears over there."

Mike looked as stunned as I felt. The men behind the bars had gone from being enemies to heroes in the course of the meeting. Even my fertile imagination had not gone that far.

I leaned across the table toward Dr. Carlson and said, "If those are our men, why such secrecy? Why bars? Why can't the people of Winslet know that heroes are right here, in our town? They would welcome them with open arms!"

"Good questions, Miss Harmony, with—unfortunately —sad answers. Those men and women who helped them while they were doing their jobs—especially those left behind—would be in grave danger if the Germans knew they were here. And there are spies everywhere. Don't fool yourself, they may even be even in Winslet. Therefore, total secrecy. Those bars are not to keep our patients in, rather they are to keep others out. I am gratified to hear that word of who they really are and what they did has not leaked out. Even most of the soldiers posted here think these men are prisoners because people are only told on a *need-to-know* basis.

"We have used other channels to drop hints that they are all German and Italian soldiers who were very combative and disruptive in hospitals, so they were herded together here. This, of course, is something the Germans would approve of—tying up American resources."

Mike's face was a bit pale as he turned to me. "I do believe Fred Flores saw something connected to these men and their secrets. Look what happened to him." He paused for a moment and then went on. "Jane, if I had realized how dangerous this could be, I never would have brought you into it. I mean it. You need to leave. Lieutenant Shrug and I will go forward."

I could feel everyone looking at me again.

"It's all right, Mike. I appreciate your concern. Truly. But I already told you, I'm staying and I'm going to help in whatever way I can. Please, let's let the idea of my leaving go."

Nothing further was said. I felt as if I'd passed some sort of test. Doctor Carlson and my brother seemed to relax back into their chairs, and Lieutenant Shrug seemed warmer

toward me, although that may have been due to the chocolate donut she had recently finished.

The doctor went on.

"Are you familiar with how battle fatigue affects
soldiers?"

Mike nodded. "I saw some cases during the Blitz, before
I was wounded and sent home."

"Miss Harmony?"

"Call me Jane, please. I've only been around a few
soldiers with diagnosed battle fatigue, but almost all the
patients on our ward had experienced severe, life-threat-
ening trauma and, from what I've read and seen, many of
their symptoms are the same.

"As a matter of fact, there is soon to be a new ward at
MGH to specifically treat patients with both physical and
mental trauma issues. I was asked to participate on the
Advisory Board."

I turned to Mike.

"I apologize," I said. "I heard about the new ward last
night and forgot to tell you this morning."

Before Doctor Carlson could comment, Lieutenant
Shrug asked, "How can you do that kind of work with no
training in mental disorders?"

This time, her tone was neutral, not condescending. She
was interested. And she had obviously discussed my background with someone, likely Hank.

"It's a new concept at MGH, Lieutenant, and we will
all be learning. Acute medical care is needed for these
patients and that's where my nurses will come in. The
patients also require psychological care and there is a well-
known psychiatrist who will be one of the three physicians
running the ward."

I turned my attention to Dr. Carlson, "Do you know Dr. Johansen, at the General?"

He nodded, adding, "I certainly know *of* him and it's all good."

"Well, he has formed an arrangement with McLean Hospital in Belmont, to which our acute psychiatric patients are usually transferred. When we plan the staffing required for the ward, we will be recommending psychiatric nurses from McLean Hospital work with the acute care nurses while the patients are still with us, so the patients already know them when they are transitioned there after their wounds are stable." I hesitated and then said directly to the lieutenant, "And, now that I know what you do here, whatever I can learn from you and your staff would be put to good use, I promise you."

She nodded and the shift in the room's atmosphere had nothing to do with donuts.

"What behaviors are you seeing in your patients?" Mike asked Doctor Carlson.

"Nightmares and reliving events, excessive fear of people and new surroundings, lack of trust, memory loss, constant anxiety. Others are easy to anger so there are always medics on the ward. Nights are the worst. We have two patients who can't sleep during the night unless we heavily sedate them, and another who has not said a single word since arriving here. He is also the patient I'm most worried about physically and would like you to see today.

"As if all that were not enough, there's another complication. Every one of these men have been living a lie for such a long time that as they recover from their head injuries, some struggle with what is true about themselves and what is the persona created for their undercover work. Few, if any, trust us or anyone else."

He left it at that, but Mike finished the thought. "So, when they give you information, you have no way of knowing if they are telling you the truth."

Doctor Carlson nodded to TJ.

"That's where I come in. It's my job to coordinate what these men tell us with other people working on the same thing. When we have three similar or identical claims, they are added to the maps. Like this."

He stood and pulled a map out from under the first one.

On the one he showed us first, square boxes each containing symbols were scattered in various locations. We all stood and bent over for a closer look. In several others, small tanks or soldiers were detailed, while yet more showed what appeared to be fireworks. Then he showed us the map from underneath—and now, we found that none of those marks were there.

"We coordinate what we've learned. The fly boys get their updated maps quickly, the rest take a bit longer."

I pointed to two of the boxes with fireworks inside them and red circles around them.

"Why are those circled?"

"Those were ammunition dumps blown up two days ago. Confirmed this morning."

There seemed to be nothing left to say after that, and the meeting ended.

EVERYBODY FILED out but I stayed back for a minute to talk to Doctor Carlson.

"It seems pretty clear from what you have said that the Germans would like to either get the information these men have, or eliminate the threat."

He nodded.

"What do you know about Mr. Flores?"

With what could only be described as a professor's look at an errant student, he said, "I know that he was likely murdered for something he saw, and it doesn't take much imagination to know it must be related to what we do. I also know that the Captain does not want you involved in solving that murder in any way."

"Yes." I coughed, adding, "Well, as long as we understand each other."

———

CHAPTER TWELVE

"It is an equal failing to trust everybody, and to trust nobody."
English Proverb

I CAUGHT up with Mike and Lieutenant Shrug as they went to the bedside of a thirty-one-year-old man. Instead of a hospital nametag over his bed, all I saw was a handwritten sign bearing the name *Alan*.

Mike read the patient's graphic sheet and then handed the paper to me: low grade fever, 100.6°; pulse, 78; respirations, 22. An intravenous drip passed into the patient's left arm, and there was oxygen running. He appeared barely conscious.

We pulled the privacy drapes around and Mike gently folded back the man's blankets to reveal a bulky abdominal dressing. There was a faint odor, the kind associated with wound infections. The lieutenant handed Mike a pair of gloves and, as he removed the dressing, the odor became more pronounced, though not overwhelming.

He looked at me. "Captain Minnigan told me about this patient. Gunshot wound to the abdomen. Not a military wound, though. A shotgun. Those red, angry-looking areas surrounding the wound are pellets that are still making their way to the surface. Since the blast did a lot of damage to his intestines, they had no choice but to remove part of his gut. His wound was infected when he arrived, and dressing changes were needed almost hourly. What we're looking at now is apparently a large improvement. Does that sound correct, Lieutenant?"

"Yes, his wound has improved but he still has not spoken a word." Lieutenant Shrug smiled at the patient and said to him, "You don't even complain of pain; we have to guess."

We were looking at a long incision starting above his waist and heading down, right through what would have been his belly button. There was healing along the top five or so inches with two gaps toward the bottom, both packed with dressing material and rubber drains. The areas Mike had mentioned were many, covering most of the tall, thin man's abdomen.

Mike went to the sink and washed his hands again, as we had both done when we'd entered the ward. Then he went back and listened to Alan's chest.

Even though Alan did not speak, he followed us with his eyes.

They were frightened, pale-blue eyes.

While Mike and the lieutenant headed to the nurses' station, I leaned over near his ear and said, "Don't give up hope, soldier. You are getting better and have good nurses and doctors who care about you. My name is Jane, and I will be back." I squeezed his hand but there was no response, his eyes closed by then.

Calvin came over to replace the dressing.

Mike looked at the front of the chart.

"Let's see—Penicillin, oxygen, IV's, and aspirin for temperature of 101° or over." He turned to Lieutenant Shrug. "You have penicillin available?" She nodded. "Very good."

Both Mike and I were surprised. While the new drug was in use for American soldiers on the battlefield and in military hospitals, civilians had very limited access as yet. It was good to know that these men could receive it, even in a temporary facility.

As he wrote a progress note including new changes to the patient's turning routine, Mike said, "Lieutenant, if his temperature does spike, I want to know. I'm concerned about pneumonia."

We went next to Fester's bed. He was more awake and pulled the sheets to his neck when Mike tried to expose his chest wound.

"Where's my doc?"

"Remember," Lieutenant Shrug said, "He told you he had to leave and a new doctor would be coming? This is Doctor Evans and his nurse, Miss Jane Harmony."

He quickly looked to me. "Harmony? As in TJ Harmony?"

I grinned, "Yes, he's my baby brother but don't tell him I said that. And please, call me Jane."

He grunted but let his hands drop.

"According to Doctor Minnigan, this soldier has bayonet wounds."

Mike pointed to the abdominal wound.

"This one missed the liver, penetrating the right lung. They did a thoracotomy to drain it. The other one," we turned him a bit to his right to see a clean-looking incision, "cost him his left kidney. He's being treated for an infection in the right kidney."

We exchanged glances. The importance of keeping his remaining kidney functioning was clear to everyone.

Trying to lighten the mood a bit, he turned to Fester and said, "Somebody didn't like you too much, did he?"

"Ouais, eh bien il n'utilise plus cette baïonnette."

The lieutenant quietly translated, "Yeah, well he won't be using that bayonet anymore."

The man closed his eyes, and our examination was over.

MIKE CHECKED his watch and headed for the nurses' station.

"It's almost three o'clock and I have calls to make at my office. Our meeting took much longer than I had planned. Any specific medical issues you need me to deal with today?"

"No, not today. We'll need some medicine renewals tomorrow, but we're fine right now."

"Jane, let's head home and plan to come back first thing in the morning."

"If Lieutenant Shrug doesn't object, I'd like to stay for a bit, meet the next shift, and read some charts."

"If you wish, Miss Harmony."

Mike nodded. "In that case, maybe you can catch me up later?"

I readily agreed and he asked us to walk him to the gate.

He had a question about the patients.

"Lieutenant, why are only the first names written above the patients' beds? Or are those names even real?"

"No, those are not their names. They were alphabetically assigned, for obvious security reasons. The first to be admitted was Alan, the second Bob, etc. There were people in command who wanted to use numbers, but both the staff and some of the patients protested so that idea was dropped."

"Glad to hear it. I think the use of numbers would be undignified, demoralizing, and unnatural. I understand the Nazi victims in Germany are given numbers, for God's sakes!"

"I agree. And while we're discussing names, I'd like to explain about the staff. On the patient ward, we use first names with each other and that's what the patients call us too."

Both Mike and I were a little confused since this was not typical practice on hospital wards. "It's the same principle as painting the walls in soft colors and arranging cozy furniture in the center of the ward—we're trying to reduce that institutionalized feeling for them."

"And do you think it helps?" I asked.

"Yes, very much. However, at the desk, on the telephone, and on base, we maintain army protocol and use rank or title. Will that pose any problem for either of you?"

We both shook our heads no, even though I had the feeling she didn't care if it was a problem or not. It sounded logical to me, but it also made me curious about Mike's time in London, working with the British Army.

"Did they have a system like that when you were in England?"

"Ha! The British? Drop rank? Not hardly, Jane, not hardly."

I could still hear him snickering as he went through checkout.

On the way back to the ward, the lieutenant asked, "Why was he in England before we entered the war?" She looked at me intently, as though something was riding on my answer.

"He was frustrated waiting for America to join with England against Germany. According to Mike, twenty or so doctors were on the hospital ship he took to Britain, along with supplies for British hospitals and any international volunteers who signed up.

"On its return to America, the ship would carry critically injured servicemen and some civilians. He arrived in London during the Blitz and the volunteer doctors worked with both military and civilian casualties. He said they never left the hospital, just flopping down onto an empty bed when they couldn't stand up anymore. After weeks of this, he was wounded and sent home. His left leg is much better now, but if you see him when he's tired, like he was during the flu epidemic, he has a very pronounced limp on the left, and needs a cane."

She nodded but made no comment.

Lieutenant Shrug turned out to be a thorough, compassionate nurse who, by the time she had finished her report, made me feel that I was beginning to know these men. They were all important to her and it showed. She was no longer openly hostile toward me, but I could tell she was holding something in reserve. I didn't know if there was another test I was expected to pass, but I was grateful that we were communicating.

"That's all the medical and nursing information I can give you. As you meet them one by one, you'll form your own opinion, I'm sure. As to our mission of gathering information, we immediately pass on any comments regarding their past to Sergeant Harmony to sort out.

"Your brother has an important job, and wears the responsibility well; he stays calm and has patience. I particularly appreciate that he has made it a priority to know each patient personally."

At that point, two male attendants and a younger nurse, whose nametag read Lieutenant Anna Polanski, came around the corner to the nursing station. She was a very attractive, tall, slim blonde with brown eyes, and a complexion that looked as though she had a perpetual tan.

Young, pretty nurses often had a problem being taken seriously at the beginning of their careers; male patients often felt obligated to flirt rather than discuss pain, weaknesses, or bodily functions with them. Nurses had to grow into the job, and each used their own techniques to do so. I had had little problem. TJ said that was because I could stop someone cold with a look that would wither... Well, whatever—it worked.

I told myself to watch and listen and maybe I could help Lieutenant Polanski.

Lieutenant Shrug introduced us.

"Miss Harmony will be joining us for a while, working as Dr. Evans' nurse and assistant. After report, I'd like you to talk with her about the evening shift while I wrap up with Dr. Carlson."

Lieutenant Polanski looked at me curiously and nodded. She didn't need to ask if I was a civilian since she and Lieutenant Shrug wore white uniforms with their Army Nurse Corp insignias—a caduceus with an enameled N superimposed on it—on their left collar, and their lieutenants' rank on their right, while I wore street clothes.

Strathmore might have been an army hospital, but it

was interesting to note that the change-of-shift report was the same as at MGH, except the patients were identified by their assigned names instead of their real ones. Their ages, diagnoses and any changes in vital signs, new orders, level of consciousness, mental status, and communication abilities were discussed.

Wound healing and dressing changes were also described in detail.

I was surprised to learn there were three patients beyond those I had seen. According to Lieutenant Shrug, these men were almost completely physically healed and ready for whatever came next. They were to be found in the second room beyond the nurses' station.

She continued, "Dr. Carlson treats the men who have told us what they remember. He is getting them ready to return home, at least for a while, trying to reduce the trauma they are bound to feel when they are out in the world on their own. Families change, the *world* has changed, and they have been away for long periods of time. Even simple things like catching up on sports, news, and the language people use these days will help them to adjust. This group is due to leave any day now and they will be given new uniforms, money, and the name of someone to contact if they need it. Obviously, they swear to not mention this hospital or any of us. As far as anyone at home is concerned, they recently got back from hospitals in England."

"Have you done this before? Sent people home from here, I mean?" I wondered.

She shook her head no.

I asked if she was nervous about it and she paused before she replied, "We all are, I think." Lieutenant Polanski agreed. "There were a lot of discussions about what to do when our patients became well—or as well as they were going to be for a while—because battle fatigue can last a long time and can come and go. That's why they have a connection outside and people will be checking on them."

"People?"

Lieutenant Polanski said, "Veterans and Army Chaplains, mostly. People who have been in battle. There is one man assigned overall but his name is not general knowledge..." She paused, I nodded my understanding, and she went on, "Dr. Carlson has a huge network out there."

"Almost sounds like being on parole."

"Yes, that's what the men say, but on the other hand, they are glad they can reach out if they need someone."

I was impressed and filed away the information for when we formed the new ward at MGH. I made a mental note to be sure to include post-discharge community follow-up.

"Will I get to meet these men? Talk to them?"

"No. Once they start truly remembering, if they are medically stable, patients are moved out of the main ward. They don't mingle with the other patients anymore; they have their own attendants. It's meant to help everyone stay safe. The sooner they forget about the people they met at Strathmore, the better."

"If there is danger to the process, either for them or us, why aren't they sent to an army post or something?"

Lieutenant Shrug answered. "That was the alternative. It was decided they deserved the chance to see family again and the hope was they would improve faster with them than around soldiers coming and going at a base. The last thing they need is to feel they are in prison—even one disguised as an army base." She hesitated and I thought she was done speaking, but she went on. "Besides, they won't all be fit for active duty again. It takes time to determine if and when they can return to what they were doing."

That surprised me.

"Do you think *any* of them will want to go back to Europe—to that danger again?"

She sighed and said, "I'm not sure if they'll have a choice."

WHEN REPORT WAS DONE, Lieutenant Shrug went to see Dr. Carlson and Lieutenant Polanski and I made patient rounds. I was impressed by how clean and organized the whole area was and how efficient the two attendants were who worked with the patients. She turned on the radio and soft music began playing. It seemed to be quiet time in the ward; several of the men who had earlier been in the center reading were now lying on top of their beds, asleep.

Lieutenant Polanski headed through the glass doors at the end of the room.

The porch was as wide as the main room, completely enclosed, with wooden walls on either side and halfway up the long wall in front. The top half of the wall was made up of large windows looking out on a snow-covered grassy field surrounded by barracks, with one small cottage on the left side. At our height, we looked down on the buildings. I wondered about privacy for the patients but realized that seeing in from below was not possible during the day, and blackout curtains were right there, ready for the dark.

Two men sat playing checkers and we went over to them.

"Hi. Who's winning?" Lieutenant Polanski flashed a beautiful smile.

Both men looked up and smiled, until they saw me. One

rose quickly enough to knock over the table, the other shrinking back in his chair.

The lieutenant never changed her calm voice as she bent to retrieve their checkers.

"It's fine. Sit back down, George, please. This is Jane and she will be here assisting the new doctor we told you about." She turned to me and nodded.

"Hello. I've been here most of the day. I saw you earlier when you were sitting in the chair reading. I don't mean to frighten anyone. I'm here to help."

While I was talking, the lieutenant squatted down to untangle the tubes leading from under George's robe to a drainage bag. From the report she gave, I remembered he'd had multiple abdominal surgeries. As a matter of fact, none of the patients had had only one organ affected. Bullets and bombs had literally torn them apart.

He looked from one of us to the other and then sat back down. She patted his arm and spoke quietly to him. What I heard was her promise that he could trust me.

I turned to the other patient, who was still cringing while he stared at me. I also squatted down to his eye level. "I'm Jane and I've been a nurse for a long time now. I see your leg is in a cast and I remember that the doctors have been trying to reconstruct your knee. Is that right?"

He didn't change position, but did nod.

"Well, I know how heavy those casts can be. Don't you think it might help if I move that hassock over here so that you can take the weight off your leg?"

"Bob and I have discussed this many times. Maybe a new nurse saying the same thing will help?" The lieutenant looked at him again with that beautiful smile of hers.

He sat up and I moved the hassock into place.

He didn't say anything, but his sigh spoke volumes.

We were standing at that point and Lieutenant Polanski said, "We'll leave you to your checkers now that you have met Jane."

On the way back to the nurses' station, she checked each patient's graphic chart at the end of their bed, counted the IV drip rate for the three patients being administered fluids, and tucked or straightened anything in need of it—all while talking to each patient who was awake.

We were headed back to the desk when I heard men's voices coming from down the hall, an area I had not yet been shown. The sound startled me.

"Hello, ladies. How are you?"

It was Sergeant Richmond and my escort, Sergeant Jenkins, both laughing and brushing off attic dust from their uniforms with their hands.

This time, there was no brilliant smile from Lieutenant Polanski. Instead, she spoke in a rather clipped tone directly to Richmond.

"What are you doing here, Sergeant Richmond, and why didn't you sign in with me?"

The sergeant kept his tone light. "I roped Jenkins here into helping me bring the Christmas decorations back up to the attic. You and the lovely Miss Harmony were busy when we came by, so we didn't bother you, right, Jenkins?"

Sergeant Jenkins nodded but added nothing. He watched.

"Next time you have an errand here, you either report in or wait at the desk. Understood, *Sergeant* Richmond?"

The temperature in the room seemed to drop several degrees and the sergeant smartly saluted, "Yes, ma'am." They left.

Once they were gone, I noticed she was shaking a bit. I

said the first thing that came to mind. "I haven't been down that corridor yet, what's there?"

She silently led the way down the short hall. On our left was the closed door to the room where the almost-ready-for-discharge patients were. On the right was an open door and she looked in. "Hello Corporal Pauling, how are you? Are you here until seven?"

I looked past her to see what appeared to be a combination pharmacy and medical equipment storage area. Along the wall on the left side was a counter, shelves with glass bottles and books, and a refrigerator, all items typical of a pharmacy. On the right side were shelves and two aisles at right angles to the door that held medical equipment. Wheelchairs obstructed the aisles. A short, nervous-looking man came toward us from the back of the room.

"Miss Harmony, this is Corporal Andy Pauling, our pharmacist. Corporal, this is Jane Harmony. She will be working with us for a while."

I held out my hand and shook his sweaty one.

"It... It's nice to meet you. M... Miss Harmony. I... I heard you were coming. Wel...welcome."

There was that smile again as Lieutenant Polanski said, "Corporal Pauling is shy and keeps to himself, but don't let him fool you, he's the best pharmacist and equipment guy I've ever met. Right, Corporal?"

He blushed.

"It's nice to meet you, too. I h... hope we can get to know each other better."

With that, the lieutenant pointed to a door about twelve feet away that ended the hallway.

"That's the entrance to the attic, where Sergeants Richmond and Jenkins came from."

"You seemed upset when you saw them."

"I don't like surprises, Miss Harmony. I always want to know who is here and Sergeant Richmond is well aware of that."

We made our way back to the nurses' station and sat down. I started to read one of the patient charts.After a few minutes of silence, the lieutenant said matter-of-factly, "You're so much more relaxed and friendly with the patients than I thought you would be. I'm afraid I let the rumors influence me. Our patients matter so much to..."

"Rumors?"

Her eyes widened like saucers, and it was easy to see she wished to retract the word but finally sighed and said, "The word around base is you are Captain Maitland's girl-friend, and he only gave you this job to keep you close to him."

What she had said was so ironic that I didn't know whether to laugh or cry and it must have shown on my face because she was looking at me strangely. Laughter won.

"Give me a minute, please."

I used the handkerchief—that my mother always insisted I carry tucked up my sleeve—to stifle the laughter and wipe away the tears that came with it. It took a minute to regain my composure. "I'm sorry, please excuse me, but you have no idea of exactly how funny that is. The short answer is that's not true, my working here was not planned, but I'm hoping it will be very helpful to me."

That earned me a frown.

"Let me try to explain. Were you given my resume to read?"

She shook her head no. "Okay, here's the short version. I am the Assistant Head Nurse on Langdon East, an ortho-pedic ward at Massachusetts General Hospital. We see only the most difficult cases, directly from the Emergency Ward or the Special Care Unit.

"However, when the nearby army or navy doctors have a patient with a need of one of our specialized surgeons, those patients are admitted to our ward. Many of our patients with orthopedic injuries also have other serious problems. We've had wound infections, knife and gunshot wounds, and patients with amputations, to name a few. I'm also very familiar with casts as well as with strange arrangements of weights and pulleys.

"Along with all the physical ailments, our patients who endure multiple surgeries and some setbacks often suffer from depression and anxiety disorders. And, while I certainly do not have your experience with patients diagnosed with battle fatigue, I have seen several cases and am very interested in the subject."

She nodded.

"When Dr. Evans offered me this temporary job, it was perfect because there's going to be a new ward at MGH that treats patients with both medical problems and trauma disorders. I hope to work on that ward, using everything I learn here."

She nodded her head again and smiled, "Ah... It's good that those patients will have the treatment they need. Please let me know if you have questions that I could answer."

Lieutenant Polanski was very observant, listened carefully, and could put things together quickly. Since childhood, I'd had a problem sharing confidences and relying on people I hardly knew. But she was easy to talk to and I had the feeling she had been through more than her age and looks would make you think. My mother used to tell me that when I was trying to decide what I thought about somebody, I should go by my feelings rather than the face they presented to the world. That advice had served me in good stead.

I stared at her for another minute and when she didn't flinch, I made up my mind—her help would be invaluable. So, I took a deep breath and plunged ahead. "Anna, are you a by-the-book soldier or do you ever bend or twist the rules a bit?"

Her smile faded, and she looked ready to run.

"If you didn't look so intense, I'd be insulted by that question and leave. Instead, you get one chance to explain. What is it you want from me? Spit it out."

"All right. I was asked to participate in solving what was likely the murder of Fred Flores, the man found in the woods."

To her credit, her facial expression didn't change. She didn't quite relax but there was no shock or pulling back.

"And why would anyone ask you to do that?"

"Because, in October, I came back to town after a long absence to help prove that my brother, TJ, was not guilty of killing the Winslet Chief of Police, Jack Connawell. People noticed."

She nodded, "Yes, yes—I remember hearing about that."

"Look, Lieutenant Polanski—Anna—I would normally take much more time to get to know you before I asked such a thing of you, but my fear is there will be more killing and we're all working to prevent that."

She looked away for a few minutes and then turned back to me.

"I would like to help you, I really would. I assume what you want is for me to funnel you any information I think would be relevant to whatever happened to Mr. Flores?"

I nodded.

"I'm sorry but what you ask is not possible right now. I

cannot risk my job by upsetting either Captain Maitland or Lieutenant Shrug. Around here, trust is everything. If they discover I'm working with you behind their backs—I'd be transferred that same day. Likely to Alaska."

I was instantly embarrassed and could feel myself flush.

"I'm terribly sorry, Anna. I'm so focused on finding out what may have happened to Mr. Flores that I never gave any thought as to what I was asking could do to you. Please, forgive me and, if you can, forget what I asked."

I LEFT the ward shortly after our conversation and passed through the security gate at the top of the stairs, exactly reversing the process we had gone through when we'd entered.

Hank had asked to see me when I was finished, and I mentioned that to the private downstairs who had replaced my friend Martha at the desk.

"I'm sorry, ma'am, but the Captain had unexpected visitors and cannot meet with you as requested. He asked me to offer his apologies and tell you he would be in touch when he could."

"Thank you, Private... Austin. If I may, I'll call my uncle for a ride home."

"No need, ma'am, as soon as I saw you coming, I called a car for you."

I tipped my head and must have looked a bit confused because he soon elaborated.

"The Captain was quite clear that you are not to be alone on the base grounds."

With that, my 'shadow', Sergeant Jenkins, came through the door and said, "I'm right out front when you are ready, ma'am."

He opened the back door of the car for me before I could reach for it.

As soon as he settled into the driver's seat, he said, "Sorry we startled you back there.

Richmond is in and out of there all the time so when he asked for my help, I didn't think anything of it."

After we went through the gates and headed toward the inn, I asked, "Why?"

"Pardon?"

"Why is Sergeant Richmond at Strathmore Hospital all the time, as you say?"

"Oh, that's easy. This is a small command and we're supposed to limit the number of non-army personnel who come on base." He looked at me in the rear-view mirror. "That means any of us with other talents get to use them. Richmond was a builder before the war. He's a jack-of-all-trades, knows some plumbing, electrical, and carpentry. He's also the chief mechanic and the drill instructor, so he's a busy man."

"Yes, sounds like it." I thought about how many places a man like that could go and how nobody would take notice. "And you, Sergeant Jenkins, what are your duties?"

"I maintain our munitions supply and teach self-defense classes along with Richmond. I grew up in a multi-cultural neighborhood, so I also teach German and Italian, and act as an interpreter if needed. But most important of all, I protect important people, like you."

This time, he stared at me in the mirror so long that I wanted to tell him to keep his eyes on the road. Instead, I turned away and thought about how hard it would be to pin down where specific soldiers were at specific times.

———

CHAPTER THIRTEEN

*"Coming together is a beginning, staying together is progress,
and working together is success."*
Henry Ford

TUESDAY, DECEMBER 28 – CARRIAGE LANTERN INN

I WAS up early the next morning, helping Aunt Ida prepare breakfast. Since Thomas was going to Haymarket Square in Boston, he left as soon as breakfast was over and Aunt Ida and I cleaned up the kitchen, dusted and hoovered the downstairs, and made a list of groceries she needed. I had two errands, one of which was to see Mrs. Fellows, so I offered to pick up the groceries.

Aunt Ida smiled and handed me the list.

I knew that she was thinking how October had changed things. Throughout my childhood, and when I'd first returned to Winslet—before the flu outbreak—Mrs. Fellows had been the bane of my existence. She had made life miserable for TJ and me and it was not until recently that we had all learned why. It had been a misunderstanding that, like many, had led to painful consequences. Still, I was not sure of the reception I would get.

FELLOWS MARKET

Besides Mr. and Mrs. Fellows, there were only two other people in the market. I waited my turn and hoped nobody else would come in before I had a chance to speak with Mrs. Fellows. When I got to the counter, she smiled at me and for the first time, I realized the woman I had been so frightened of for so long was an attractive woman.

"Miss Harmony, I had heard you were back in Winslet. I wish you Happy Holidays and I also wish there was not another murder to greet you."

I nodded and said, "Happy Holidays to you, too."

Mr. Fellows left the register and came to join us. I was not sure who he was aiming to protect, but his presence increased my comfort level.

"I have my aunt's grocery list but, in addition, I was wondering if maybe we could have a word, Mrs. Fellows?"

She handed the list to her husband and some private signal must have passed between the two of them because he relaxed and went about gathering the items for Aunt Ida.

She motioned me into the back room, which was just as chaotic—with boxes stacked in crazy piles—as the main store was neat, everything in its proper place.

I plunged right in. "For Christmas, my Aunt Ida and I went through a large chest filled with old photo albums and mementos. We found a picture of my aunts and uncles in younger, happier times and framed it as a gift for Aunt Margaret."

I was talking fast and tried to slow down as I put the knitting bag I had commandeered from my aunt on top of a box, then removed a book-sized album wrapped in tissue paper.

"While we were searching, we found this, and thought you should have it."

I handed it to her, and she recognized it immediately. At first, she was surprised, then delighted and, finally, overcome by tears. "Oh! Oh! I've always wondered where this went!"

The sounds brought her husband running. He looked from her to me and back, sized up the situation, and brought his wife a chair. She clutched the book to her chest and rocked back and forth as if cradling a baby, while I quietly told him what it was and how we'd found it.

The pictures were old, each labelled with names and dates, and they had been remarkably well preserved. I turned to leave and give her some privacy, but she reached out and put her hand on my arm. "Thank you, Miss Harmony, thank you so very, very much."

A new flood of tears came with this declaration, and I could only nod because I was filling up, too. Why was it I cried so much whenever I was in Winslet?

Our order was ready, and I picked it up at the counter. As I reached the door, I heard Mr. Fellows call my name. I walked back and rested the carton on the counter.

"Thank you, Miss Harmony. That was a kind thing for you to do, especially after..."

I waved my hand to hopefully avoid a discussion of the past.

"I'm trying to put all that in the past where it belongs.

We thought the pictures would bring some comfort and during these times, we all need that."

He nodded and then cleared his throat. "I've heard that Micah enlisted you to look into Fred Flores' death. Is that so?"

"Yes, did you know Mr. Flores?"

"No, not really. I saw him at church now and then, speaking with Father Fitz. But there was one strange thing he did a day or two before... well, before he died. He brought in a piece of paper with a list of groceries on it and wanted to know if I knew who it had belonged to. I looked at it and told him no, I'd never seen that list before. I would have remembered it because we don't sell ice cream."

I nodded and showed him the copy of the list that I had.

"Yes, that's the same list." I thought he was done, but then he added, "I did tell him I'd seen that fancy writing before, though. Occasionally, I get a list from the army base, things they've run out of until the next supply run, mostly. And sometimes, that list is written in that hand."

"You're sure?"

He nodded and handed it back to me. "A man who reads lists all day long appreciates a clear, legible hand, Miss Harmony. I'm positive I have seen that writing before."

I brought the groceries back to the inn.

It had started snowing again but I was so focused, I didn't feel the cold.

Did Mr. Fellows' information mean the grocery list was a clue leading to a soldier at the army base? I made a mental note to ask Martha who wrote the lists of groceries needed.

CLARENCE'S FIX-IT SHOP

After leaving the groceries with my aunt, I went back out, down the front steps. I was headed across the street but had to stop. I waved and waited for the horse-drawn trolley to go by but, instead, Hiram Merriweather, one of the two brothers who operated the transport, pulled to a stop to say hello.

"Miss Harmony! Nice to see you again. Can I take you anywhere?"

"No, thank you, Mr. Merriweather. I'm only crossing the street. How are you feeling after the flu?"

"Fit as a fiddle. Take more than that to stop an old bird like me." He wagged his finger at me. "Now I heard a rumor that you're getting involved in whatever happened to Fred Flores. Is that true?"

I sighed and thought, *what?* Was it on the front page of The Chronicle? *Jane Harmony at it Again?*

"I'm only assisting the Chief and Captain Maitland with this case. Don't you worry, I'll be careful. I promise."

He grunted. "Well, the Chief told me to keep my eye out for any strangers and I haven't seen none. He also asked about that friend of Fred's, name of Cede or something funny like that. Haven't seen him either."

I thanked him for the information, said goodbye, and watched the former streetcar, now painted a patriotic blue with white stars, disappear around the corner. As I headed across the street, I remembered Thomas saying that there wasn't much that went on in Winslet that the Merriweather 'boys'—two eighty-something-year-old men—didn't know. Even so, I hoped to fare better with Micah.

Clarence's Fix-it Shop had been in the same location in downtown Winslet since I was a child. It had been closed when I was in town in October because Clarence the 3rd, the current proprietor, had signed up right after Pearl

Harbor, along with many of Winslet's young men and some not quite so young.

Aunt Ida told me that Micah had written to Clarence and offered to 'man the place' for him and Clarence had jumped at the chance for his business to keep going while he was away.

I entered the small, dimly lit store that smelled of dust, time, and old memories. The shelves held everything from toys to toasters, radios to shoes. There was a sale table near the front of the store filled with an assortment of refurbished lamps. Along one wall, a large space was filled with used suitcases piled high and more on the floor besides. They came complete with stickers from cities like New York, Chicago, Washington D.C., and Paris, France.

I went to the counter and rang the small dinner bell for service. Beyond the counter was

the largest rolltop desk I'd ever seen. On the open writing surface sat a collection of clocks and watches. The cubby holes meant for envelopes and bills were instead jammed with small tools, and two goose-necked desk lamps —one on each side—were shining down on the silver and gold timepieces.

A minute later, Micah came into the room through a curtained doorway beside the desk. He carried an alarm clock in one hand and a screwdriver in the other. His face lit up when he saw me. I was afraid he was hoping I had come to the store to give him news of Mr. Flores' murderer and my suspicion was confirmed right away.

"Oh, hello, Miss Harmony! Do you have news for me? Didn't mean to make you wait. Needed somethin' back there."

"That's fine, Micah, I wasn't waiting long. I'm sorry to disappoint but we've found few clues." He nodded. "This is an interesting store, a little bit from everybody's attic I'd say." He laughed and put the clock he'd been working on down on the counter. "Do those bells ring?"

I pointed to the two that sat atop the clock.

"Do now I've replaced the mainspring. Hard to get these parts nowadays."

He set the clock and a minute later, a small hammer hit first one bell then the other, back and forth, until he shut it off. The sounds would certainly wake a person up. I thanked him for showing me and then got on to my reason for coming.

I took Mr. Flores' grocery list out of my pocket and handed it to him.

"Mr. Flores forgot his backpack at the library, and we found this in it."

He looked at it.

"Now, we all know Mr. Flores had no use for a grocery list, but Miss Smithers thinks it was some sort of coded message he was trying to figure out. We wondered what you thought?"

"Fred never let that backpack out of his sight, so if it was at the library, there was a reason." He gave me a meaningful glance. "And Miss Smithers knows as well as I do that Fred didn't make this list. He never wrote anything, always printed."

"Yes, she said that." I waited for him to say more.

"It's some sort of message, all right. I don't know from who to who but if Fred was interested, it must be important."

"Mr. Reddy saw him studying it and said he was very evasive about what it was." He nodded and handed me back the list. With fingers crossed, I asked my next question, "Do you know anything about breaking codes?"

To my disappointment, he shook his head and said, "No, that was the kind of thing Fred was good at, not me. But I'll give you a piece of advice, if I may?" I nodded and he continued, "I wouldn't go flashing that list around town. Get people all riled up about spies and such."

"That's exactly what the Chief said."

"I'm surprised he let you have it. How'd you manage that?"

"Miss Smithers actually did it. I saw a new side of her today." I started to laugh. "She's a force to be reckoned with."

"Then you two make quite a pair, birds of a feather, I'd say. I almost feel sorry for Chief Fielding."

I chose to take that as a compliment and asked my next question. "Has this man Cede turned up anywhere since word of Mr. Flores' death got out? Have you seen him?"

"No, and Johnny and I been looking and asking around. Nothing. I got a feeling like he don't *want* to be found."

CARRIAGE LANTERN INN

By the time I returned to the inn, changed into what I thought of as my 'working clothes'—a pair of dark-blue gabardine trousers, white blouse, and light-blue sweater— Mike had arrived to go to Strathmore and there was no time for lunch.

Mike was in a quiet, sullen mood. There was no conversation all the way to the hospital. Sergeant Jenkins joined us at the gate, walked us to the door, and waited until we entered before leaving. Mike nodded, but didn't speak to him, either.

·   ·   ·

STRATHMORE

Martha was at her desk and smiled at us as we came through the door.

"Jane, Captain Maitland is waiting for you. I called Lieutenant Shrug and told her I was pretty sure you would be eating lunch with him." She winked.

I turned to Mike to ask if he minded but he waved me off without saying a word and took the stairs, two at a time, to go see the patients. I had no idea what was bothering him, but I planned to find out later.

"Martha, I have a question."

"Is this cloak-and-dagger or regular stuff?" She wiggled her eyebrows a la Groucho Marx and I laughed.

"Might be the former. Do you know who writes out lists that go to Fellows Market when extra groceries are needed? Lists like this one?"

I reached into my bag and pulled out the list from Mr. Flores.

"Oh sure, this was written by Sergeant Richmond." My heart skipped a beat. I was so excited until she said, "But that doesn't mean it was *his* list. His writing is so much better than most of the men around here that he copies things all the time. And he doesn't change a thing." She pointed to one word on the paper. "Look. See how *tomatoes* is spelled wrong here; he left it the way it was."

Feeling a bit deflated, I knocked softly on Hank's office door and went inside when he called out *enter!* He stopped writing, smiled, got up, and came over to wrap me in strong arms. Neither of us spoke and we stayed that way until he finally pulled away.

"Hi. You hungry?"

Before I could respond, my stomach growled and we both laughed.

"That's what I like, a woman of few words. C'mon."

We went across the hallway to a door I had only seen closed. It turned out to be a small conference room with a round table in the center, covered with a white tablecloth and set with two places. Hank seated me, said he'd be right back, and he was. He returned carrying a tray. I could smell turkey vegetable soup. Stacked beside that were toasted cheese sandwiches and, finally, dishes of vanilla pudding with fruit for dessert.

My stomach growled again, and he sat down. "Cookie had this waiting. Let's eat first, talk after."

One large bowl of soup and three halves of toasted cheese sandwiches later, I was full enough to sit back and pause before dessert.

"That was so good! I always thought of army food as blah but that was anything but."

"The food here has been great," Hank said as he also sat back. "You're right about blah in many army places but we're spoiled. It kills me to give him credit, but I think your Uncle Albert pulled strings. You should see our Sunday dinners."

"Speaking of that 'dear' man, have you heard any more since he left?"

"First, I want to apologize again for the way you and Mike were treated by him. If he were a soldier... well, I doubt we'll be seeing much of him now anyway."

"Really? Why? How?" I was genuinely excited.

"When he came downstairs, he continued to carry on and threatened again to tell the President about my incompetence until Paul went to the telephone and called *his* senior officer. He began explaining what had happened until Albert ripped the phone right out of his hand and started with, "Now you listen to me..." I'd never seen Paul so angry.

"Albert didn't get to say very much. Whatever he was told, we watched as his face went from beet red to no color at all in a matter of seconds. He hung up the phone, mumbled something about calling the President, and left without another word.

"I don't envy my friend that trip back to Washington, I'll tell you. I had all I could do not to sock him. Your uncle, I mean."

I laughed. "Well, don't hesitate on my account. I'm glad he's gone; the man gives me the creeps. And what about Joseph Hoffman? I heard he was in your office, too."

He looked at me askance. "Looks like I may need to have a little chat with a certain private at the front desk..."

I started to plead her case, but he laughed.

"I'm teasing, Jane—mostly. Hoffman is helping the men who are almost ready to go. He is the one who will help them settle in at their homes and follow up with them."

"You trust him that much?" I couldn't keep the surprise out of my voice.

"Yes, why?"

"Well, I heard he was going to come back to Winslet, demand Catherine and the baby live with him, and... and Catherine left town because of him!"

"What are you talking about? And who did you hear this from?"

"Albert told..."

"Albert again! Listen, Hoffman is working with those men and TJ, too. He's great with them. As far as trusting him goes, when the three of us went to Italy, he had many opportunities to kill us or have us captured. He did the opposite—he risked his own life, family and friends. *And,* as far as Catherine goes, he showed me the divorce papers when he got here. I hadn't understood their arrangement before, but he said he planned to stick to it. Catherine had signed the papers a while ago and he signed them in front of our notary. They should have gone out with the last mailing, as a matter of fact."

I was so relieved I leapt up, sat in his lap, and gave him a long, passionate kiss. It was a few minutes before we pulled apart.

"God, I wish we were someplace else!" He physically put me back on my feet. "You can't kiss me like that where anybody could walk in."

He ran his fingers through his hair and straightened the tie I had messed up. I laughed and sat back down, thinking that had been the highlight of our discussion. I was so wrong.

"We haven't had any quiet time together like this in such a long time, Hank. I had almost forgotten how nice it is to share a meal and talk with you." I reached over and we squeezed hands.

"Same here." He let go of my hand and sat up straighter. "And that brings up the reason why I wanted to talk with you yesterday and today, again."

His voice became sober, his eyes serious.

I also sat up straighter and could feel myself tense.

"Jane, I've been thinking a lot about our conversation in the park Christmas Day and about how we seem to be at odds with each other all the time."

My throat started to feel dry.

"I've come to some conclusions. First, I was wrong about your job. Dismissing it like I did. You wanting to work at what you're trained to do, and are needed so desperately for, makes perfect sense. It's basically the argument Paul made to get me into the Italian campaign and this assignment—and I even left you at the altar to do it."

He certainly had my interest.

"Second, you seem to have both a need and a desire to do investigative work." I tried to interrupt, to explain, but he asked me to let him finish. "I confess I don't understand it, but I do trust you, so I need to curb my natural protective instincts and stop objecting." I started to jump up again until I heard, "HOWEVER, the only way I can truly accept it is if I work with you on the investigation and know exactly what you are up to. In that way, I may still be able to prevent harm from coming to you."

My mind raced as he waited for the questions he knew would come.

"What's your definition of working together Hank? You direct and I follow?"

He sighed. "I suppose I deserved that. No, the way I see it is we would have to be partners, equal partners, and that partnership is based on trust. The only thing that could limit what I share with you is that some of the information I have, I can't talk about."

"Top Secret stuff?"

This time, he laughed a bit. "No, I'm talking more like *Confidential*—at least so far."

Again, I took a few minutes. "So how would all this work in your mind? Do we get married at some point?"

"Absolutely. After the war is over, the first Saturday it can be arranged, we have a date to get married." Once more, he squeezed my hand. "Until then, you continue your nursing work in hospitals, I continue with the army, we work together on any investigations, we sneak in whatever private moments we can, and we take a lot of cold showers. At least I do."

"Are you sure? This sounds like quite an about face."

"Yes, well, I've thought about it a lot and I realized I'm the person who must adapt to some changes here, Jane. Since I was in my early twenties, I've been taking care of the people I love. When our parents died, I became responsible for my brother and sister, seeing to their safety and education. Our family business was in tough shape, so I had to work on that before a lot of people we knew and cared about lost their jobs. And now, I'm in charge of an army base with an important mission. When it comes to you, my brain goes right into protection mode, maybe over-protection mode, because no one and nothing has ever been as important to me."

After a hug, a long kiss, and a few tears from both of us, he went on.

"Knowing I needed help, I asked for advice."

"Advice? About me? How many people did you ask? *Who* did you ask?"

"TJ, Father Fitz, and I called your friend Margie, who I like very much, by the way." I swear he blushed. "I tried to plead my case to more objective people, but they cut through the years of tradition that had formed my thinking and asked one question.

"They all asked if I loved you, and when I said yes, they all told me to stop trying to change you because I would lose you. I knew what they said was true, and I also knew I would have gotten around to the same conclusions eventually, but time is not on our side, Jane, so I took a shortcut. Are you angry?"

"No, no I'm not."

My heart felt full. I wanted to cry or laugh. Instead, I tried to understand how things would work.

"Do you want to know what I know so far... partner?"

"Shoot."

Hank already knew a lot of what I knew, so I focused on the grocery list and the fact that nobody could find this man Cede. I repeated my conversations with Mr. Fellows about other lists in the same writing coming from the army base, that Miss Smithers and the Chief thought a possible code was hidden in the list that had the German word for tomatoes on it, and the fact that the man called Cede likely did not want to be found, according to Micah.

I finished with Martha's revelations.

He nodded. "You've been busy. What if you continue working on that list, and I see if anyone around here knows this Cede? That work?"

I agreed with the plan and knew he would think it over and get back to me with any ideas he came up with. That was how his mind worked, careful and precise.

I took a deep breath and said, "That's basic investigative stuff, but now I'm going to test your resolve."

I told him about approaching Anna Polanski, and her response. He reached over for my hand again and what he said washed over me like a spring shower.

"Well, it's done now. Let's see what she does when she has time to think about it. Look, Jane, I don't expect this new arrangement with us to go smoothly all the time. What does? All I know is I love you and don't want to lose you because I tried to force you into being who you are not. If you're willing to take a risk on me after some of the not-so-nice things I've done, I stand behind what I've already said."

This time, I didn't bother to try to hide the tears. He helped me stand and hugged me like he would never let go. At the rate I'd been crying since arriving in Winslet, I would soon need to be treated for dehydration.

We stayed locked together until there was a tap on the

door. With a sigh, Hank let go of me and opened it. "Sorry to bother you, Captain, but Major Genese would like you to call him at this number as soon as possible." Martha handed him a piece of paper.

And in a second, my fiancé was gone and the Captain was back. He flashed me a quick smile and said as he walked to the door, "I'll call…" He stopped talking, told Martha he needed one more minute, and closed the door. "Jane, in order to do this right, I had to tell the Chief that I was going to be helping you."

"What did he say? And does he know Mike is helping me, too?"

Hank nodded. "He was actually relieved. I also had to enlist Martha a bit. So that's five of us, which is a lot, but it can't be helped. You will find an envelope from me in your bag when you leave. That's one way we can communicate." And he was gone.

I'd been summarily dismissed.

I wasn't even in the army, but it was beginning to feel that way.

As soon as Hank was gone, Martha said, "Jane, you are positively glowing."

"Am I? Oh Martha, it's like this heavy weight is gone. I'll tell you about it when we can have a few minutes."

Martha and I were walking toward her desk as Mike came back downstairs.

"I wrote the orders needed. And the staff up there are busy doing some sort of inventory. The lieutenant didn't say it, but I think she would prefer us to skip rounds today. And it's okay by me. Take the afternoon off, Jane."

At that point, he turned to Martha.

"Do you think the Captain would have a few moments to talk with me?"

"Yes, Dr. Evans; if you can wait until he finishes the call he's on, he has some time." She turned to me. "I'll call for a car to take you home, Jane. See you tomorrow."

"Mike, ask Hank about Joseph Hoffman. He has some news you'll want to hear."

The door to Hank's office opened and Martha went to speak to him for a minute, then Hank gestured for Mike to come to see him.

I left them to talk, waved to Martha, put on my coat, hat and boots, picked up my bag and headed out the front door to find Sergeant Richmond standing there.

"Do you want to sit in the back all alone, Miss Harmony, or would you rather sit up front with me where it's warmer?"

He delivered the question with a rakish smile. I couldn't decide if he was flirting with me or not, but didn't want to encourage him if he was.

"I'd prefer the back, thank you."

He opened the back door and reached for my bag. "I'll take care of that for you."

"Thank you, Sergeant, but it's not heavy. I'll keep it."

We drove around the loop, past the woods and the garage, to the front gate where the guard stopped us and signed me out.

Once on the road, the sergeant looked in the rearview mirror and I was once more intrigued with his dark eyes. "What do you think of our little hospital? And our patients?"

Instead of answering him, I asked a question of my own.

"Do you work at the hospital, too?"

"It's a small base, Miss Harmony. Some of us function in multiple ways. My main duty is managing the garage, but my father was a builder and I learned a lot by going on jobs with him. It comes in handy here.

"And what about you? I hear you're a nurse. Why would they need a civilian nurse to help with the crazies?"

My eyes locked with his in the mirror. He wasn't flirting, but looking for information.

"Those patients are *not* crazy, and I think we both know it. As for me? I'm here for the same reason they need an auto mechanic to help with the electricity, I suppose."

He laughed, but there was little humor in it. I was trying to think of how to bring up Mr. Flores when he beat me to it.

"Don't mean to seem nosy, Miss Harmony, but everybody around here has been on edge since that old man was killed and then you and Dr. Evans show up and..."

That was it and I gave in to the irritation that had been building. "You may not know it, Sergeant, but *that old man* was a decorated war hero."

He said, "Sorry, ma'am," but I didn't think he was.

We were silent for the rest of the trip to the inn. It was obvious I would need to be more careful in the future—there were people who would be very interested in what I said and did at Strathmore Hospital, for their own reasons. I decided to mention the conversation to Mike and Hank, first chance I got.

———

CHAPTER FOURTEEN

"There is always a pleasure in unraveling a mystery, in catching at the gossamer clue which will guide to certainty."
Elizabeth Gaskell

WEDNESDAY, DECEMBER 29 – WINSLET LIBRARY

AS SOON AS Sergeant Richmond dropped me off, I said a quick hello to my aunt, left the knitting bag at the inn, and headed straight for my second trip to the library.

Mr. Reddy was coming down the stairs at the front entrance as I was walking up the path.

He touched the brim of his cap and said, "Hello, Miss Harmony. Have you had any thoughts about that list I told you about? Did you talk to anyone who knew what it was?"

I looked around to see that we were indeed alone.

"I think it may be important, but for now, I think we need to keep it to a limited number of people, don't you?"

"Right, right you are. I haven't told a soul except you." He patted my hand in reassurance. "Oh, and that soldier, but of course, he's safe. Told me he was part of their security team at Strathmore."

It felt as though my stomach dropped to my knees and it took all my self-control to stay calm. "Um, where did you see this soldier? And which soldier was it?"

"I was at the base, to go over the blackout rules. The lights there have been seen on at night a few times and we can't have that. Captain Maitland assigned a nice fellow, a sergeant, to review them with me and said he would make sure everyone was up to snuff. After we finished, we got to talking about Fred's murder and how everybody was anxious to figure out who did it."

I waited.

"Well, I told him about that time with Fred, when he was so focused on the list. He thought that was very odd but interesting. I told him you and the Chief thought it was, too."

"Was this sergeant's name Richmond?" I held my breath.

"No, I know him." He waved the idea away. "Seen him at the Post Office. No, the name was Irish... or English... Jenkins. That's it! Yes. Sergeant Jenkins. Nice fellow, and smart, too. If you were not already spoken for by your captain, I'd..."

I didn't hear the rest. I mumbled something about being late, said a hasty goodbye to Mr. Reddy, and fairly ran up the library steps.

Miss Smithers was not at her desk, but I found her in

the room to the right of the door, shelving books. There was nobody else in the room.

"Ah Jane, glad to see you. I was wondering how you were doing with your inquiries."

She indicated a chair. I removed my coat, hat and gloves, sat down, and told her about my conversation with Mr. Reddy.

"I must say, I'm surprised that Augustus talked to that soldier about the list. He must have the sense it's important. Problem is, if that soldier spreads the information around the base, it could warn the killer, if the killer indeed is a soldier."

I let out a long breath. "That was exactly what I thought as I listened to him. I did ask him not to tell anyone else but I'm afraid the cat's out of the bag now."

"Agreed. And did you see Micah?"

"Micah is no help with coded messages, says that was Mr. Flores' strength. I also asked him about this Cede person. He said he and Johnny have been asking after him and can't find him. He thinks he doesn't *want* to be found."

Miss Smithers was quiet for a minute and then said, "I only saw him that once, you understand, but I've seen Fred with Micah and Johnny. They joked and teased each other. I told them they were like mischievous little boys who never grew up." She smiled briefly. "But he wasn't like that with Cede. No banter. No conversation at all. I'm not sure what, if anything, that means."

I switched the subject. "On a different note, my friend Martha explained who wrote the grocery list, but it's not very helpful." I related the details and Miss Smithers was as disappointed as I had been.

She shook her head. "As far as decoding that message, I've tried various basic codes and they don't work."

"I have a free afternoon. Want some help?"

She grinned and retrieved a file from her desk, along with several books. As patrons came and left, she took care of library business, while I read enough to develop a healthy respect for both those who created and those who deciphered codes. After a few hours, my eyes were crossed and we were no closer to learning what—if any—message had been contained in the grocery list.

It was time for me to leave but I had one more question. "Do you know a Sergeant Richmond or Sergeant Jenkins?"

She shook her head no. "I understand they have quite an extensive library at the base, I rarely see any soldiers."

CARRIAGE LANTERN INN

I took my time walking back to the inn, stopping in front of the park for a few minutes to watch some children trying to build a snowman bigger than they were. I felt the same kind of comfort I did when I watched Aunt Ida cook, or when I helped with the laundry; normal activities, not related to war or murder, were a gift to be treasured. As much as I knew coming to Winslet was the right thing to do, I found that I missed going to work at MGH, the staff and, most of all, our patients. My job there was also 'normal' and something to be treasured.

Mike and I arrived at the inn at the same time. Thomas and Aunt Ida were in the parlor listening to the radio when we entered so we stopped to talk with them.

"Hello. Don't mean to interrupt. Mike and I need to talk for a while and, unfortunately, it's nothing we can share with you."

Aunt Ida asked why.

Thomas put down his newspaper and answered for me.

"Army bases are private places, Mother. People who work there usually have to keep what they see and do to themselves."

"That's right, Aunt Ida. Sorry. I would like your input, but we signed an official paper today saying we would not talk about what goes on there."

"All right." She looked as though she wanted to say something else but thought better of it. "We ate early tonight but there's dinner in the oven on warm for you. We won't bother you."

She went back to knitting socks for soldiers as we left our coats in the front hall closet. I went to my room to pick up my notebook and a red pen. On the way back, I could hear Aunt Ida and Thomas talking softly but couldn't hear what they were saying. Mike had gone ahead to the kitchen and was already eating when I joined him.

Before we started, I asked about his conversation with Joseph Hoffman.

"Seems that any trouble regarding Hoffman has been coming from your Uncle Albert. Hoffman signed the divorce papers, said he and Catherine had always intended to honor the agreement. He also said he cared for Catherine very much, as a friend, and I'd better treat her right or he'd come find me." Mike grinned.

"Why are you grinning?"

"The man loves her as a sister and is not planning to ruin her life the way Albert Winslet implied. Catherine can feel safe to come home with Elizabeth any time she wants. Hoffman will be leaving soon on his job assignment and he'll be stationed in Boston after that."

The difference in Mike's mood since his meeting with Hoffman was amazing. A total turnaround, from sullen to happy. I hadn't seen him smile like that in a long time and I was sorry to have to go on to less pleasant subjects.

I repeated my car conversation with Sergeant Richmond word for word. Mike said he had already asked my friend Martha about Richmond who reported that he was popular on base, the main reason being that he knew all the gossip and shared it in tantalizing tidbits.

Next, I caught him up on what I had learned from Mr. Reddy and Miss Smithers and showed him the documents Hank had left for me in the knitting bag.

There was a list of the men on base at the time of the murder, as well as the names of those men who had found Mr. Flores' body. Hank added that two 'unofficial' entrances on the far side of the woods that Mr. Flores had used had been located and blocked, that he had ordered Mr. Flores' hut torn down, and that the two army gates were now kept locked.

We looked at the names of those who had been on duty Thursday, December 23rd. There were sixty-one soldiers out of the base complement of 120. I checked off the people I knew or had met already: Hank; Martha; Avis, Anna; Corporal Pauling, the Pharmacist; Sergeant Jenkins, my escort; and Calvin, the medical tech. Dr. Carlson was also there. I didn't say anything to Mike, but was disappointed that Sergeant Richmond's name wasn't listed too.

I had grown to dislike or distrust the man—I wasn't sure which. It was then that I realized he reminded me a great deal of Charles Connawell, Winslet's former bank manager who had been killed in October. Both men thought they could talk their way in or out of anything.

On the list of the four men who'd found Mr. Flores' body, I knew two: Sergeant Richmond and Sergeant Jenkins. Privates Hershey and Macaulley were new names to me.

I asked if Mike knew any of the soldiers I didn't, but he shook his head no. While he finished his meal, I opened my notebook and we updated the list of clues I had written.

Case List
    Frederico (Fred) Flores (FF): Age: 53. No family.

1. Bad left knee, needed walking stick.
2. Veteran—never same after war. Distressed that Germany was again the aggressor.
3. Locals knew him by sight, some gave food or temporary shelter. Library, Micah.
4. Lived rough in lean-to shed in the Strathmore Hospital woods, another in South Winslet woods. Police found gun in good working order in shed.
5. Had sometimes companion called Cede, who stayed with him—man was mute?
6. Micah, FF's good friend, identified body. Johnny, Father Fitz, Thomas, Mr. Reddy and Aggie's grandfather knew him.
7. Aggie's grandfather thought FF had continued to work for government. Mr. Flores was researching secret codes at library.

MURDER:

1. Pathologist said victim was stabbed. Could have

been killed by either man or woman.

2. Chief Fielding originally thought was an accident because body reeked of alcohol, dressed in old clothes, alone in woods, looked as though tripped and fell while running. Reversed decision after visiting scene, listening to Micah.

3. Micah sure death not accident from the beginning: FF didn't drink, needed walking stick for balance. Stick found—broken as if FF had hit someone with it.

4. Fr. Fitz saw ~~regular~~ civilian shoe prints and smaller soldier boots at the clearing.

5. FF's pockets contained four dollars, change, train schedule, handkerchief, pair of socks.

6. FF ~~tossed~~ war medal into nearby bush. Micah believes that was a message—a warning—to him from his friend.

7. Mr. Reddy mentioned a grocery list FF had. A coded message?

QUESTIONS:

1. Where is FF's other hut? Anything important there? Ask chief.

2. Who is this Cede? Was he there the day FF killed? No luck finding him. Hiding?

3. What sort of meeting in woods on army base between at least two people (2 sets footprints) would get somebody killed? Illegal? Info about patients? Does it involve hospital?

4. ~~What, if any, secrets are there to know at Strathmore?~~
5. ~~Who are the patients behind those barred windows?~~
6. Is grocery list important? Some kind of code? Chief and Miss Smithers working on it.
7. How can I get Hank to let me talk to Strathmore soldiers? Hank now helping. Plan to interview? Need meeting with Chief, Hank and us.

MIKE READ THE LIST OVER, then said, "So, at the moment, it looks like we want to know about this Cede character, whether the grocery list is some kind of code, and who—if anyone—at Strathmore would sell information?"

I hesitated to say this out loud but decided it was time. "I think it comes down to three suspects: Cede, and Sergeants Richmond and Jenkins."

"Why them?"

Mike sat back, lit a cigarette, and waited. He reminded me of Mr. Jankowski, the lawyer who had helped me with TJ's case.

"Nobody seems to know anything about this Cede man. He's like a shadow or he's trying to be mysterious. If he were a real friend of Mr. Flores, I think he would have come forward by now, don't you?"

"I'm not sure you can accuse a man of murder because you're curious, Jane. What are your *facts*?"

I paused, unable to come up any more reasons to explain why I thought him guilty. I knew talking about *women's intuition* would get me nowhere.

"And you put Sergeant Richmond on the list when he wasn't even at the base when Mr. Flores was murdered. I hope you have more evidence on Sergeant Jenkins. Do you?"

By now, Mike was looking at me over his glasses and I felt like an errant child. I shook my head.

He went on. "And what about the other man?"

"What other man?" I had no idea why he was introducing another name to the list.

He sighed. "Whoever left the smaller footprints in the clearing. Whoever Mr. Flores saw that day. All three of your 'suspects' are tall men who could have left the *larger* print but not the smaller ones."

Doubt in my investigating abilities hit me like a hammer. My mind immediately went back to the other time I'd had the same feelings—when I had gone to the bank and accused Charles Caldwell of murder. I shivered.

I couldn't sit still anymore. I stood up, cleared the table, washed and dried the dishes, put them away, and finally returned to the table with coffee for both of us.

After a fortifying few sips, I told Mike he was right, that I was letting my feelings cloud my judgment and I said there was obviously a lot more work to do.

I also added 'mystery man' to the case list.

At that point, he reached inside his suit jacket and brought out an opened envelope. "This was at my office when I got there."

As I'd hoped, it was the autopsy results on Fred Flores.

There was no alcohol in his blood; it had been splattered on his clothing. He had died from a knife wound to the back. No surprises, only sad confirmation.

Micah had been right about his friend all along.

Fred Flores had been murdered.

"It says what we all thought." Mike lit another cigarette. "Except for one thing—Mr. Flores was dying. He had advanced stomach cancer and since he must have been in considerable pain before he died, I think he knew it. That tells me that whatever he was doing in those woods, he considered it important enough to spend the limited time he had left doing it."

My eyes filled up with tears quickly.

That news somehow made the murder even more gruesome to me.

"There's more. The knife used to kill Mr. Flores was a stiletto. Do you know what that is?"

"No, I've never heard that name."

"It's a blade that's more dagger than knife, long and narrow with a needle-like point."

"Sounds very dangerous." A chill went through me as I thought of Mr. Flores.

"It is and Jane—the *only* reason someone would carry it is to kill with it. We are dealing with a professional here. I called both Hank and Chief Fielding to let them know."

AFTER A FEW MINUTES OF CONTEMPLATION, I needed to change the subject and asked Mike what he thought of Strathmore Hospital and the patients.

"Now that I've had time to think about it, if the people who called me had been upfront about what I was walking into, I probably would have turned it down."

I hesitated to ask but finally decided it should be out in the open if we had a problem. "Does it hit a little too close to home, Mike?"

"To be honest, yes. When we were told what they're trying to do there, all I could think about were Catherine and Elizabeth. But later, I started remembering. After I was injured in the bombing raid, I spent three months in British hospitals, sometimes mentally out of it, sometimes in and out. After discharge and coming home, I spent three more months dealing with nightmares and drinking to try to forget the war, the devastation I'd seen in London, and the endless patients we treated at the hospital. If I hadn't been offered this job in Winslet and met Catherine... well, I don't know what would have happened to me. I still hear the air raid sirens in my dreams."

He removed his glasses and cleaned them with his handkerchief. "And again, I'm going to say it. I'm damned sorry I got you into all this. You may not have been in a war, but your life with the man you thought was your father and his death..."

I leaned over and squeezed his arm and spoke straight from my heart.

"As to Strathmore, I'm not upset. I have a different perspective than you. It seems to me that both of us are a good fit for that place. A perfect fit because we can understand and hopefully not judge the patients there for their behavior.

"So, please don't worry about bringing me into it. As to my father and the shooting? I've talked to several people who knew different parts of the story about how my mother met John Harmony and what our lives were like. They knew those involved. Mike, I now realize my mother was caught in a terrible situation and did the best she could.

"The one person—Albert Winslet—who could have helped her and changed everything, *didn't*. As far as I'm concerned, he's as guilty about the result as if he'd planned it. And now he's here to wreak more havoc and I will not let him scare me away from Strathmore!"

Mike paused while I took a few breaths to calm down. Then he said, "Okay, point made. Getting back to Strathmore Hospital, we need to be on our guard. Something there is not right, but I can't put my finger on what it is. And when it comes to your investigation efforts, you need to be extremely careful who you say what to."

I told him about Anna Polanski and my botched interview with Sergeant Richmond. Like Hank, he said what was done was done, but cautioned me to be very careful going forward.

When I went to bed later that night, I still had strong doubts about my ability to help in the investigation into Mr. Flores' death and I wanted to talk with Hank.

THURSDAY, DECEMBER 30 - CARRIAGE LANTERN INN

The next morning, I set the breakfast table with four places but changed it to five when Mike arrived with Father Fitz in tow.

"Ah, muffins!" the priest said as he handed Aunt Ida what looked like a one-pound bag of sugar—a gift as valuable as gold since the war began. "This is from a very grateful parishioner and I thought you would put it to better use than I."

Now and then, my aunt got flustered and such a thoughtful gift did that to her since she was used to being the giver rather than the receiver.

She thanked him and asked him to join us for breakfast.

Father Fitz removed the lid on the serving dish in the middle of the table and the smell of my aunt's spiced sausage, potato, and egg casserole filled the air.

After saying grace, we all slathered butter on the hot

bran muffins as Aunt Ida passed around generous helpings of the casserole. There was silence while we tucked into the delicious food, like hungry truck drivers. Lots of cranberry juice and coffee filled out the meal.

"That was perfect, Mrs. W, thank you," said Mike.

The rest of us echoed the sentiment. Aunt Ida was a wonderful cook who had the enviable talent of knowing what foods lifted the general mood and when they were needed. Her skills were a godsend during a protracted war when it was easy to get discouraged.

One of the ways she was different from other cooks I knew was that she grew herbs I was not familiar with and used them liberally in her food. The original plants were shared with her on a friend's return from Italy, before the war. I was used to mostly plain foods, dressed up sometimes with gravy or ketchup that my mother made.

I didn't have mustard until I went to nursing school and ate in the hospital cafeteria. Vegetables were spiced with salt and pepper, parsley, and butter—when available—both at home and at the hospital. One special treat I remember was that my mother liked to serve garden peas with warmed cream and butter.

But Aunt Ida used spices with names strange to me, such as oregano, thyme, and basil. Thomas told us that one guest, at the beginning of the war, had asked my aunt if she thought it was patriotic to use Italian spices when we were fighting the Italians.

My aunt had simply replied that spices were nonpartisan, but if he would prefer, he could have his food plain. Thomas said that ended the discussion.

Father Fitz added, "I had these spices when I was in New York City earlier this year. Italian immigrants brought over a dish they call a *pizza pie,* but it's not a dessert. There was a small restaurant in Times Square that sold only these pies and there was a line out the door."

"Does it look like my pies? What is it made of?" my aunt asked.

"Well, it's not like an apple pie. No, the one I had was square and had a dough crust, covered with tomato sauce or fresh tomatoes with those spices, then cheese and some-times a meat-like salami topping. Mine had more than one kind of cheese. It was delicious and very filling. Soldiers and sailors loved it."

"Sounds good to me!" Mike looked ready to head to New York and we all laughed.

Everybody settled back over coffee to digest the meal and catch up. The men lit cigarettes while Thomas prepared his pipe. My aunt and I, in a rare change of pace, sat for a few minutes before rising to clear the table and clean the kitchen.

Father Fitz asked if we were able to discuss our jobs at Strathmore Hospital. Mike kindly saved me the problem of replying.

"Unfortunately, as we told Mrs. W and Thomas last night, we signed a paper to not discuss anything we see or hear at Strathmore."

Father Fitz whistled. "That says it's serious business going on behind those bars, eh?"

He directed his comments to Thomas, who nodded and said, "Figured it had to be important to get my brother back here from Washington, but he won't want to be away long, so I think he'll leave sooner rather than later".

Sounds of "Hear! Hear!" echoed as we all lifted our juice glasses in agreement.

———

CHAPTER FIFTEEN

"With method and logic, one can accomplish anything."
Agatha Christie

THURSDAY, DECEMBER 30 - WINSLET POST OFFICE

THE BRICK BUILDING that housed the post office was two doors down from Mike's office, past Rexall Drugs. As I entered, a small bell announced my arrival and the woman, who by size and personality dominated the space, stopped putting mail into slots and turned to see who had come in.

"As I live and breathe, it's Jane Harmony!"

She put the pile of mail she'd been holding down on the counter and came over to engulf me in a huge hug. Mrs. Irene Gagnon had not changed a bit since my childhood.

She was a short, stout woman with curly gray hair and glasses that sat perched atop her head. She wore a flower print dress with a green apron over that and smelled of the butterscotch candies that always filled her pockets.

Once I could catch my breath, I said, "Hello, Mrs. G. When I was here in October, I missed seeing you, but was glad you stayed healthy during the flu problem."

"I heard all about what you did when you came back! You didn't miss me, dear; I wasn't here. I was visiting family in Canada for the month of October—always go when the leaves turn color, you know—and when I returned, I heard about the flu, Chief Connawell, TJ, and you solving crimes. I had a long chat with Ida. She's so proud of you and, at the same time, so worried that you took such chances."

I was waiting for her to pause but she rushed right on. "Are you here to stay? Are you leaving Boston finally? Are you going to marry that nice young man and raise a family here? Tell me!"

With that, she sat on the stool behind her high desk and motioned me to the only chair, but I shook my head and remained standing. "As far as my plans go, things are up in the air, what with the war and all. And I'm not sure how long I'll be here." She sighed.

"I came to say hello and ask a few questions, if you don't mind."

"Questions? Jane, are you playing detective again?"

"I'm not playing. I'm working with Chief Fielding." Even though that was a stretch, my conscience stayed quiet. "I'm working to find out more about the man named Fred Flores."

Now she looked genuinely sad. "Oh, yes, poor Fred. Terrible thing that you serve your country and end up murdered."

I wasn't surprised she was already aware it was murder.

Western Union could learn a thing or two from the small-town grapevine.

"So, you knew him?"

"Oh yes, of course, for a long time. Every other Friday, he came in here, regular as clockwork, and picked up his mail. He would visit for a while and we would have a lovely chat. Only man I know around here who appreciated a good cup of tea." She pointed to a small table with cups, saucers, and a tin marked *tea leaves*. "I will miss those visits terribly."

"Do you know why he came every other Friday specifically?"

"Certainly. He picked up a letter. As a matter of fact," she walked over to one of the cubbies and reached in, "Here's one, right here."

She looked at it and then said, "I suppose I should give this to the Chief." She paused, then nodded her head. Decision made, she handed the letter to me. "Since you're working with Chief Fielding, why don't you take this on over to the station and save him a trip? He knows where I am if he has any questions."

I wanted to hug her, but settled for a smile and a thank you. I was about to leave when another question occurred to me.

"Mrs. G, does the mail for the Strathmore Army Base come through this post office?"

She shook her head. "That comes on average once a week from an army sorting station and goes directly to Strathmore. The only soldiers who would come in here are those who want to send and receive mail privately."

"And do any?"

"Several. Their boxes are in that bottom row, right there, beside Fred's."

I looked at her and said as casually as I could, "I suppose it would be unethical for you to let me see who those soldiers are?"

She held my gaze for a long time, and I was afraid I had overstepped the bounds of friendship. I was about to apologize when she headed to the door beside the rows of cubbies and opened it. "I need to restock my envelopes, Jane. If you would be so kind as to help anyone who comes in, I'll be back in two minutes."

With that, she left. I rushed over to the cubbies, took my notebook out of my bag, and noted the names of those receiving mail and the places from which they were postmarked.

She came back in exactly two minutes, gave me another hug, and cautioned me to be careful because there were some very bad people out there.

WINSLET POLICE STATION

I'd been into the police station for the first time in October and being there had made me uncomfortable, since it had been the scene of Chief Connawell's murder *and* my brother had occupied one of the small cells in the back at the time. To return because of another murder made me feel sad—and angry.

Desks had been rearranged. The Chief's desk was no longer directly behind the waist-high counter in the main room, facing four others. The officers' desks, two of which were occupied, were now spaced farther apart and a new bank of file cabinets sat along the far wall. The small switchboard was still located to the right of the front door.

Officer Jean Hemp came over to greet me, a big smile on her face. "Jane! I heard you were back. How are you?"

Jean was slim with dark hair and light brown, almost hazel eyes. She wore her hair pulled back off her face, small silver earrings, and no make-up. She looked professional, competent, and attractive. She had been a great help in October, even when she was sick.

"Hello, Jean. It's so nice to see you looking healthy."

"Thanks to you and Dr. Evans, I am. I'd had no idea how bad the flu could be before it knocked me right off my feet." She hunched her shoulders and trembled a bit, a milder version of a dog shaking off water.

"We were very fortunate that the town virtually shut down and people listened about staying at home and doing what they needed to help stop the flu from spreading. If they hadn't, we probably would have had another 1918 outbreak on our hands."

"Amen! While it's wonderful to see you, I doubt you are here to reminisce. Am I right?"

She smiled when she said this, but it felt as though she could see right through me.

"Right. I'd like to see the Chief if he's in." I looked around but didn't see him.

She pointed to her right. "He moved into the conference room; it's now his office as well as the place we meet with families."

"Did he keep...?"

"Chief Connawell's desk? No. It was shipped out to a station in Boston where they don't know the story. Truth be told, it's a relief not to look at it every day." I could understand that. "He's in there. Let me go ask if he can see you."

Chief Fielding stood when I entered his office, stepped in front of his new desk—a somewhat smaller version of the one that had been relocated—and walked past the conference table where TJ and I had sat two months ago.

"Miss Harmony. Should I assume this is not a social call?"

"Now, please don't get upset with me, Chief."

He sighed, closed the door, indicated one of the chairs at the table, and sat beside me.

"Confession is good for the soul. Tell me what you've done and don't leave out any details."

I reviewed my visit to the post office and handed him Mr. Flores' letter. I omitted the part about the soldiers' letters because that was not suspicious—yet.

"Hmm. I've dealt with situations like this before and know I have the legal authority to open this letter."

He looked at me and tapped the envelope against his hand as I sat there and stared back.

Mind made up, he got up and went to the door, opened it, and called Jean.

Once she had joined us, he said, "This letter was mailed to Mr. Fred Flores. I am going to open it in your presence. Please note the date and time in his file."

With that, he used a letter opener to slit the envelope and shook it.

We all gasped but I was the first to speak.

"What does this mean? Why would someone mail an empty envelope?"

The Chief looked at the envelope itself and then carefully peeled off the stamp. Nothing underneath it. Mr. Flores' name and the town were spelled correctly; there was no return address and the envelope looked like one you could buy at any stationery store.

The Chief stood up. "I'm afraid this meeting is over, Miss Harmony. If I'm right, there is more going on here than the murder of a man who pretended to be a homeless drifter. Now, if you will excuse me, I need to speak with Captain Maitland."

"Chief, as you know, I'm now working at Strathmore Hospital. I was under the impression that Captain Maitland had informed you that he is now working with me on the investigation into Mr. Flores' murder and I am going to continue doing that. As a matter of fact, Mike Evans and I need to meet with him for an update. I wish you could join us, but it involves Strathmore Hospital and..."

We stared at each other for at least a full minute and then he sighed. He went back to the other side of his desk and reached for the telephone, asked the operator to connect him with Strathmore, and then said, "Captain Maitland, please."

When the call was put through, my mouth dropped open at what he said. "Hank, Chet here. Your Miss Harmony is with me at the station and feels you, she, and Doc Evans need to meet. I think it's time I sat in, too. Four p.m. at Strathmore?" He looked at me with one eyebrow raised. I nodded.

"That will be good. We'll see you then."

He hung up.

"But how..."

"Miss Harmony, I did not transfer from the Boston Police Department only to take what I thought was going to be a less complicated job. I've known about the patients in Strathmore Hospital and what they have been through since the beginning. It was me, working with the army and the BPD, who arranged their transportation to Winslet. What I didn't know was that a murder would occur and involve me with the safety of those patients."

. . .

MIKE'S OFFICE

I walked into Mike's office to find the waiting room empty except for Ginny, Mike's nurse, who greeted me warmly.

"Hi, Jane, how are you?"

"Good. And how are you feeling?"

"It's so much better now that I'm staying in the office. Some of that is thanks to you since you're going to Strathmore Hospital with Dr. Evans."

I waved that off.

"Truth is, nobody around here is used to seeing nurses expecting a baby. And heaven help us if anyone should use the word 'pregnant'". She laughed. "They think women should stay home, knit booties, and remain 'confined'.

"And I've heard it's even worse in the manufacturing plants, where the bosses are either firing the women who get pregnant, or looking the other way until the women can't do the job anymore, but not adjusting anything for them."

I nodded. "I know a couple of nurses who secretly got married and had to leave as soon as it was obvious that they weren't just gaining weight. There's not much this war doesn't touch."

We both paused to think about that and when I asked if Mike was available, she nodded, and I knocked on the door of the combined office and examining room. He called *come in* and was sitting there with a huge smile on his face.

I laughed. "Let me guess. The letter was good news and you spoke to Catherine?"

"Yes, and yes. As soon as the divorce is final, we're getting married and you are invited!"

He gestured for me to sit, and we discussed how happy Catherine was for a while and then went on to what I had discovered that morning. The empty envelope intrigued him.

The six private post office boxes included one for Sergeant Richmond and Anna Polanski. The rest of the names we didn't know.

"Do you have a theory what the boxes mean? Did you mention them to the Chief?"

"No. We can discuss it with him and Hank later." I explained about the four-o'-clock meeting.

"Well, it'll be good to compare notes." He stood up, "Let's get a quick lunch—my treat—and then head back to Strathmore and make rounds before the meeting."

REXALL DRUGS

When I went to the Rexall in October, I was greeted with suspicion and anger. The town regulars saw me as someone interfering in a murder investigation that they thought they had already solved by deciding that my brother was guilty of killing Chief Connawell. I disagreed and the visit was an unpleasant experience. On this occasion, as Mike and I took seats on the red leather-topped stools at the marble counter, we were greeted with both smiles and friendly greetings.

Mabel came over with the plastic-covered menus and a big smile.

"Hello Jane, Doc. What's going on? Have you figured out who killed Fred Flores yet?"

Mike shook his head and I smiled back. Hearing that question at Rexall's proved that it was all over town that Fred Flores had been killed. I wondered if there was information to be had from this group who spent many noontime hours discussing town issues.

"Can't do that, Mabel, until we figure out why anyone would want to kill a helpless old man."

I had added the word 'helpless' to see if I could get a rise out of anyone and I certainly did.

A bunch of men sputtered and competed to tell me how wrong I was. Finally, Mike intervened and said, "Let us order our lunch and while we wait for the food, one of you tell us what you all want to say."

We ordered ham sandwiches and barley soup and Ernie, the unofficial spokesman, started talking.

"Miss Harmony, Doc, you are smart people, but you are way off base here. Fred was homeless, true, but that was by choice. He gave away his home to someone he figured needed it more than him. After his Iris died, he didn't want it anymore.

"And homeless isn't the same as helpless, no sir." A chorus of agreements followed his statement. "He came to town every couple of weeks. Saw Micah and Johnny, often helped them out with odd jobs."

Oscar, our local dairy farmer, spoke up at that point.

"Last spring, when I sprained my ankle—remember, Doc?—he took over the milk delivery for a whole week. Tended the cows, too. The wife and I were very grateful. Wouldn't take any money for it but he did stay in our barn and took his meals with us." He paused, looked down for a minute, and then looked up with a smile. "I swear, the cows missed him when he left. The milk has never tasted quite as sweet since."

Everyone laughed at that.

"And another thing," back to Ernie, "Fred read a lot of books and could always answer a politics question. I kept the local paper for him, and he came by my house for dinner one night on each visit and we discussed news. He was always interested in the goings on at Strathmore and what we thought about it all. It may have been an unusual arrangement, but Fred Flores was as much a part of this town as all of us."

Men called out "Yes! Yes!" and banged their spoons on the counter until our lunch arrived, and the conversation went back to what was going on in town.

When we tried to pay our bill, Mabel pushed the money away. "Your money is no good here. After what you two did for the town, there's no charge. And please, find out who killed one of us."

We tried to argue the point, but Ernie said nobody could win an argument with Mabel, and besides, she would have them all chip in for the bill anyway.

Mabel reached out for my arm to stop me leaving and leaned a bit closer.

"The last time I saw Fred was the day before he died. You should know, he was upset about something, but wouldn't tell me what. Instead, he asked me a funny question. He wanted to know if the week before, on a Wednesday, I had seen any of the soldiers dressed in civilian clothes rather than their uniforms."

"What was your answer?"

"No, I hadn't. Truth is, I wouldn't recognize too many of them, in or out of uniform."

"Have you told the Chief this?" She shook her head. "I think you should."

We left after that, more determined than ever to keep digging up information.

———

CHAPTER SIXTEEN

"I am not what happened to me, I am what I choose to become."
Carl Jung

THURSDAY, DECEMBER 30 – STRATHMORE HOSPITAL

IT WAS GROWING COLDER, and snowflakes had started falling by the time we arrived at Strathmore. We were in a pattern of snow squalls, followed by cold, then more squalls. There were piles of mounting snow everywhere.

We passed through the gate, parked our car, and Sergeant Jenkins appeared at our side.

"Miss Harmony, Doctor Evans, how are you today?"

Mike didn't answer so I did.

"We're good, Sergeant, and you?"

"I'm well, thank you. I love snow; everything looks so pristine. And how are you liking your jobs so far?"

That seemed like an odd question for the sergeant to ask and the way he went from snow to work surprised me.

I was about to ask him why he would ask when I felt Mike's hand at my elbow, urging me forward. We were at the front door. The sergeant said goodbye and left.

"What was that all about?" I asked Mike.

"He's fishing. He's seen that something is up, and wants to know the story, I suspect."

I hoped it was that innocent.

Martha was at her desk when we entered.

"Hi Jane, Doc Evans. Oh, is it snowing again?"

"Off and on."

I gave Martha my knitting bag to place out of sight.

As we headed for the stairs to go up to the hospital, TJ came out of Hank's office. He signaled for us to wait for him.

"Hi. Listen, after you two make rounds, could you help me with something?"

"Do you need me or is it Jane you'd like to see?" asked Mike.

"Primarily Jane but your input is always welcome."

"All right." He turned to Martha, "Is the Captain alone in his office?"

She nodded.

"Would you call and see if he'll give me a few minutes?"

She did and told Mike to go on down the hall. He turned to TJ again. "Why don't you two go ahead while I see Captain Maitland and I'll join you when we're done?"

TJ and I went up the stairs, through security, and met Lieutenant Shrug at the door leading to the wards.

He told her Mike would join us in a bit but as she

turned to head down the short hall to the nurses' station, he stopped her.

"Lieutenant, what I want is for Jane and me to comb through the patient files and see if anything looks amiss. We think Fred Flores was killed because he saw something he wasn't supposed to see and we're wondering if maybe there were papers with information about the patients involved. I want to know if anything is missing or out of place."

"Do you want my help?" she asked.

"No, thank you. I spoke to Captain Maitland. He prefers it appears, for your safety, that none of the staff is 'investigating'. He's worried word would somehow get out and you could be in danger. I know the set-up of the files really well and since we don't have that many, it shouldn't take too long."

"That's fine. Do what you need to do." She turned to me and smiled. "Miss Harmony, I'll go ahead and start afternoon rounds and direct you and Dr. Evans to those patients you need to see."

The patients' records were filed by assigned names in the top drawer of the filing cabinet behind the nurses' desk. The cabinet was positioned so the long, flat side was against the wall behind the desk, and the fronts of the drawers faced people entering the area. TJ wanted to start with the first two records; I pulled the top drawer out so both TJ and I could reach in. He removed the file for Alan, the largest, while I reached in for Bob's. They were each at least two inches thick with papers stuffed into them and I almost dropped my folder. While I juggled it, the extended drawer stayed open.

That was when it happened.

Corporal Pauling rounded the corner from the pharmacy carrying a large box, saw us with the charts, stopped short and said, in a shaky voice, "Are you going somewhere with those f...files? I... I need them."

I could see Sergeant Richmond leaving the pharmacy right behind him, also carrying a box, but he wasn't looking ahead at Corporal Pauling; he was looking at Lieutenant Shrug who had called to him from the doorway of the ward. I saw what was going to happen but couldn't warn him in time because it happened in a second or two.

The sergeant bumped directly into Corporal Pauling, pushing him and the box he carried into the cabinet, which meant the sergeant and his box landed on top of the smaller man. Bottles of IV fluids flew out of the open box in the corporal's arms. The weight of the two men tipped the file cabinet over, hitting TJ who was knocked to the side as the cabinet fell, scattering the contents of the folder from his hand. The files in the top drawer flew in all directions as the cabinet tipped. Those pages blended with the ones TJ had been carrying. I tried to jump out of the way, slipped on some papers, and fell onto the desk at the nurses' station, scattering pens, pencils, the telephone, the nursing Kardex and the file I had in my hand. In a Groucho Marx movie, the scene would have looked funny, but it was not, and neither were the consequences.

The file cabinet had landed with a loud bang and several patients immediately began screaming. Two ran down the hall, toward the security door. Three curled up on their beds, pillows over their heads. Dr. Carlson came rushing out of his office, and the guard turned the corner with Martha and Hank right behind him.

They brought the two patients back to the ward with them.

I stood up, a bit shaky, and looked at TJ, who was unconscious. Mike went to him. Lieutenant Shrug, Dr.

Carlson, and one of the medical attendants went into the ward.

A man was screaming, "Don't! Don't! Oh God, not again!" Other voices joined him.

Hank went to the second ward to make sure those patients were all right.

I asked about TJ but got no answer from Mike who, with one of the attendants, was moving him to the vacant bed in the ward. I stumbled over to examine Sergeant Richmond and Corporal Pauling; I was a bit dazed myself. The sergeant was back on his feet almost immediately and helped me get the corporal into a chair. He was bleeding from a deep gash on his forehead, his glasses were broken, he looked ashen, and his side was tender to the touch. His pulse was rapid. The sergeant got the first aid kit from the pharmacy, and I cleaned and dressed the corporal's head wound. Any stitches or x-rays needed would have to wait until Mike was free.

Martha and the guard somehow wrangled the cabinet back into an upright position.

As soon as I could, I left Corporal Pauling with Martha and went into the patient ward. Several patients had hurt themselves trying to run from what they had thought was a bomb. There was broken glass, IV fluids, and blood from patients who had yanked their IV's out of their arms to run.

As soon as one of us approached any patient, they either jumped or hid their heads with their hands. One patient had reverted to speaking French only; most were not speaking at all.

The only patient who had not responded to the sudden noise was Alan. His eyes were still closed, and he hadn't moved. I went over, squeezed his hand, told him he was all right and then went through the chaotic scene in the ward to the porch because all those in the ward were being tended to and I had not seen either Mike or patient Bob. They were both there.

Mike was leaning over the patient, who was lying on his side on the floor. It looked as if he had attempted to curl into a ball, cast and all.

Mike looked up. "Jane, can you get a stretcher and someone to help us pick him up? We need to x-ray this knee. And he's going to need morphine."

Bob was not speaking but he was shivering; tears were leaking from closed eyes, running down his cheeks. I put a cushion under his head, a lap robe over him, and left.

Avis told me where the stretchers were. I returned with Martha, Hank, and Sergeant Richmond. They waited for me to give him an injection and then we managed to lift him up and strap him onto the stretcher, propped up by pillows. When he screamed this time, it was from pain rather than fear, even though we had tried to be gentle.

It seemed Mike knew how to use the portable x-ray machine, as did one of the medical assistants. We maneuvered the stretcher as carefully as we could through the congested ward.

Bob's leg was out of alignment. The cast had split and was now cutting into the man's leg. I assisted Mike as he removed the cast, repositioned the knee, and propped it in place with sandbags on each side that extended from above the knee to below it. They took several x-rays.

Fortunately, it took little manipulation to get the knee back in place and the morphine had started doing its job. Everyone left and Mike said he'd send help to bring him back to the ward as soon as possible. I asked him to check Corporal Pauling's head injury and side.

My attention went back to Bob. "Are you still in pain?"

"Much better; keeping it still helps. What... what was that noise?"

"That big metal filing cabinet behind the nurses' station was knocked over onto its side. The noise frightened all of us."

He looked at me and tried to say something twice but couldn't seem to find the words. Then, so quietly that I had to lean close to hear, he began to talk. "Two women—partisans—and I blew up a section of tracks when we knew a German supply train was coming. We stayed around long enough to see the engine go off the tracks and then we ran for what seemed like miles and hid in the remains of a village church. I don't even know where we were at that point—some of the towns were no bigger than a church and a bakery.

"Suddenly... suddenly, there was this loud bang—louder than today—and next thing I knew, the remains of the steeple collapsed down into the sanctuary where we were hiding and pinned us. S*woosh,* it happened so fast! We tried... we tried to dig ourselves out, but the next blast hit the altar directly."

He was getting sleepy from the pain medication. I told him to rest and that we could talk later, but he said he could remember now and didn't know about later.

"We were right behind the altar and large pieces landed on top of the steeple remains. We lay there, stuck, for at least two days, in pain with no food or water. Our weapons had been lost in the blasts. My ears were ringing awful but every now and then, I heard a weak voice, more like a kitten than a person, and I tried to answer because I thought it was one of the women. My eyes were so filled with dust and dirt I couldn't tell if it was day or night. I figured it was the end and made what I thought was a last confession to an empty church. And I'm not even Catholic."

He stopped talking and closed his eyes. As I added another blanket to keep him warm, he finished. "We waited for the Germans to come back and finish us off, but it was an American squad that found us. They took the two crying women away first. I had to be carried out on a litter and I saw a sign on top of a pile of rubble out front. It said *St. Jude, Patron Saint of the Impossible,* in French. I remember whispering a thank you and then I must have passed out because I woke up in an English hospital and have no idea how I got there."

IT WAS two hours before things were close to normal again, aside from a large stack of paperwork that needed sorting. Corporal Pauling was in his quarters with a male attendant. Mike had examined him, stitched his head wound, and diagnosed bruised—luckily, not broken—ribs as well. He was to be monitored for signs of concussion. All the ward patients were back to bed, most had been medicated, and a few had eaten. The men in the next room, ready for release, were fine and would be leaving the next day.

TJ was still in bed in the ward, but he had woken up and said a few words before he went back to sleep. Mike said he needed time but thought he would be fine. I whispered a prayer of thanks.

Lieutenant Shrug quietly turned to me. "Do you feel as if you understand battle fatigue better now?'

I nodded, still too disturbed to talk.

She looked over at the patients. "For most of them, this condition will go on for a long time. Someone will say something, or they will see something, or a noise will frighten them like today—any of those things can send them right back to a battlefield." She paused to wipe her eyes. "We can only do so much in a short-term hospital setting. I hope the new ward you are going to be part of can put them into a program where they are not forgotten. This is not their fault —their minds just finally reached their breaking point."

It was at that moment that I realized what Dr. Eldridge's new ward needed was Lieutenant Avis Shrug.

———

CHAPTER SEVENTEEN

"The measure of intelligence is the ability to change."
Albert Einstein

THURSDAY, DECEMBER 30 – STRATHMORE HOSPITAL

ANNA and the evening shift had arrived during the clean-up and she and Avis were moving patient records into Dr. Carlson's office when I told Avis I was going to speak to TJ for a moment.

He looked more like himself—his sleepy self, not the ghostly pale man he had looked like a short time ago.

"How are you doing?"

"Good, don't worry. Mike's being over-cautious because he likes telling me what to do." Typical TJ. "What about you? Are you sure you're all right? You landed hard on that desk. Did Mike check you out?"

"I'm good. A few bumps and bruises."

"Glad to hear it, sis." His voice drifted off as he went back to sleep.

I found myself smiling as I headed back to the nurses' desk. TJ hadn't called me 'sis' for a long time. He probably didn't realize it, but he had only ever called me that when we had gotten past one of the many episodes with our father.

It was time for my meeting. I found Lieutenant Shrug in the pharmacy, preparing medications for the patients. I waited until she had finished and then said, "I've got a meeting I'm scheduled to attend, but I'll stay here if you still need me."

She looked at me for a minute, and then put her arms around me and hugged me. I made sure she didn't see me wince with pain and hugged her back.

When we separated, she said, "I'm not afraid to admit when I make mistakes. And I made one about you when I misjudged you. Jane Harmony, you are a fine nurse and exactly the kind of person I want beside me in an emergency—calm, caring, more than competent, and efficient. I apologize for my attitude when I first met you."

"You're not so bad yourself, you know. I saw how you quietly directed all of us to the most needed places and how you spoke with such calm authority and compassion that even frightened men responded. As far as maybe getting the wrong first impression, well, I've done that often enough to not judge when someone else does it. Let's forget all that and move on."

She smiled and stepped around me to look up and down the corridor.

"And the rumor is that you are helping investigate Mr. Flores' murder. Yes?"

Surprised, I nodded.

"Well, I'd like to talk with you about a few odd things around here when we can have some privacy."

She turned back to her pills. "Right now, I've got to pass out these medications and you have a meeting to go to."

Before going downstairs, I made a quick stop at Dr. Carlson's office, where he was reassembling charts. I reported my conversation with Bob and the memories the sound of the cabinet crashing to the floor made him remember. He said several patients had had the same thing happen to them and TJ had better get well in a hurry because he had work to do! He laughed as he said the last part, but we both knew the urgency of using accurate information.

I headed downstairs, surprised and a bit humbled that I felt like a part of this talented team of health care professionals so soon.

HANK'S CONFERENCE ROOM

When I got to the foot of the stairs, Martha greeted me with, "Are you okay?"

I nodded, "And you?"

Her eyes filled with tears. "Jane, I've never seen a group of men that upset. I'm glad you and Lieutenant Shrug kept your heads and could let the rest of us know what to do. I really felt bad for those guys."

I gave her a hug and made a mental note to talk with Dr. Carlson and Father Fitz. I could offer to set up sessions, private or group, for us to talk with anyone who had witnessed the chaos upstairs and needed to talk with people who could help. Margie and I had had a lot of success at MGH with group sessions for the staff and ourselves after we'd lost patients.

She wiped her eyes. "Thanks, that helped."

"Me too."

"Now you'd better go, they're waiting for you in the conference room."

Hank, Chief Fielding, and Mike each had papers in front of them. Martha had handed me the knitting bag I used to carry things back and forth and I took a seat and removed my notebook. Hank smiled at me and then started the meeting.

"Everything quiet up there now, Jane?" he asked. "Are you and the staff all right?"

All three of them looked at me intently.

"We're all doing what needs to be done and we'll deal with feelings later, thanks. The patients are settled now, most of them in bed. Lieutenants Shrug and Polanski are there."

Hank nodded.

"Good, then let's get this meeting going. The purpose is to be sure we are all up to date on the investigation and see if we can put the pieces together. Chief, would you like to start?"

"We've been to Mr. Flores' other hut in South Winslet; it was about the same as the one here but no Cede and no gun. We asked around but people only knew Mr. Flores, not the other man. Every person we spoke to was mighty sorry to learn what had happened to Mr. Flores. Seems like he would help people out whenever they needed it, like he did here, and never asked for anything in return, except maybe a meal."

He paused for a few seconds and then continued. "I talked with our Station Master. I was wondering if everyone on leave for the holidays was really gone and asked if any soldiers had arrived back in Winslet at the time of the murder. Of course, since it was before Christmas, the station was busy, and he couldn't tell us specifically who arrived. However, he did say a soldier named Richmond goes back and forth to Boston at least once a week, and sometimes wears civilian clothes. That means if he had come back, he would blend in with the other passengers."

Hank nodded. "I know about those trips; the sergeant is on army business. But I don't know the exact time he comes or goes."

"Last thing I've got is this." The Chief picked up the envelope I had brought him from the post office. "Apparently, Mr. Flores got a letter at the Winslet Post Office every two weeks. I checked at the South Winslet Post Office—he got one there on the alternate weeks." That was news to me. Hank took the envelope the Chief offered. "As you can see, the envelope is empty and that is the way we found it." He looked at me. "Miss Harmony was there when I opened it."

Hank passed the envelope to Mike, who then passed it to me.

Hank then looked at each of us and said, "Theories?"

Almost as one, we said, "Some sort of message."

The Chief spoke again. "Postmarked Boston. I went back to see Mrs. Gagnon at the post office and asked if she could remember anything about the other letters. She said they didn't all come from Boston; they were usually heavier than this one, and Mr. Flores paid any postage due. She added that every now and then, the envelopes were too large to fit into the P.O. Box."

"Where else were they postmarked from?" asked Mike.

"That's the interesting thing. All local. All from neighboring towns except one. Mrs. Gagnon teased him that one envelope had cost the mailer money when they could simply have asked her to hold it for him. You see, it was mailed in Winslet, pushed through the slot into the night basket. That's almost the same thing they told me in South Winslet. Most of the letters there were postmarked from Winslet."

Before I realized it, I was saying out loud what I had been thinking. "What safer place to keep private information for a man who comes and goes than at a U.S. post office?"

The Chief nodded. "So, whatever Mr. Flores was up to, it looks like he had accomplices, one in Boston and one or more local."

"What do you think Mr. Flores was 'up to', Chief?"

"I don't know, Miss Harmony, but I certainly wish I did."

There were grunts of agreement around the room and the smokers lit up while I rubbed the quarter-sized wooden disc Mr. Flores had carved for me.

Mike went next. "All I have to add is that the autopsy reports confirm Mr. Flores was murdered and that he was a very ill man. Stomach cancer."

"Would that have killed him in time?" asked the Chief.

"Sooner rather than later, I'm guessing," Mike replied and then told them what he had said to me in his office. "Frankly, I'm surprised he was still able to move around as much as he did and to me, that means whatever he was doing mattered to him very much."

Hank responded by saying exactly what I was thinking. "And given the man's past behavior, I believe Mr. Flores was once again serving his country. That alone connects this murder with the patients we have at the hospital."

Hank nodded to me to share my information.

"Miss Smithers and I spent a lot of time working to try

to break the code we believe is buried in that grocery list, but with no luck."

"What language did you look for words in? English?"

I nodded.

"Try German."

"Yes, Miss Smithers is trying that now. It's hard because some of the words I would like her to look for I can't say without giving away the hospital mission."

Hank nodded. "After this meeting, you and I can try again."

"Good. Thank you. I went to the post office also."

"Irene must be thrilled with all the attention," Mike said. As was often the case, Mike tried to lighten a mood, even a little.

"I discovered that several soldiers have private P.O. boxes there, right beside Mr. Flores' box. The two connected with the hospital are Anna Polanski and Sergeant Richmond, who doesn't work there but pops in on a regular basis."

The Chief asked Hank, "Why would they need a private P.O. box? Is there any problem or delay with the army mail drop?"

Hank shook his head but added to the notes he had been keeping since the start of the meeting.

"Last thing. Avis Shrug would like to talk privately with me. Says she has been noticing some odd behavior lately."

"Shouldn't we have her come down here now and talk to all of us?" the Chief asked.

Before I could answer, there was a quick knock on the door and a very pale Martha came bursting into the room. "Captain, someone has tried to kill Corporal Pauling."

All four of us were up and running immediately, Hank in the lead. He called over his shoulder to Martha, telling her to put the base into lockdown, and have Lieutenant Edward Wellesley, Hank's second-in-command, conduct a roll call on the parade grounds.

CORPORAL PAULING'S APARTMENT

Once we went through the back door of the building and onto the path leading to the barracks, it seemed as though armed soldiers were joining us from every direction. We were all running toward Corporal Pauling's room on the first floor of the barracks to our left, arriving pretty much at the same time.

Sergeant Jenkins and a soldier I didn't know were on guard at the door and were totally dressed in black instead of their uniforms. We didn't stop to ask why. Everyone made way for Hank and the soldiers spread out around the outside of the building.

Hank went through the door and the rest of us followed.

The corporal was in a single bed in the left corner of the room, opposite from us. The area around it was in chaos. A table and chair were upended beside the bed and an alarm clock, glass, and water were on the floor. The bedspread was half on, half off the bed. An easy chair, small table with two chairs, lamp and bookcase on the other side of the room looked untouched.

Mike listened to the corporal's heart and checked his pupils with the beam of a flashlight. He didn't respond to our voices but did move his hand reflexively when Mike tested it with a pin.

I readjusted the oxygen mask that had fallen off and increased the liter flow.

Mike turned to address the others in the room.

"He's unconscious and needs to be admitted into a

Special Care Unit. Before you ask, I have no idea when or if he'll come around."

Hank turned to Calvin. "Are you all right?"

Calvin, bleeding from a nasty cut on his cheek, answered, "Yes, sir."

"What happened?"

"I went to the bathroom sink to refill the ice bag for the corporal's head wound. I was only gone a minute but when I came out, a man dressed in black was leaning over the corporal, trying to smother him with that."

He pointed to a pillow that had landed on the floor.

"I jumped him, yelled for the guard outside, and we fought. He got in a good punch but as I fell to the floor, I managed to reach the phone that had fallen off the bedside table and holler to the operator that I needed help in room 101. He ran.

"I left everything the way I found it so you could see it."

"Why are Sergeant Jenkins and the other soldier on guard dressed in black, too?" I asked.

Hank answered me. "Voluntary commando exercises in the woods tonight which means there should be twenty or more men around here dressed in black. Finding this guy will be tough." He turned back to Calvin and said, "And where *was* the guard while all this happened?"

"Knocked out cold. He's in my room, next door, curled up to an ice pack if you want to see him. He feels pretty bad that the guy got past him, sir, and I do, too."

MIKE PICKED up the phone and called Sedgewick Hospital in South Winslet. After a few connections, he finally talked to the medical director of their Special Care

Unit and explained the situation. They discussed a specific room for the corporal and then Mike hung up.

"No bed tonight but he thinks they can move a patient after rounds in the morning and we would be able to bring the corporal there before noon. It's a private room in the SCU that they keep for patients who need attendants or guards, so a soldier can go with him." He asked Hank, "Is that acceptable to the army?"

"I'll call Major Genese and discuss it with him. That sounds good for tomorrow, at least until he's stable enough to move to an army facility. But what about tonight? I'm reluctant to put him in with our patients here, especially after what they've been through today."

I spoke up quickly. "Why can't we move him to the inn? I'm sure Thomas and Aunt Ida wouldn't mind. Mike, Calvin, and I can handle his medical care and you can post as many guards as you think you'll need."

Mike nodded. "Yes, that's a good idea. It worked for our sickest flu patients in October and the transfers to the hospital went well."

"I can give you police coverage for the night, too," added the Chief.

"Jane, could you ask Thomas and Mrs. W?"

I went to the phone and asked the operator for the inn. Before she rang the number, she wanted to know if everything was all right at the base. I told her yes to avoid a long list of questions. Aunt Ida answered. I explained what had happened to Corporal Pauling at the inn and she agreed he should come there, as I knew she would.

"Aunt Ida, I know this is a scary time. There's a killer out there who is getting desperate. The army will have guards there, and Calvin, Mike, and I will be there. Please be honest. We could figure something else out if needed."

"Jane, we want to help, and we trust you and Captain Maitland. Please, just bring him here."

I told Hank and the others the news and Calvin started preparing for the move. When I got closer to Hank, to satisfy my curiosity, I asked, "Why does the corporal have a private phone in his room?"

"In case there are any pharmacy needs when he's off duty. Avis Shrug and I have one, too."

CARRIAGE LANTERN INN

The move from Strathmore was handled in a quick and efficient manner. Corporal Pauling was moved from his bed to a litter and put into the back of an army truck, on a pile of blankets. He was carried upstairs at the inn on the same litter and tucked into bed. I rode in the back with him, Mike up front with the driver, and four armed soldiers in a jeep behind us. Our patient had not stirred during the trip. Fortunately, it was past sunset and the whole downtown area was empty of questioning eyes.

Mike examined Corporal Pauling again. His pupils still responded to light sluggishly. He did not respond to voice commands, his breathing was irregular at times, and he had an elevated but steady pulse. Calvin, who refused the offer to be off duty and get some rest, took the first shift sitting with him while Mike and I went downstairs to eat the meal my aunt had prepared.

I swear, she could feed everyone at Strathmore on a moment's notice.

Three guards stayed at the inn, two out back and one on the front porch, all in the shadows. Aunt Ida would feed them and Calvin when we were done, and Thomas and

Mike would be on guard while I went back to Corporal Pauling.

As we started eating our soup, the doorbell rang.

I answered it to find Father Fitz standing there.

"Captain Maitland thought you could use an extra hand inside and I got elected. Since I knew it came with Mrs. W's food, I agreed."

He grinned like a little boy, hung his coat on the rack by the door, and followed me to the kitchen.

"Look what the smell of your soup and corn bread dragged in, Aunt Ida!"

We all laughed and made a place for him.

It was awkward to sit and eat with my aunt and uncle and my favorite priest and not be able to tell them what they wanted to know—what had happened to the soldier upstairs, whose name they didn't even know. I hated feeling that I was holding something back, but I had signed that paper...

There was another knock on the front door. Thomas answered it and returned with Hank, who removed his coat and hung it on a peg by the back door. He kissed my cheek before taking the seat my aunt offered.

"Are you hungry, Captain? There's soup and corn bread."

"Thanks. I'll pass on the food, but I'd like coffee, if you have it?"

"Thanks to you, we do."

The rest of us finished supper quickly and my aunt and I cleared the table. It was obvious Hank was there for a reason. He removed some papers from his inside pocket.

"Unusual problems call for unusual solutions. Mrs. W, Thomas and Father Fitz, while Corporal Pauling is a patient here, I'm considering the inn an extension of Strathmore Hospital. As such, I am offering you temporary hospital employment with the caveat that you sign this confidentiality agreement. Do you accept?"

Thomas and Aunt Ida looked at each other, nodded, and accepted their forms, as did Father Fitz. They read them and signed them.

"Good, thank you. I've taken the liberty of asking the Chief to join us." As if Hank had conjured him up, the Chief knocked and then came through the back door. He was settled in a minute and Hank continued.

"Because of your new status, we are able to discuss the investigation of the murder of Fred Flores with all of you. That may be stretching the term *temporary employee* a bit, but since we don't know if the attack on Corporal Pauling is related to Mr. Flores' murder and you could be in some danger, I think it's justified."

Hank briefly explained to them the purpose of Strathmore Hospital and how they were using the information obtained.

Father Fitz whistled. "Imagine, all that in quaint little Winslet!"

My aunt and Thomas murmured their agreement.

Hank looked at Mike. "What is the corporal's status now?"

Mike stood up. "Actually, I'm going up to check on him right now. I'll be back shortly."

Father Fitz also stood. "It seems Corporal Pauling is Catholic. I'd like to say some prayers for him."

They went upstairs and the rest of us moved around. Hank and the Chief went out to the back porch to talk privately, Aunt Ida and I washed the dishes, and Thomas went downstairs to the basement to stoke the furnace.

Everyone was seated at the table again about fifteen minutes later.

"There's no change in his condition."

"When do you think he will be able to talk to us?"

"We don't know how long that pillow was stopping his intake of oxygen. His condition could last hours, days, or even months. We're giving him oxygen, keeping him hydrated, and monitoring his breathing and level of consciousness. We hope to transfer him to Sedgwick Hospital tomorrow..."

Hank shook his head. "Plans on that have changed. I've got orders that if he doesn't wake up tonight, I'm to make arrangements to drive him to Massachusetts General Hospital tomorrow." He turned to me. "The army has some sort of arrangement with the hospital, right?"

"Yes, they do. We had soldiers on our ward now and then, and another ward is being planned that will have more."

Mike's face was beet red. "And where do you think those orders came from?"

"Major Genese didn't tell me, but I know he disagreed, like I do. We both know Corporal Pauling should not take such a long journey yet." He looked at Thomas. "This is pure speculation but your brother Albert may still have more to say about Strathmore than we thought. I know he has the President's ear but... well, let's pray that Pauling wakes up tonight."

"And are the *brass* aware that such a long ride could be dangerous for him?"

"They are. That's why I was told to ask you to go with him, personally."

Mike swore.

What followed was a silent contest of wills. Both men knew Hank could not change his orders. Both men knew that the bouncing and jostling inevitable in a truck would not be helpful for the corporal. They also both knew that if an emergency occurred while in transport, there was little that could be done, even with Mike there. The room felt as though it was getting smaller and warmer as the rest of us waited for a decision.

Each man looked torn by their duty—Hank to country, Mike to his patient—but it was Mike who gave in, knowing he had no other choice, really. "I'll go."

The Chief spoke up. "You can borrow Winslet's ambulance for the trip. There's nothing modern about it, but it's a better set-up—more comfortable for the patient—for transport than the army's trucks, I think."

Mike nodded his thanks.

"And four soldiers will follow you in an unmarked car. Three will stay in Boston, one will be with the corporal on guard duty for each shift, the other can bring you back," said Hank.

Mike lit up a cigarette and I put my hand on his arm. "Once you get your patient settled, you could go see Catherine and the baby."

Again, he nodded. His shoulders relaxed a bit and it looked as though he'd accepted the decision as well as he could.

The Chief waited a minute, and then said, "Now that the plan for Corporal Pauling is set, I'd like to ask a question." Hank nodded. "Why would someone want to kill the corporal? What does he do? Is he that important?"

Hank answered. "He is our Pharmacy Technician which means he dispenses medications, mixes solutions, orders drugs, and maintains the narcotic records. He also stores and maintains all medical equipment. His role is important."

"In that capacity, would he have access to the patient charts and records?"

"Absolutely."

"Which means he would have access to what those patients at Strathmore Hospital are telling us?"

"I see where you're going with the question. I thought the same thing at first, but if someone wants information, killing the corporal isn't going to get it from him."

The Chief agreed, Thomas grunted, and everyone else stayed silent until Father Fitz said, "Chief, what if it's the other way 'round? The corporal is injured—in a more vulnerable position, you could say. More likely to say something he wouldn't otherwise. In that case, the person who attempted to kill him could have been trying to *stop* the corporal telling us what he knows."

I knew Father Fitz well enough to be sure he had something else to say, so I asked,

"And do you have any thoughts on how that theory would fit with Mr. Flores' murder?"

"Yes, darlin', I do." He winked at me. "You see, Corporal Pauling has small feet—about the same size as the second man in the clearing, where Fred Flores witnessed the meeting that cost him his life."

———

CHAPTER EIGHTEEN

"It is better to offer no excuse than a bad one."
George Washington

THURSDAY, DECEMBER 30 – CARRIAGE
LANTERN INN

THE MEN WERE STOIC; my aunt and I gasped. Was
Corporal Pauling one of the missing links? Was that why
someone wanted him dead?

"If your theory is right, it would follow that the man
who did this is the same man who killed Fred Flores."

The Chief wasn't asking a question; he was thinking out
loud.

"Everyone was present and accounted for at the base, so
it's a soldier we're looking for," Hank added.

"A soldier dressed in black, like the guards?" I asked.

"When Wellesley checked, the black clothes idea got

more complicated. When he asked which soldiers had been a part of the exercises in the woods, twenty men still in black stepped forward but then twenty-seven more who had put their fatigues on over the black clothes they wore for the exercises also stepped forward."

He sighed. "Usually, these events are assigned and there's paperwork to be filed about how long the men participate, but this one was voluntary, and Richmond and Jenkins were more lenient. Seems men were going in and out all day for an hour or two at a time, practicing for tonight. Most could prove approximately when they went into the woods, but few could prove when they came out."

My aunt spoke up next. "Captain, do you think whoever already tried will try to kill that young man again?"

"I don't mean to alarm you, but I believe that depends on how desperate he is feeling right now. We need to know what Corporal Pauling knows."

People were getting restless, I could tell. Like me, they wanted to *do* something.

"I mentioned before Martha came in that Avis wanted to talk with me. Should we call her or have her come here so we can all hear what she has to say?"

Hank was the only one who didn't say yes. Instead, he stood and went to the phone. I heard him updating Martha on the corporal's condition and then asking to be connected to the hospital. It was a short conversation with the lieutenant, first asking how the patients handled the noise and activity surrounding the attack on Corporal Pauling, then asking her to come to the inn.

Everyone moved around again. My aunt and I relocated the group to the dining room since there was not enough room at the kitchen table for Avis to join us. We set up coffee, tea, and a platter with bread, cheese, and apple slices. After that, I updated my notebook with the latest events. Mike went upstairs to check on Corporal Pauling, Hank went out back to talk with the guards, the Chief called the station, and Father Fitz went out onto the front porch.

It was early evening by the time all of us, plus Avis, sat down to finish our meeting that had begun what seemed like a very long time ago.

Avis was introduced to those she didn't know, and I explained that if something she had seen or heard could help us find out who had tried to kill Corporal Pauling, we all needed to hear it.

"Yes, I understand. What I wanted to talk with you about was Sergeant Richmond and Sergeant Jenkins." She paused, as if looking for the appropriate words. "You know by now that Richmond is in and out of the hospital for various reasons—repairs, trips to the attic, etc., and lately, Jenkins is often with him. Well, yesterday, Corporal Pauling was leaning over my desk, telling me how worried he was about his sick mother. He'd had another letter from his sister asking if he could get leave to come home to see her. He was very intense."

She stopped talking.

"Go on, lieutenant, tell us what you came to say."

Hank spoke in what I would call a 'soft' command voice—not authority filled but leaving no doubt that he meant it.

"I hate talking about a fellow soldier like this, but the two sergeants came down the hall from the attic at that point, and when the corporal saw them, he broke into a sweat, straightened up, and stuttered a thank you when his language had been perfectly fine beforehand. He rushed into the pharmacy. Sergeant Richmond watched him, but the two men came toward the desk and left the suitcases for the men who are leaving from ward two.

"Later, I asked Anna if she had noticed that Corporal Pauling got nervous around Sergeant Richmond and or Sergeant Jenkins and she instantly became jittery herself, stood up, and left the station, saying over her shoulder that there was something she'd forgotten to do."

"And what did you do about this, lieutenant?"

"I spoke to Dr. Carlson. We decided we would get Andy Pauling and Anna together the next day—today—and ask them what was going on. We never had a chance to do that."

"Thank you, Lieutenant. You may return to Strathmore."

Hank was about to wrap up the meeting when I said, "One last thing. What about Cede? I think he remains high on any list of suspects."

"Why?"

"It's all the suspicious behavior. First, nobody knows anything about him. Mr. Flores never mentioned him to anybody. Next, he was supposed to be a friend, but nobody in either Winslet or South Winslet has seen him since word of Mr. Flores' death got out, and Micah thinks he's either missing or hiding. And last, he could have been the second man in the clearing since he wears regular clothes and shoes, not boots, on the days he travels."

As I spoke, another thought occurred to me, and I turned to Father Fitz. "You said you'd been to the hut where Mr. Flores and Cede stayed. Which side did Mr. Flores sleep on?"

He looked a bit confused and asked what I was thinking and then I saw his expression change as he understood.

"Mr. Flores slept in the bed on the left and this man Cede in the bed on the right—where the gun was found."

Hank stood up. The meeting was over. "You're right, Jane, he stays on the list. I think

we're done here at this point. I need to get back to base. Chief, do you want to come with me? I intend to find Sergeants Richmond and Jenkins and talk with them."

"Yes, I would very much like to come with you. Let me make a call first and then I'm ready to go."

Hank turned to the rest of us. "Thank you all for your time and, please, be extra careful. This killer is getting more desperate."

Everyone thanked my aunt and uncle for their hospitality. The Chief made his call while Hank went out back and spoke to the guards. A few minutes later, Hank gave me a hug and told me he'd call as soon as he had the chance. He and the Chief left through the front door; I would have liked to go with them but knew that was not possible. Father Fitz spoke softly to my aunt, she nodded, and he followed Mike and I upstairs.

Calvin was turning the corporal from his side to his back as we entered the room. The corporal was moaning and thrashing his legs, as if in a bad dream.

"I was about to come get you, Doctor Evans. This all started after I turned him on his side, so I was turning him back. He doesn't respond to his name, and I couldn't understand anything he said."

When I put my hand on his wrist to take a pulse, the leg movements slowed and then stopped but his pulse was racing.

Mike nodded. "I've seen this before. We can't read into it—it may or may not mean he's waking up. Calvin, you look tired. I'm sure Mrs. W. has food for you downstairs. You too, Father. Jane and I can handle this."

"Actually, I'm going to join you, if you don't mind," said Father Fitz with a smile. "I've no doubt the boys outside are capable, but a little extra security never hurt, right?"

Since we both knew the kind of security Father Fitz could provide, Mike and I were grateful.

Mike turned to me. "In that case, Jane, why don't you see if you can get some sleep? We'll call if we need you."

I started to protest and then realized I really was dog tired. I went downstairs, told my aunt I was going to lie down for an hour or so, went to my room and snuggled under one of her homemade quilts.

FRIDAY, DECEMBER 31 - CARRIAGE LANTERN INN

When I awoke, the house was quiet. I looked at my watch and was shocked to realize I had slept until almost 3 a.m. I washed up, changed my wrinkled clothes, wolfed down a glass of juice and a cold muffin, and went upstairs to see our patient.

I tapped softly on the closed door and Mike came out to the hall.

"Why didn't you wake me up? I could have relieved you. How is Corporal Pauling?"

"He's the same as far as sporadic movement of arms and legs. His pupils are reacting better, less sluggish, his pulse has slowed down, and his other vital signs are stable.

"As far as waking you, you obviously needed the rest. I was about to wake Calvin, but if you can take a shift, we can let him sleep." I nodded. "Hank called to let us know that they can't find either Sergeant Richmond or Jenkins on base. Around midnight, he sent guards to relieve the ones who were here, and Chief Fielding has the night cruiser parked out front."

I offered him the muffin wrapped in a napkin, and juice that I had brought upstairs for him, but he said no. All he wanted was some sleep. Mike left and when I entered the room, Father Fitz's soft voice came from the darkest corner. "Were you able to get some rest?"

"Yes, thank you, I was. Why don't you go do the same while I'm with the corporal?"

He chuckled. "No, no. I learned to live without sleep a long time ago, dear girl. I'll be here if needed."

He did, however, gratefully accept the muffin and juice.

At about 5 a.m., Corporal Pauling opened his eyes and seemed to be looking at me, but they were open only a brief time and when I tried speaking to him, I got no answer. I let Mike sleep and sat back down to continue waiting.

Father Fitz spoke up from his corner. His voice sounded a little eerie, coming from the dark like that. "When our boys started opening their eyes, it was a good sign. Might take a bit o' time, but it's hopeful time."

Not for the first time, I wondered about exactly what kind of experiences Father Fitz had had in Ireland with 'the boys.'

A while later, I opened the blackout curtains to let in the early morning sun. I was standing beside Father Fitz's chair, looking out at the peaceful view of a snow-covered park, when I heard a weak voice.

"W... where am I?"

Father Fitz passed me quickly on his way to the door and turned left toward Mike's room when he got to the hall.

"Hello, Corporal, you're at the Carriage Lantern Inn in downtown Winslet." The corporal tried to sit up but I gently placed a restraining hand on his shoulder. "Please don't move until Doctor Evans comes. You've had a rough evening and night."

His pulse was steady, and I was fitting a blood pressure cuff around his arm when Mike came into the room wearing striped pajamas, a plaid bathrobe, bare feet, and a stethoscope dangling around his neck.

The corporal's blood pressure was a bit low, but better than it had been, and his pupils now reacted normally to the light. Mike held up three fingers and asked how many Corporal Pauling could see. He answered correctly. Rather than sit him bolt upright, we added a pillow behind his head and shoulders, propped him up a bit, and gave him a sip of water at his request. He complained of a throbbing headache where his head wound was, but otherwise, he was in stable condition. And able to talk.

"Corporal Pauling, we'll give you something for that pain after you answer a few questions for Captain Maitland, who is being called right now and will need to talk with you first."

Mike turned to me. "If Mrs. W is awake, could you ask her to put together a light tray for the corporal? Maybe some tea and scrambled eggs?"

Father Fitz and I passed on the stairs. "The Captain is on his way. I don't think he slept last night, either."

Half an hour later, Corporal Pauling had eaten, and his complexion was less pasty. Despite the ever-present headache, he was rapidly improving and asked if he could change into the clean uniform Hank had brought and sit at a table to talk. Calvin and I helped him get dressed and Calvin and Mike assisted him down the stairs.

. . .

CARRIAGE LANTERN INN

We all met in the dining room at 9 a.m. Chief Fielding had come with Hank, Mike, Father Fitz, Corporal Pauling, Calvin, Aunt Ida, Thomas, and me. I brought my notebook and made a notation as the coffee and tea were served.

Hank turned to Mike. "Do you have some medical questions you need to ask?"

Mike nodded. "Corporal, what do you remember from yesterday?"

"I kn... know I fell into the filing cabinet and hit my head. I heard people screaming from someplace far away and I remember you helping me, Miss Harmony. Thank you. I remember Doctor Evans examining me but not what he said. Then I was moved around until, finally, I was in my own bunk. At that point, Calvin told me what had happened, why my head hurt, and he told me to lie still." He reached up and touched the bandage on his forehead and then gulped down a whole glass of water. "I drifted off and had an awful nightmare that someone was trying to suffocate me, and this morning, I woke up here."

He looked around at the dining room and the people sitting there. I was sorry he had to learn the truth.

"That wasn't a nightmare, Corporal. Someone knocked out the guard at your door, went inside, and tried to suffocate you with a pillow. If Calvin had not wrestled him off you and called for help, you likely wouldn't be here right now."

It was Hank who had spoken, and I thought he was a bit harsh considering what the young man had been through in the past twenty-four hours. I was about to say that when that small voice in my head, that I attributed to my mother, told me to be quiet. It said that Hank had one murder and one attempted murder to solve, as well as a base to run, not to mention an important mission. He had to get Corporal Pauling to talk—quickly.

As if he'd heard my internal conversation, Hank said, "I don't mean to sound unsympathetic to what you've been through, Corporal, but you need to understand the urgency here. We think the person who attacked you is the same person who killed Fred Flores in the woods, and we need you to help us catch him before he kills again."

Corporal Pauling lost any color his face may have had and he began sweating.

As he got out of his chair to see to his patient, Mike said, "That's enough for now. We need to get him back to bed. You'll have to talk with him later." Mike was checking his pulse when the corporal pulled his wrist away.

"No." He held up a hand. "No. I want to end this. What do you need to know, sir?"

Hank looked at Mike who shrugged and returned to his seat.

"Were you one of the two people meeting in the woods the day Fred Flores was killed?"

"Yes."

I could hear the collective intake of breath.

"And who was the other man?"

"Sergeant Richmond."

And those breaths came out in a whoosh.

"Why were you there?"

This time, the corporal hesitated, drank more water, and then started speaking slowly.

"I had a severe back injury three years ago, when I g... got thrown from a horse and fractured several vertebrae. For a while, they thought I might be paralyzed but thank God that didn't happen. I spent two months on bedrest and during that time, I became addicted to morphine."

He paused again. "My addiction continued when I finally went back to work at my last post, and I've been trying to detox since I was transferred here. Somehow, Richmond figured out what was going on and he has been blackmailing me ever since."

"What did he want?"

"He knew that the patients here were spies and that they all had injuries and were diagnosed with battle fatigue." Hank cursed under his breath. "What he didn't know was who they were, where they had been placed, and what they had told us."

With that, the corporal started to cry, as if the enormity of it all was too much for him.

This time, when Mike stood up, his tone said he would not take no for an answer.

"Okay, that really is enough for now. He needs to rest and have something to eat after this session. If he's up to it later, he can finish his story."

Nobody with eyes to see could possibly argue with Mike that Corporal Pauling needed rest, except the corporal himself.

"I have one more thing to say before we put this on hold." He wiped his eyes and looked directly at Hank. "Sir, you have to believe me, the papers I gave Richmond were pure fiction. I made everything up—names, nationalities, overseas assignments, and notes basically saying how mostly unsuccessful the men had been against the all-powerful Germans. I made them sound like these spies were as stupid as the Germans think they are.

"I wrote that we were hoping they would recover enough to go back into the field and if they did not, we had not yet decided their fate. My plan was to make it sound believable to the German mind without laying it on too thick." He sat up straighter and managed to smile a bit. "You see, I grew up in Pennsylvania with many German immigrants, the majority of whom were good, hard-working people. But I directed these 'official papers' to the types I had heard all about from them—like Hitler, the SS, and anyone else who does his bidding."

With that, Mike, Calvin, and Corporal Pauling went upstairs.

Hank shook his head and then turned to the rest of us, sitting there stunned, and said, "I don't know whether to recommend the man be hung for treason or to be given a medal for brilliance in confounding the enemy while under duress."

———

CHAPTER NINETEEN

"It is a capital mistake to theorize before one has data.
Insensibly
one begins to twist facts to suit theories, instead of theories to
suit facts."
Sir Arthur Conan Doyle

FRIDAY, DECEMBER 31

WHILE CORPORAL PAULING RESTED, Hank went to Strathmore to call Major Genese and to check on the search for Sergeants Richmond and Jenkins; Mike and the Chief went to their offices. The rest of us had a quick lunch and then I went upstairs to relieve Calvin.

At 2 p.m., we all gathered to conclude Corporal Pauling's questioning, except Mike. A baby had decided to come into the world early, and Mike was busy delivering the newest Winslet citizen. Hank led off.

"The decision has been made to move you back to Strathmore Hospital to continue your detoxing under Dr. Carlson's supervision. Obviously, any further information you remember will be passed on to me.

"As you know, soldier, your addiction and theft of medicines would in most circumstances automatically lead to discharge from the army and maybe criminal prosecution. However, as with everything connected with Strathmore Hospital, this is a special situation. In other words, nobody is sure what to do with you."

"Will I possibly be able to return to work, sir?"

"I don't know about that except I can guarantee you will have no further access to narcotics. Dr. Carlson and a disciplinary board will determine if and when you can return to duty.

"Right now, we need to wrap this meeting up. The most important question I have left for you is, did you see Sergeant Richmond shove Fred Flores, ultimately causing his death?

I sat closer to the edge of my seat.

"No sir, I did not. I ran the other way." He paused. "And I... After we heard a noise in the bushes, I'm not sure how much time went by before Mr. Flores was killed. That's important because on my way out of the woods, S... Sergeant Jenkins ran past me. It could have been either one of them."

"Captain, how is the hunt for Sergeants Richmond and Jenkins going?" asked my aunt.

"No luck yet, so I'm keeping the guard here even after the corporal is back at Strathmore until they are found and we can question them."

"Are you willing to have them stay?" he asked her gently.

Aunt Ida looked at Thomas and they both nodded.

Hank thanked them and then shook his head. "Strathmore is not that big. I can't figure out where they are."

"Maybe they're both off base," said Thomas.

Hank shook his head confidently. "No chance. We went right into lockdown, and they were there for rollcall. We locked the gates to the woods and those two entrances at the back of the woods that Mr. Flores had used to get to his hut were blocked the day we went to the scene of the crime."

Thomas lit his pipe and quietly asked, "And what about the other way in and out of Strathmore?"

He had everyone's attention.

"What other way in and out of Strathmore?"

Hank was standing at that point, poised like a hunting dog.

Thomas also stood. "Come downstairs with me, Captain. I don't believe I've ever shown you my diorama of Winslet, including the Strathmore estate, before it was converted into a temporary army base."

The Chief, Father Fitz, and I followed them downstairs.

Thomas led us to the converted pool table that was the base of his diorama of Winslet in the year 1915. Each time I saw it, I was more impressed with the detail. Thomas had already added the new buildings we had given him for Christmas.

He pointed to the section that was Strathmore. In the past, I had paid most attention to Main Street and individual houses, so I was surprised at the size of the estate in its original form, with only the main residence and stables where the garages now stood. There were no additions to the mansion and no barracks out back. There had been more bushes and trees near the house than the army kept, except between the house and the road, where it looked as though the thick greenery was undisturbed. I thought Thomas would point to that area for a secret entrance and exit but he didn't; he directed us instead to the back of the stables where there was more dense greenery. It was easy to see that the entire area had once been woods and the estate was carved out, leaving three sides of trees and bushes intact.

"When I first started the diorama, some of the workmen who'd built the estate were still around. They said it had taken three years to clear the area and erect the buildings to Colonel Strathmore's exact expectations. They also said he had one peculiarity—he didn't want any rubbish going out the front gates. In his words, he 'didn't want people picking over his castoffs'. Instead, behind the stables, there was a rutted path and the men had to use that."

We all turned to Hank when the Chief asked, "What's behind the garage that's there now?"

"I haven't been back there in a while but it's where we have compost heaps for use in the gardens and extra oil drums for garage use. The area backs up to the trees and bushes on that side of the estate."

"And if that path remains in some form, where would it lead?" I asked Thomas.

"Behind St. Agnes' Church, there are more woods, not deep, but enough to block a view of the old landfill, where everybody used to dump cuttings and dirt. It was in use for a long time. Once it was filled in, the town built a park over it right beside the river, a park that connects to the land behind your woods, Captain. Same place where Fred Flores went in and out of the woods."

"I'll check that path myself when I get back to Strathmore. Thanks, Thomas, your diorama may have saved us a lot of time. Chief, I'd appreciate it if you would join me."

It was agreed that Thomas and Father Fitz would stay at the inn, in case someone still thought Corporal Pauling was there.

We transported Corporal Pauling back to Strathmore with a guard and me in the back of the army truck with him since Mike was still at the delivery. Our patient was silent and calm. Mike had spoken with Dr. Carlson and, for the time being, they were continuing to wean the corporal from morphine with smaller doses than he had been taking, administered at more frequent intervals. "Only enough to take the edge off," Mike had said. There were more questions coming for the corporal and they needed his head to be relatively clear when Dr. Carlson conducted the interviews.

When we brought the corporal upstairs, Lieutenant Shrug met us. She was kind but firm with him, establishing his change in status quickly. He was to be kept in one of the patient isolation rooms, under her staff's supervision. Instead of turning toward the patient ward, we went straight to the first room on the right of the short corridor. That and a second door were opposite Dr. Carlson's office. Instead of an isolation unit, the room would now be used for protection, as evidenced by the prominent new lock on the door.

Like the general ward at Strathmore, Corporal Pauling's temporary living quarters did not resemble a hospital room. The walls were painted a soft shade of yellow and you could almost see yourself in the gleaming wooden floor. The furniture consisted of a hospital bed, two comfortable-looking armchairs with a table between them, and an illuminated lamp that gave a soft light. Clothing could be kept in a closet with built-in drawers.

I wondered about the possibility that Corporal Pauling

might attempt suicide but stopped worrying when, once we'd settled the corporal, a corpsman stayed with him in the locked room. And directly over the head of the bed, I noticed a red square with the word *emergency* written in white above a button in the center.

"Captain Maitland told me about the interview, Sergeant Richmond, and the blackmail. Was there anything after that I missed?" the lieutenant asked when we were outside the room.

"He's not sure who pushed Mr. Flores—Richmond or Jenkins."

"The idea that Sergeant Richmond could do such a thing doesn't surprise me so much, but I would never have thought of Clark... Sergeant Jenkins... being involved."

She looked crestfallen for a minute before she recovered her composure, so I tried to reassure her. "Look, we don't *know* that he was involved. He could have arrived at the scene after it happened, panicked, and left. We don't know yet."

I didn't think she believed Sergeant Jenkins would panic any more than I did, but we let it go at that. We had patients to see.

CONSIDERING the disruptions to their routines, the patients were doing remarkably well. The big news was that Alan was now watching when staff spoke to him, and he appeared to understand. He could follow commands, such as squeezing a hand, though he still made no effort to speak.

I leaned in close and said, "It's all right, soldier, take your time. It's enough for now to know that you can hear us."

His response was unexpected. He flashed a smile that

turned him into a very handsome man. It was gone as quickly as it came, but seeing it lifted my spirits.

We stopped at each bed and at the furniture arrangement in the center of the room to make sure we talked with the patients individually. The noise and fears had brought back memories for several of them, and they required a lot of reassurances that they were safe.

Patient Gene, an older man with gray hair and stormy-looking eyes, who'd had several abdominal surgeries, came through the filing cabinet incident looking unaffected, but during the night, he was found huddled in a corner, sweating and crying. This morning, he was again sitting up, looking calm. I wondered what the night would bring.

Bob was in his bed. His leg was in good alignment and his pain was in control.

"How are you doing?" I asked.

He kept his voice low when he said, "The name is Jackson, Jackson Philip Logan."

Avis joined us in time to hear his declaration.

"I was sent to France in '42."

"Have you told this to Dr. Carlson?"

He nodded. "He was here late last evening when I woke up and remembered it all. He and a medic moved my bed out to the hall near his office, he pulled up a chair, and we spoke quietly. He told me what you folks are trying to do here and I told him everything I could think of that might help."

He paused.

"Funny, it wasn't until I could almost see and feel that altar crashing down that I could remember anything, including my name. Before that, it was flashes, some of them terrifying."

Avis and I talked a bit more about the patients, and I

added notes to the charts of the ones I had spoken to and wrote down the patients and medications Mike would need to review in the next day or two. After that, I left and went downstairs.

HANK, another soldier, and I reached Martha's desk at the same time. He introduced me to Lieutenant Edward Wellesley, Mike's second-in-command who had been on sick leave and had returned to the intrigue now at Strathmore.

I asked Hank if the path through the woods was still there.

He nodded, "And there are some broken branches that verify someone has been using it.

I posted a sentry in case he comes back."

"So now we're looking for Jenkins?" asked his second.

"Have you checked Mr. Flores' hut?" I asked.

"It's not there anymore. Remember? I ordered it taken down."

"No, you didn't," said Martha. Hank gave her an odd look. "Well, sir, I mean *you* did but then Chief Fielding called and said to leave it alone so that's what we did."

If the situation had not been so grave, I would have laughed and said something like "Oops", but Hank's face was a peculiar shade of red and I kept silent.

He was not having a very good day.

He picked up the phone and asked for the police station.

"Chief, Maitland here. Can you tell me why you changed my order about tearing down Fred Flores' hut?" He listened. "I didn't think you would do something like that, but after I ordered it torn down, Private Billings tells me you called and countermanded the order." He listened more and then said, "Yes, certainly, we'll wait for you."

He gave Martha back the phone.

"Chief Fielding is on his way—he never countermanded any order."

"I'm sorry, sir, but he swore it was the Chief."

"Who did?"

"Private Willis, who relieved me at noon that day. He said it was a short call, but the Chief was very insistent."

"It's all right, Private Billings. It's not your fault, we'll get to the bottom of it."

Hank said it probably wasn't necessary for me to go to the hut but changed his mind when I told him we had no idea who had called and why they wanted that hut. It was possible someone there might need medical care. While we waited for the Chief, I ran upstairs and got an emergency medical kit.

STRATHMORE WOODS

Two armed soldiers led the way with Hank and Chief Fielding behind them, weapons drawn. It was eerily quiet as I waited back a way with Lieutenant Wellesley. The man radiated a calm confidence, which I appreciated.

The soldiers burst into the hut and immediately called for Hank.

In seconds, we were all inside, staring at Sergeant Jenkins, gagged, hands bound to his feet, and looking... well, mad.

———

CHAPTER TWENTY

*"The only thing that should surprise us is that
there are still some things that can surprise us."*
François de la Rouchefoucauld

FRIDAY, DECEMBER 31 – STRATHMORE WOODS

WHILE THE SOLDIERS worked on the ropes binding the sergeant's wrists and ankles, Hank removed the gag. Words started to pour out of Jenkins' mouth immediately.

"It's Richmond. He killed Flores, tried to kill Pauling, and I'm only alive to use as a hostage, if he needs one. Hurry! He could be back any minute. He's planning some sort of explosion today, before he leaves for good."

The sergeant tried to get up as soon as he was free of the ropes but swayed and fell back on the cot. One of the soldiers helped him sit up while the other kept his rifle pointed at him.

"Not so fast," said Hank. "What's your name? And don't bother with Jenkins. You don't sound or act like any sergeant I've ever known, and your skills are at a much higher level."

"May we have this conversation in private, sir?" He looked first at the Chief, then the soldiers, and finally rested his gaze on me. "It's confidential."

Hank dismissed the soldiers. The Chief now held his weapon on the sergeant.

"Chief Fielding, Lieutenant Wellesley, and Jane have been vetted and have signed the confidentiality statement. They stay. Now, how do we know that you aren't in this with Richmond and this Cede guy and us finding you tied up isn't all part of the plan?"

"No disrespect, Captain Maitland, but if I weren't so mad and sore, I'd laugh."

I had my first glimpse of how raw and painful-looking the rope burns at his wrists were, but he seemed to totally ignore them. "First thing, you're completely off-base about Cede."

"Why?"

"Cede can't be helping him because I *am* Cede. I was working with Fred Flores and took on that persona the few times we needed to meet in person. We usually got in touch by mail."

"Wait a minute. What were you and Flores 'working on' and who were you working for?"

"We were monitoring this facility. And this will help explain." He started turning toward the wall side of the bed, but the Chief stopped him. He looked at Hank and said, "May I?"

"Help me stand him up." You could feel the tension in

the room as Hank and the Chief pivoted him to the other bunk.

Hank and the lieutenant moved 'Cede's' bed.

"Feel under the bed, near the top. There's a sealed envelope attached to the cot springs."

Chief mumbled something that sounded like a swear word, which would have been very much out of character. "When we found that gun, we should have flipped the cot over".

Hank answered him. "Unless it's been planted there since."

He found it and brought it to the door for more light. He opened it to find a very official-looking piece of paper with a large seal at the top. Hank and the Chief read it and then showed it to the rest of us.

OCTOBER 15, 1943

TO WHOM IT MAY CONCERN:

Let it here be known that Special Agent Clark A. Johnson, of the Federal Bureau

of Investigation, is working under my direct orders and in conjunction with the United States Army while at the Strathmore Army Base.

If proof of identity is needed, Mr. Johnson has a birthmark in the shape of a bell on the outside of his left thigh. Any hindrance to his achieving his mission will be considered an act of treason against the United States in time of war.

.   .   .

SIGNED BY: J. *Edgar Hoover*
    Director, Federal Bureau of Investigation

I TURNED AWAY and Hank and the Chief verified the birthmark.

"I've never heard of the FBI working with the army."

Hank still did not sound convinced, letter or not.

"Captain, in this war, where you work or the initials beside your name do not matter so much anymore. There's a lot of crossover and sharing of resources and people. Trusted individuals are being tagged for sensitive jobs, as were you and Miss Harmony's brother, and many others, when help was needed bringing Italy into the war on our side."

Hank looked as shocked as I felt.

"But how... how did...?"

"How did I know? Major Paul Genese is my army contact. He was Fred's, too. Please call him to satisfy yourself about me, but hurry, we have no time to lose."

STRATHMORE

After hearing that, while Hank went to make that call, we brought Agent Johnson back to Strathmore to tend his wounds. Avis and I took care of him or, more accurately, she cleaned and bathed his wounds while I watched. The budding affection between the two of them was obvious, and in different circumstances I would have left them alone, but not now. That man was not getting out of my sight.

Before he'd left for the main building, Hank had ordered the guards to stay hidden and inform him if Richmond returned.

Twenty minutes later, Hank, Agent Johnson, Chief Fielding, Mike, and I, with the addition of Dr. Carlson, gathered for what was hopefully the last strategy session. After quickly reviewing recent events, Hank started the meeting.

"I spoke to Major Genese, Agent Johnson. He confirmed what you said and told me I'd best show a little respect." Hank flashed a brief smile. "Seems you've been in and out of some tough scrapes, and the Major is not prone to exaggeration."

"I can usually handle myself, but Richmond snuck up on me when I went back to the hut to get that letter. And may I suggest that it would work better if you all continued calling me Sergeant Jenkins for the time being? I'm used to it now and that's how people around here know me."

Mike jumped in at this point. "Pauling said he saw you in the woods the day Fred Flores was killed. How do we know you didn't do it?"

Jenkins nodded, "I was there. Passed Pauling on his way out, running fast. When I found Fred, I realized he was dead, not hurt. I didn't chase Pauling because he had too big a head start." The sergeant's face showed his regret when he paused. "Leaving Fred like that, face down, was the hardest thing I've ever done. I liked and respected the man, but I had no choice. I didn't want to disturb what was a crime scene in case the police could prove who had killed him. And if they couldn't, I knew the best I could do for Fred was to find him myself.

"So, I started hanging around with Richmond because he was always up at the hospital, near Pauling, and I could watch the two of them. I had already been suspicious of Richmond's absences anyway and things started to add up. As for Pauling, I had met him a couple of times. He may be many things, but a murderer is not one of them. I'd stake my life on that."

Mike's shoulders relaxed. Due to our various jobs, the people in that room were adept at determining true emotion from someone putting on an act. Sergeant Jenkins was telling the truth.

Hank nodded and asked him the question on the tip of my tongue. "So, was there anything else that put you onto Richmond?"

"Well, Fred found a grocery list with…"

"This one?" I reached into my pocket to remove the paper I had been carrying with me everywhere, hoping inspiration would strike.

"Yes." He didn't seem surprised I had a copy. "It wasn't hard to figure out the code. Spells out: SPIONS."

"German for spies," Hank interpreted for the rest of us. "That means he figured out that our patients are not prisoners."

"Right." He borrowed a pencil from Mike and circled letters on the list. "Two, two, and two. Pretty simple, really."

Baked Beans Last Letter: **S**

TurnipLast Letter: P

Ice CreamFirst Letter: I

OnionsFirst letter: O

TomatenLast Letter: N

Cranberries.Last Letter: S

"HE MADE TWO AMATEUR MISTAKES. He asked for ice cream from a grocery store with no frozen foods *and* he used the German word for tomatoes. Richmond is not very good at codes, I'd say."

Nobody wanted to mention that he had fooled us.

"Sergeant." Chief Fielding looked more concerned than I'd ever seen him as he asked, "You mentioned something about an explosion? What exactly did Richmond tell you?"

"He kept going on about how Americans were as stupid as he had been raised to believe and that he was insulted by the jobs he was ordered to do while in the army.

"He said he was used to sabotage, not flirting with women for information. However, at the same time, he was so proud of how he'd outfoxed the United States Army—getting you all to trust him so he could go about anywhere on the base—that he bragged. Another amateur mistake. Frankly, I think he was looking for congratulations.

"Look, my brother-in-law is what the doctor called a manic-depressive. What the family sees is that he's sometimes okay for periods of time, but then he can go to extremes where he acts like he's either higher than a kite or depressed to the point where my sister has to watch him in case he tries to commit suicide. Richmond was on a definite high, as though he was drunk or taking too many of the amphetamines the army gives you to help you stay awake." He turned to Dr. Carlson. "I got the feeling he thought he could do just about anything."

Dr. Carlson agreed with him. "The man needs to be found. There's no telling what he will do when in a manic state."

Jenkins was silent for a moment, and then said, "On his way out the door, after tying me up, he spoke to himself in German. He said, 'Today, at last, the spies will get their payback.' All I heard after that was crazy laughter."

Everyone turned to Hank and each of us asked our own version of 'What now?' at the same time.

I looked at the serious faces of the men around the table: Sergeant Jenkins looked like a racehorse anxious to get out of the gate; Mike was plain angry and had trouble lighting a cigarette because his hands were shaking; Dr. Carlson looked very concerned; Chief Fielding wore absolutely no expression, his face a mask; and Hank was in full leadership mode—he sat up straighter until he was almost rigid, his jaw set. I watched as he squeezed the grocery list Jenkins had handed him into a tight ball held in his clenched fist. But it was his eyes that always showed me what he was thinking, and they were blazing.

My heart was racing and it took all my willpower not to run into the front foyer and up the stairs, yelling for the staff to evacuate the patients. All I could think of was those men and how they would react to an actual explosion rather than a file cabinet crash, or even if they would have a chance to react.

At that moment, there was a knock on the door. It opened and Martha came in, pushing a cart with a food tray loaded with sandwiches, a bowl of apples, and several non-alcoholic drinks.

"I figured none of you thought to stop for food and it could be a long night, sir. This way, you can eat while you talk."

Hank somehow maintained a calm voice when he thanked her. She left quickly, and, surprisingly, most of us did grab a sandwich and drink. At least Richmond wouldn't be warned off by growling stomachs. Then we went right back to the subject at hand.

"We have police watching the train station. Soldiers guarding the entrance and exit to the path. Do we arrest him if he comes back?"

Jenkins shook his head. "I've had plenty of time to think about this. He's unlikely to have the explosives with him. No, I think they are either already in place or ready to go.

And there's another thing. What if he's not working alone? What if you were right and he does have an accomplice, just not me?"

The air turned blue as Mike swore. Hank held up his hand to stop him.

"Captain, I think I should go back to the hut, and it should look like I'm still tied up. You can have people nearby, but not too close. I think, since he didn't kill me, he and maybe any partner he has will return there before whatever he's planning, if for nothing else than to finish me off."

He spoke as if he was talking about a trip to see a friend. It made me wonder exactly what kind of 'tough scrapes' Sergeant Jenkins had been through in the past.

"A partner? Who?" asked Mike.

Once more, my mouth spoke before my brain had time to warn it.

"What about Hoffman? He..."

"Jane, it's not Joseph Hoffman. He and his patients ready for discharge were on the early train to Boston this morning."

After a pause, the Chief asked Jenkins, "And what if he doesn't come back?"

"I'm open to other suggestions."

There was total silence in the room. I missed Father Fitz. He always seemed to know the right thing to say.

Hank looked from person to person, lingering on my face for an extra second, and then decided.

"All right, we'll go with your plan. It sounds logical and I suspect you've had more experience with a situation like this than the rest of us."

Sergeant Jenkins nodded.

"Well then, if you will tell us what to do, we'll do it."

It only took a few minutes to get our assignments and we all got up to leave.

Hank needed to order the sentries not to detain Richmond, to call Major Genese regarding the plan, and to catch Lieutenant Wellesley—who was upstairs guarding the patients—up on the plan.

Mike and Sergeant Jenkins headed for the hut to set the scene.

The Chief went to call his men and tell them to let Richmond through if they saw him and then he would join the two soldiers in the woods as backup for Jenkins.

My job was to go upstairs with Dr. Carlson and start preparations for evacuating the patients. Hank would join me as soon as he could.

————

CHAPTER TWENTY-ONE

"Let us accept truth, even when it surprises us and alters our views."
George Sand

FRIDAY, DECEMBER 31 – STRATHMORE HOSPITAL

THE ATMOSPHERE UPSTAIRS WAS TENSE, as if there had been a microphone in the conference room and they knew there was imminent danger. Dr. Carlson told Avis, Anna, and Lieutenant Wellesley that we needed to prepare the patients for evacuation when Hank determined it was necessary and that he would be upstairs shortly to explain more.

"Come look at this, Jane."

Avis went to the nurses' desk and took out a red folder marked Evacuation Plan from one of the drawers.

"This is our plan for natural disasters. It's updated monthly. What needs to go with us, which patients go first, and where to go when we leave—it's all right here."

"This is wonderful. Let's start gathering these supplies."

Anna spoke up immediately. "I'll take the pharmacy list. After Corporal Pauling was hurt, I did an inventory so now I know where everything is."

"Good. Here." Avis handed her a single sheet of paper with the medications and equipment needed. We were going to travel light.

Hank came upstairs at that point and caught everyone up on what had happened so far and our plan to deal with it. Then he said, "Lieutenant, come with me. I'd like to look around in the attic. Richmond spent a lot of time up there." He and Lieutenant Wellesley left.

Anna went to the pharmacy, and I picked up the phone to call Martha. Nobody answered.

"Avis, aren't the phones working?"

"I haven't called anyone yet but if there's any problem, Martha would let us know. But don't worry, the pharmacy is on a separate line." As soon as she finished speaking, the phone in the pharmacy rang. "See? You can use that phone."

I was about to do that when patient Dexter came to the desk, dragging his IV bottle and pole with him.

"Are we all going to die?" He looked at me. "I heard Captain Maitland say *evacuation*."

There were two more patients behind him, looking agitated.

Dr. Carlson put his arm around the man's shoulders and gently turned him around. "You know, we've never had an evacuation drill at Strathmore and for some strange reason, the higher ups think it would be a good time tonight. What do you think of that?"

As he directed him back to the ward, he signaled to us to go stand by the others.

"As a matter of fact, I was about to announce it so everyone would know what is going on."

We guided the standing patients to chairs rather than their beds. They would be walking out, with help. The psychiatrist stood in the center of the room.

"Gentlemen, some of you are asking what is going on with so many people around tonight. Well, I'm here to tell you."

His voice was calm, almost matter of fact, as he explained about a practice drill. Some of the reading that Dr. Eldridge had given me included the kind of training these men had endured before their overseas assignments. Practice drills should be nothing new to them.

I watched their faces as he spoke until Anna tapped me on the shoulder.

"Dr. Evans called. He wants some of the patients to have mild sedatives along with their regular medications. None for Corporal Pauling, but would you mind giving him his evening pills? It takes a while to open his door and I need to get the rest of these out so they can take effect."

Normally, I would never have given a medicine I hadn't prepared myself, but this was not a 'normal' time, and I knew the drugs the corporal was taking. The patients were calling out questions now to the doctor, and I knew they would need help from all of us soon.

I took the metal tray with two medicine tickets and a small paper cup containing two pills. Anna gave me the key to the corporal's room, and I headed down the corridor.

Something she had said was bothering me, but I couldn't figure out what.

"Jane! G... good to see you. Do you know what's happening? Will I be getting out of here? What..."

"Hold on, Corporal. You and everyone else will be out of here soon. We're having an evacuation drill tonight and..."

He stared at me as though he was trying to read my mind and then blurted out, "Drill, my foot! Something big is going on. I can feel the tension and people were whispering at my door, and then they took my guard away. Look, I know what I did was wrong, but can't I help? Please!"

He did look much better than the last time I had seen him. And he sounded sincere.

"I'll ask Captain Maitland, Corporal, that's the best I can do."

There was a noise behind me as the door opened and crashed against the wall. I turned to see Hank, Wellesley, Dr. Carlson, the guard from the top of the stairs and the corporal's room, and Avis, all coming through the door in a rush, protesting loudly.

"Stop talking or I will shoot!" The room became silent. "Jane Harmony, you come out here, now."

I could not believe my eyes. Anna was standing there with a gun in her hand.

"Move. Now."

Hank tried to argue that she should take him instead of me, but Anna's answer was to point the gun directly at Pauling.

"One more word and I shoot him. I do not want to, but I will."

That was when I noticed her hands were shaking as she

held the gun. It wasn't hard to believe it could go off by accident. I left the room. She closed the door, and locked it.

"Go over to the top of the stairs and call Martha. Tell her to hurry. And know that I will use this gun if you force me to do it."

The gate was open; I went to the top of the stairs and called out, "Martha, we need you up here!"

She responded immediately. I wanted to say something, to apologize, but Anna raised the gun, pointing it at me, so that Martha could see it. Martha sized up the situation very quickly.

The shock on Martha's face reflected what I had felt. "Anna, think what you are doing! Think about your family!"

That was the only time Anna's voice had risen since I'd come upstairs. "I *am* thinking about my family, more than you know!"

In less than a minute, Martha joined the others in the former isolation room.

WE WENT DOWNSTAIRS. Anna ordered me to put on my coat, hat and boots while she did the same. She wanted us to look 'normal'. I kept waiting for her to let her guard slip, but she maintained a lot of space between us. A realization came to me as I put on my hat.

"That wasn't Mike who called you; it was Richmond."

Her expression didn't change.

"Anna, how can you work with a man like that? He killed Mr. Flores and tried to kill Corporal Pauling. And he has something horrible planned for those patients upstairs —*your* patients! How can you do it?" The more I said, the higher my voice rose.

There were tears streaming down her cheeks as she said, "It's either them or my mother's entire family in Poland! Which would *you* choose?" She wiped her cheeks angrily. "No more talking. Go. Out the side door by the cafeteria."

Because of the blackout rules, the base was very dark with only faint lights scattered near doors to the house and the garage entrances. Anna removed a small flashlight from her pocket, the kind the night nurses used to make their way to and from work in the dark these days. As we walked down the path toward Mr. Flores' hut—Jenkins had been right that they would return there—I tried to think of an argument to sway Anna and finally came up with what could be a very slim chance.

I turned and said, "Anna. What if you could save both?"

"I can't. Go. Walk."

"But if you could, would you?"

"Of course. But no more foolish talk. Richmond is on his way here now."

We were at the hut. I went inside with Anna following, and with one quick swishing sound, the gun was on the ground, Anna's arm was behind her back, and I could hear her breathing heavily. I lit both candles on the bedside table and the Chief and Mike came into the hut. Jenkins was still in position on the bed, looking tied up.

A man dressed from head to toe in black, who had emerged from the dark shadows in the corner of the hut, released Anna and removed his knitted cap.

"Hello ladies, fancy meeting you here."

"Father Fitz. I should have known." Relief flowed through me as he simply nodded. "Listen, Richmond is on his way here now and I don't know how long we have. Anna is helping him because he is threatening her mother's family in Poland. She doesn't want to hurt anyone."

Anna, who was now crying again, said, "I'm a nurse! I want to help, not harm, but what do I do? Let them all perish?"

I took the gag from Jenkins' mouth but he stayed in position so the rope wouldn't unwind. It was to him that I addressed my idea.

"Look I've got an idea. What if we do both? What if we let Richmond think he got away with it, give him time to send a message to his boss, and then grab him?"

"How?"

"It would mean trusting Anna to communicate that he couldn't risk being seen because everyone is on to him and that he should get away. She'd have to ask him what to do to explode the device or devices. When he's not too far away, we blow something up so he can hear it, and see if he makes a call from somewhere or gets on the train."

"Where is Captain Maitland?" Jenkins asked.

Anna told him and gave the keys to the Chief, who immediately left the hut.

"What exactly is Richmond planning to do?" Jenkins asked.

"He has dynamite to blow up the Strathmore Estate. It is positioned at the back of the building, I think."

"You *think*?"

"He did not discuss this plan with me much. He did say he had trouble getting the dynamite and ended up with much less than he wanted, but could still do the job. He said the original building will stay but the entire addition, including the hospital and the cafeteria, will be gone." Her voice, which had been trembling, changed to an angry tone.

"He said he could do this because he was an expert at sabotage. And he said every time people looked at the front of the building, they would remember that he was the best."

We all digested this for a moment.

"How long do we have before he gets here?"

She looked at her watch. "Another ten minutes, at the most. He has an abandoned barn he uses about half an hour's walk from here. That is where I was to meet him after... after the blast."

Jenkins looked at Father Fitz and said, "I've heard you're somewhat of an expert in these matters. Is that true?"

He sighed. "Until I entered the priesthood, God forgive me, I was an expert in ambush and sabotage. I know dynamite."

This time, there was no joking or hints from our small-town parish priest; he'd finally admitted his past.

"Do you think he can do what he says he can?"

"If he is as good as he says he is, yes."

Hank and the Chief came into the hut and got caught up.

"Does anyone have a better plan?"

No response.

"Are you willing to do this, Anna?" I asked and she nodded.

"It's not if she's willing," said Father Fitz, "Richmond won't trust her. She's helping him under a threat, not because she believes in what he's doing. I would not have trusted her back in those days, and *he* won't trust her now."

Mike and the Chief agreed with him.

Hank took a minute and then nodded. "So, what do we do? Arrest him when he comes?"

"If we do that, they will send someone else. They need

to either get the information these men have in their heads or make sure we don't get it," said Jenkins.

"So..."

It was the saboteur-turned-priest who responded. "I'm so sorry to say this, Jane, but the only way I see is that the lieutenant takes you with her and tells Richmond to keep you hostage until she joins him at the barn."

Father Fitz somehow sounded sorry yet firm at the same time. My heart went racing again and my breath was coming in small catches.

Hank's reaction was swift and predictable. "Absolutely not, we can't ask her to risk..."

"We are running out of time." Anna looked at the hut doorway as if she expected Richmond to appear at any moment.

"And Hank, I'm going. Nobody is *asking* me—I'm offering. None of us can come up with anything better and we need to hurry."

It was a pivotal moment for Hank and me, and we both knew it. Finally, Hank nodded his agreement.

Jenkins threw off the ropes and stood up. "Captain, you need to come with me and help with the explosives and evacuation of the patients if we can't find that dynamite."

Father Fitz looked at me and said, "I'll be right behind you, darlin', all the way."

"And me, too," said Mike. Hank started to argue with him, but he held up his hand. "I got her into this mess with my brilliant idea of an assistant and I'm going to damn well get her out. Besides, with all these guns, someone might need me." He raised his medical bag.

The Chief spoke up next. "I know the barn you're talking about. I'm going to get my best officers and we'll be there when you arrive."

Jenkins turned to Anna. "How does Richmond enter the woods?"

"He comes in through the back, near the water."

"Those entrances were closed off," said Hank.

Anna shook her head. "Richmond said he had removed the barriers the soldiers put up."

Father Fitz said, "Here's your gun back. The bullets are in my pocket. We don't want any accidents now, do we? Let's go."

He and Mike left first, then Anna and I.

Hank came out after, squeezed my hand and said, "You come back, that's an order, soldier." He then kissed my forehead and left.

Anna walked beside me and set a fast pace through the woods, first on the path where Mr. Flores died, and then the long, straight path to the right. She used her flashlight again, focused on the ground ahead of us. The trees were so dense that there was little snow on the ground and we could move easily, but still had to be careful not to trip on tree roots. I tried to keep my mind as blank as I could but for such a cold night, I did notice how much I was sweating.

From the start, I had no sense of being followed. Father Fitz and Mike could have been anywhere. We kept going until I could hear the Housatonic River and I was thinking that we'd reach the beach soon when Richmond stepped out in front of us, scaring us.

"What are you doing here, Anna? We were to meet at the hut."

His voice sounded cold, threatening. He didn't seem manic now; he seemed mean.

"I came to find you and bring her here. They know about you and there are guards all over the estate looking for you. They'll be in the woods any minute. I only got out because someone said they found Sergeant Jenkins at the hut, and we were sent to give him medical care."

I thought that was quick thinking on her part and it was clear she was not going to turn us over. I didn't know how to swear in German, but I was pretty sure that's what I heard spew out from Richmond.

He paced back and forth until he decided. "There is nothing to be done. My superiors are waiting for confirmation of a job well done. It must happen now. Kill her and come help me."

He started to walk away when Anna said, "Wait, I've thought of another plan."

"*You* have a plan?"

The sarcasm that he put into that one word spoke volumes, but it didn't stop Anna, although her voice was a bit shakier than before.

"It's you they are looking for, not me. You could take Miss Harmony back to the barn as a hostage. I can do what needs to be done to b... blow up the hospital and join you at the barn when it's all over."

He sneered as he said, "And how would I know you did it? Take your word for it?"

"You don't have to trust me. You would hear the sound as you walked away."

There was no response, but he started pacing again, and I hoped his next plan did not include killing me.

"All right. That sounds like the best choice we have, but you remember, if my superiors do not hear from me tonight, all those relatives die. Not to mention what will happen to the Captain's fiancée."

He proceeded to explain to Anna where the charges were hidden and what she had to do. It all sounded shockingly simple and that made my skin crawl.

He grabbed my arm roughly and pushed me in front of him, headed toward the water.

Anna left without a word, and I was all alone with Sergeant Richmond—or whatever his true name was. Well, not quite alone. I had my two dark guardian angels.

———

CHAPTER TWENTY-TWO

*"Often when you think you're at the end of something,
you're at the beginning of something else."*
Will Rogers

FRIDAY, DECEMBER 31 – STRATHMORE
HOSPITAL

WE WALKED on for what seemed like hours in silence
before he stopped at the edge of more woods.

"You'd better hope Anna does what she is supposed to,
or it will go badly for you."

He was trying to frighten me; I had the absurd thought
that I should assure him that was not necessary as I was
already frightened enough. He now had a gun in his hand
that he carelessly waved around as he spoke.

Suddenly, there was one loud bang followed quickly by
another. Light and flames were visible above the tree line. It

looked as though all of Strathmore had been blown up. I sucked in my breath and prayed.

"Es ist vollbracht! Es ist vollbracht!" He grabbed me and kissed me, hard. "A great thing has happened here after months of planning! It is finished! Now, when I go home to Germany, it will be as a hero!"

He again grabbed my arm and pushed me ahead of him.

I could only assume he was turning around to see if anyone was following us, and I still marveled that my guardians were not seen.

Soon, we were going through dark neighborhoods, getting farther from the water. But we were no longer alone. People were outside—on porches, in yards, in the street in small groups, with flashlights pointing downward. Some cars with their dimmed headlights were leaving the street. The sound of the volunteer fire wagon's bell screamed through the night. People were rushing to help at Strathmore.

"Keep your head down. Speak to nobody or I will shoot them."

I pulled the collar of my coat up and rearranged my scarf to cover my face so no one would recognize me. Richmond did the same.

When we came to the side street that would lead us to the barn Anna had referred to, I started to turn, but Richmond grabbed my arm and kept us going forward, to Main Street.

"What about the barn?" I asked. "Anna will be expecting to find us there."

He kept his voice low and said, "Then Anna will get more than she is expecting."

I wanted to ask him what he meant but he squeezed my arm painfully once we reached the main road and turned us right. We stayed on the side of the street with trees that overhung the sidewalk so that we blended in with the dark as he increased the pace. The police station was across the street but there was no visible activity and nothing they could do to help, yet.

It was clear now that he was headed for the train station.

The church bells rang out that it was eight o'clock, and the last train out of Winslet tonight left at about eight twenty if it was on time.

WINSLET TRAIN STATION

When we got to the station, I was out of breath and panting but Sergeant Richmond looked and sounded as if we had been out for a casual stroll. He directed me to the station itself. I opened the door and the station master, Mr. O'Leary, stood up from his desk to greet us.

"Why, Sergeant Richmond, aren't you needed at Strathmore, what with that explosion and all? And Miss Harmony, why are you..."

He didn't get to finish his sentence because Richmond hit him with his gun, and the station master collapsed. I managed to grab hold of him before he hit the floor.

"Help me drag him over to that corner."

I did as I was told and noticed that a lump was already forming on the right of Mr. O'Leary's forehead. His pulse was strong though, and he was dazed.

"Be quiet, old man, and you will live." Richmond went to the desk. "You come over here and ask for the long-distance operator. And remember, I will have the gun trained on both of you. Hurry, the train should be here soon."

I picked up the phone and groaned inwardly when I heard Clara's voice asking what number I wanted. Clara was the most talkative of the Winslet operators. Richmond put a paper in front of me with a long-distance telephone number on it.

"Clara, this is Jane Harmony. I need a long-distance operator quickly. It's an emergency."

"Jane, what are you doing at the station at this time of night? Why didn't you call from the inn? I thought you were working at the hospital—why aren't you there? What..."

I took a deep breath and prayed that what I was about to do would work.

"Clara, I got a call from Uncle Chester. Mother is not well. I came here so I could take the last train out. Please, put me through."

After only a second's hesitation, she said, "Yes, yes Jane, I'll take care of it. Right away."

As soon as the long-distance operator came on the line, I gave her the number and then Richmond took the telephone. He started speaking in rapid German, smiling and laughing in a fiendish way. There was little doubt in my mind as to what they were talking about.

I went over to Mr. O'Leary who was stirring more, looking as though he was going to try to get up. I sat down beside him and whispered, "Please don't move. Richmond will kill you without a second thought. Believe me."

"Miss Harmony, leave him, I hear the train. You will come to Boston and not say a word for the entire trip. If you do that, I may set you free."

"Another deal? What about the one you made with Anna? You said I was supposed to go free if she did her part. What about her family?"

"I lied." That laugh again. "Her family left their farms two weeks ago, in the middle of the night, and we do not know where they are—yet."

Then he raised his arm to shoot Mr. O'Leary but I had been ready for such a move, and kicked his right knee with all my might. He fell to the floor, but recovered quickly and we both scrambled to reach the gun he had dropped.

As the door to the train platform burst open, I heard Father Fitz yell, "Roll out of the way, Jane. Now!"

Richmond had almost reached the gun when Father Fitz sent a shot into the floor right in front of it, sending splinters flying everywhere. Richmond screamed and put his hands up to his eyes. My ears were ringing, loudly, and I could hear nothing.

Police officers came in through the door we had entered. Everyone had their guns trained on Richmond, and I went back to Mr. O'Leary's side.

The Chief and two more men arrived.

"Chief—don't go to the barn, it's a trap. And Anna..."

He answered me but I couldn't hear him, so he went to the desk, wrote a note, and handed it to me.

Anna fine. Clara called station—warned us that you were here and thought you needed help. A device was rigged to go off when someone opened barn door. Jenkins will take care of it.

———

SATURDAY, JANUARY 1, 1944 - CARRIAGE LANTERN INN

The next morning, I slept late and was amazed when I awoke and saw that it was eight-thirty. I moved Vic aside and got out of bed, washed up in the bathroom, and changed into my favorite dark blue slacks and light blue twin set. A quick brush of my hair and two barrettes to hold it back finished my preparations.

"Good *morning*, Jane. Happy New Year!"

They sounded like a kindergarten class addressing their teacher and had silly grins on their faces. Many of the people I loved best in this world were sitting right in front of me at the dining room table—Hank, TJ, Thomas, Aunt Ida, Mike, Chief Fielding, and Father Fitz.

Hank got up and gave me a hug and kiss, as did TJ, only with his cracked ribs, it was a very gentle hug. Aunt Ida hugged me on her way to the kitchen. I suspected that my breakfast was being kept warm in the oven and a minute later, I was proven right. Not to be left out, I turned to see Mike, Father Fitz, and Thomas lined up.

By the time I sat down, I was the one with the silly grin.

"And a Happy New Year to all of you. I raised my juice glass in a toast. And may this year bring peace."

Everyone joined in the toast.

"I don't remember much after you shot at the floor, Father Fitz. Can someone fill me in?"

"That's because we brought you right here, I gave you a mild sedative, and you went off to sleep," Mike answered.

Hank caught me up with events.

"After you and Anna left, Jenkins and I went back to Strathmore. We found the dynamite bundles right where Anna said they were and moved them. We knew we had to fool both Richmond and the Winslet people who would come running as soon as they heard the noise. After getting out the few important things I had in there, we blew up my cottage."

"You did what?"

"We needed to have a real crime and a reason to arrest

Richmond. Everybody around here thought he was a nice guy."

"What about the patients? How did they react?"

"Dr. Carlson made it all sound like it was part of the drill. He said the cottage had water damage and would have had to come down anyway." Hank laughed. "He should go into theater, he's that good. The patients were mostly good about it and Avis was great with them."

"I think I remember that the Chief, and the police officers and Anna are okay?"

"Thanks to you and Clara." Now Thomas was laughing. "Clara will be talking for years about how you talked in code and she saved the Chief."

The Chief added, "And she did indeed do that. She knew your mother had passed away years ago, and that I was not your uncle, so she called the station. They got hold of us by car radio. When we looked carefully at the door, we found the device he had rigged. That's when we knew he wasn't coming back there. Since Anna was safe at Strathmore, I left guards at the building until Jenkins could deal with it, and I headed to the railroad station." I thought he was done but instead he said, "What you did took a cool head under pressure, Jane Harmony. Anytime you want to change careers, you let me know."

That brought a loud chorus of groans from everyone.

"And where's Richmond now?"

"On his way, under armed guard, to Boston. And he'll go from there to a maximum- security prison. After he's been tried in civilian court, the army wants him but it's up to the lawyers to fight over him. Our job is done."

Father Fitz ended the conversation on a more somber note. "Richmond likes to think he's tough. Well, he'll get a chance to prove it where he's going."

Nobody laughed at that, but nobody expressed any sympathy, either.

The rest of the breakfast was talk of war news and plans for New Year's Eve.

Eventually, Aunt Ida and Thomas shooed everybody out.

"Jane, you and Captain Maitland go into the parlor. You've had no time to yourselves at all. Thomas and I will handle this. Go." She smiled and started clearing the table.

HANK and I sat on the couch in the parlor. The Christmas tree and the decorations were still up, it was snowing outside, and there was soft music playing on the radio. I reached down and removed the Claddagh ring from my right hand. I handed it to him and nodded.

He slipped it onto my shaky left hand.

Hank Maitland was once again my fiancée. He put his arm around my shoulders, and I wanted these precious moments to last forever. I knew that wasn't possible with a war on and the awful backlash of it, but something had changed in the past few days.

When I'd arrived, I had been frightened Hank and I would never work things out. Now I knew we would—even if we had to bend and twist a few rules here and there.

THE END

EPILOGUE

YESTERDAY WAS the long-awaited beginning of the end
of the war. Newspapers used large, bold print to scream out
the word **INVASION**—allied troops had landed on the
northern coast of France, at Normandy. Radios broadcasted
up-to-the-minute details as they received them. President
Franklin Roosevelt told Americans about the staggering
numbers of troops, ships, and planes involved in a battle the
likes of which had never been seen.

Everyone reacted to the arrival of the anticipated battle.
Some were happy, almost manic, convinced the war was
just about over. Others, less sure, continued praying that the
war would end soon. All of us worried about how many
soldiers would never come home.

. . .

I WAS BACK in Boston working on the recently opened Veterans Rehabilitation Ward that Dr. Eldridge and his colleagues had envisioned. After my experiences at Strathmore, I felt more prepared, and, when I needed her, Avis Shrug was my "Personal Consultant".

I received my salary from the physicians in charge, not the hospital. Because of that change, my contract did not restrict me to being single.

Hank would be retired from the army when Strathmore Hospital closed at the end of July.

He had another job to do. He would be returning to Boston to join a group of businessmen charged with working with the army to prepare homes and jobs for the thousands of veterans who would be returning when the war finally did end.

After his retirement, we planned a small, simple, candle-lit wedding at St. Agnes' Church in Winslet, one that everybody except me had known would happen one day.

Hank and I had come through our 'detective' activities well. Stronger, more united. At the end of our last discussion about the "case", we had looked at each other and said, "Really, what were the chances we would ever have to get involved in solving another murder?"

———

HARMONY SERIES CHARACTERS

MAIN CHARACTERS:
   JANE HARMONY: Assistant Head Nurse, Langdon East, 4th floor, Surgical Ward, @ MGH (Massachusetts General Hospital); amateur detective.
   CAPTAIN HENRY (Hank) MAITLAND: Commanding officer at Strathmore Army Base and Hospital in Winslet and Jane's on and off again fiancé.

BOSTON CHARACTERS:
   DR. ELDRIDGE: Chief of Surgery, MGH (Massachusetts General Hospital).
   MARGIE MALONE: Jane's best friend and Head Nurse, Langdon East.

FAMILY:
   ALBERT WINSLET: Jane's uncle – oldest of the four WINSLET siblings.
   MARGARET (Winslet) and FRANK McCARTHY: Jane's aunt and uncle, who raised Jane and TJ after their mother's death.

THOMAS and IDA WINSLET: Jane's uncle and aunt. Owners of *The Carriage Lantern Inn*. Sons in the service, Russ and James

HANNAH (Winslet) HARMONY: Jane and TJ's mother. Married John Harmony.

CATHERINE (Winslet) HOFFMAN: Albert's daughter, Jane's cousin.

SGT. THOMAS JAMES HARMONY (TJ): Jane's brother.

WINSLET CHARACTERS:

AUGUSTUS REDDY – Air Raid Warden – "Reddy's always Ready"

AGNES (Aggie) LIDDINGS: TJ's fiancé; manages *Winslet Daily Chronicle* for her grandfather.

CHIEF FIELDING: New Chief of Police.

DR. MIKE EVANS: Town doctor, covering Strathmore, too. Catherine Winslet's fiancée.

FATHER FITZ: Priest at St Agnes' Church.

IRENE GAGNON: Postmistress.

JOHNNY BIRDCAGE: Tends Victory Gardens, does odd jobs for people in Winslet. Good friends with Micah.

MICAH: Friend of Thomas, Johnny, and Fred Flores. works at Clarence's Fix-it Shop

MISS SMITHERS: Librarian.

OFFICER JEAN HEMP: Only female officer on Winslet force.

VICTOR: Cat at *The Carriage Lantern* Inn.

STRATHMORE CHARACTERS:

CEDE: Stayed in hut with Fred Flores on occasion.

DR. CARLSON: Resident Psychiatrist, Strathmore Hospital.

FRED FLORES: Victim.

JOSEPH HOFFMAN: Catherine's legal husband.

LIEUTENANT ANNA POLANSKI: Evening Charge Nurse, Strathmore Hospital.

LIEUTENANT AVIS SHRUG: Head Nurse, Strathmore Hospital.

LIEUTENANT EDWARD WELLESLEY: second in command to Captain Maitland.

MAJOR GENESE: Hank Maitland reports directly to him.

PRIVATE MARTHA BILLINGS: Jane's friend – assistant to Captain Maitland.

SERGEANT CLARK JENKINS: In charge of weapons and security.

SERGEANT JOHN RICHMOND: In charge of garage, jack of all trades.

ACKNOWLEDGMENTS

When you write a book, it starts with you and the blank page. You need to come up with an idea, develop it, and present it in a manner that others will follow and, hopefully, enjoy. It would be easy to feel alone during what is, for me, a long process. However, I never did because I had the help of the same people who helped with my first book: my writing group (Terri, John, Scott, and Michael), friends (Dana, Bobbi, Susan, and Carol) and, of course, my family. Much love and appreciation for the thoughts, good wishes, encouragement, and knowledge they shared with me.

Professionals helped give the novel that 'finished' look. Annie Jenkinson, www.just-copyeditors.com, edited this book, as she did the first; and the book cover design was by JD&J Design. Thank you both!

With this second book, I also received help from a new source – feedback from readers about my first book, *Harmony in Winslet*. Thank you so much!

ABOUT THE AUTHOR

Gail Balentine, who lives 30 minutes outside of Boston, is a retired nurse who always wanted to write novels, like the many she read and enjoyed. It was natural for her to combine her favorite genre – mystery, with her favorite era – the 1940's and her favorite location – New England.

Her first story – *Harmony in Winslet* – focused on the main character – Jane Harmony – returning to her hometown to prove her brother innocent of murder. While trying to investigate, old ghosts and repressed feelings emerged to make her quest more difficult.

Her second novel – *Harmony at Strathmore* - takes Jane Harmony into a world where the stakes are larger, and the risks go beyond Jane. The war raging around the world seems to come home to tiny Winslet and Jane is determined to win this battle.

Gail has been gratified by the response from readers and interested in their comments about what she's written. She would greatly appreciate either a review of the book on Amazon or direct contact from you with your comments at gbalentineauthor@gmail.com. Thank you.

Made in the USA
Monee, IL
12 January 2022

88770326R00164